Alameda's Awakening

By Tara Pegasus

Purple
Pegasus
Publishing

Art direction and design by Derek Nelson

Cover artwork by Ashley Walters

ashleywalters.net

ISBN-13: 978-0692453636 (Purple Pegasus Publishing)

ISBN-10: 0692453636

Fiction / Coming of Age

ACKNOWLEDGMENTS

I would never have published this book without the help, encouragement, and brainstorming abilities of my beautiful wife, Jordan Pegasus.

Special thanks are due to Lenora Rain-Lee Good, Steve Wallenfels, Maureen McQuerry, and Jeff Copeland for their support, comments, and critiques. I am grateful to Ashley Walters for creating outstanding cover art and to Derek Nelson for his design.

Thank you, J.G., for helping me in a time of crisis. You provided the seed that grew into another reality.

Alameda's Awakening is for anyone who has struggled with cognitive dissonance between what they have been taught to believe and what they experience in life. Never be afraid to change. Never despair of others changing.

ALAMEDA'S AWAKENING

CHAPTER ONE

Sometimes the smell was so bad it gagged her. Ada remembered one school recess when she'd inhaled the fecal odor, wafted to her on a spring breeze, and vomited on the school steps. Even on Sundays, when factory work was put on hold for the Sabbath, the smell, smoky and bright as blood on the tongue, lingered.

Everyone else seemed accustomed to it, but Ada had never succeeded in desensitizing herself. Ever since she toured Worden's meatpacking plant as an eighth grader, she knew that what she smelled was death.

As Ada walked past the rural district into the countryside, the stench dissipated under the earthy scents of thawing soil and new greenery. She took a deep breath and shifted the position of the cake box she carried. Today her best friend Naomi Gentle turned eighteen, and in a few months Ada would as well. In anticipation of fulfilling their childhood dream of joining St. Cecilia's Convent when they were both of age, Ada had decorated the cake with a cross. She couldn't wait to see Naomi's smile when she surprised her by arriving early.

Her arms were stiff from holding the box, even though she'd traveled only a mile. Snow had melted from the pitted road, but it lay in thin sheets like tissue paper across the fields and hills around her. Gingering across a patch of mud, Ada glanced up the drive. Dennis Gentle's Chevy Fleetline Fastback, a gleaming new model, was parked by the front gate. Last fall, the railroad had stationed him in Worden, and he had moved in with his brother's family. Now that he was courting the mayor's daughter, Ada doubted he would be on the farm much longer.

Ada unlatched the gate. It was unusual that none of Naomi's five siblings played in the yard. Ham, a spotted brown mutt, snuffled her feet as she ambled up the walk. When no one answered her knock or hello, she tried the door. It was unlocked, although the front room was empty. She eased off her boots and placed them in the corner, which hosted a dirty sock and two sets of footwear—Naomi's boots and a pair of men's shoes.

The family must be out for a Sunday stroll, or perhaps a calving. Naomi had mentioned a heifer that was in danger of giving birth early. Simmering beans and onions flavored the air, so Ada guessed they'd be back soon. Naomi might be watching the food while the others were out.

She deposited the cake box on the table, which was already set for the meal. Where was Naomi? The unexpected silence made her stealthy as she crept down the hallway to the room her friend shared with her youngest sister Mattie. Naomi could be napping; she needed the rest. Recently, it seemed she caught the slightest glance of disapproval like a physical blow, and she had removed her eyelashes, painstakingly and perfectly. Ada said nothing, but she noticed and worried.

Behind the slightly ajar door she heard a scuffling noise, like one of the dogs was inside. Without knocking, Ada started to open the door. She froze. Naomi lay on her back on the small bed, her skirt pulled up past her knees. In front of her were two hairy, naked legs. The bottom of a Sunday vest brushed against fleshy buttocks.

Ada's cry stuck in her throat. She reeled from the room. At the front door, her hands trembled as she thrust on her boots. Then she was outside, through the yard, past the gate. Her legs failed. She collapsed next to the fence, not realizing until then that she was suffocating. Her fast breaths whined in her ears. She closed her eyes and hugged her arms around her chest until at last she could breathe.

When she opened her eyes, she saw a wooden train with a broken wheel upside down on the grass. Bile rose in her throat. She picked up the toy and flung it as far away as she could.

Ada thought of her friend's wisp-thin, pale blond hair, her swollen eyes, her thin bones jutting through the plain fabric of her dress. Naomi was unhappy, and this was the reason why.

Feeling she might be sick, she rose unsteadily. She glanced at the front door, wishing and dreading that Naomi would appear to answer her questions. There were a thousand things she wanted to ask, but doing so would make what she saw real. She wanted to forget it. Now. Forever.

She turned away. At first she walked, and then she ran. When she reached the footbridge over the creek that marked the edge of the property, she stopped and looked back again. The house was hidden behind a line of trees that pushed up from the ground like gnarled necromancer's knuckles.

In the distance, a cow lowed in pain.

♫

Ada knew she should have told somebody. She should have told her mother. It would have been easy enough when Sybil asked why she had come home early. Instead, she escaped to her bedroom with the excuse that she felt ill. She should have told her father, Rev. Silas Williams, the pastor of Worden's Reformed Christian Church. He would have taken the matter to the elders immediately. Or, if she'd wanted a second opinion before doing anything rash, she could have consulted Jon. Her twin brother was out with his meatpacker friends, but she was still tossing restlessly when he returned late in the evening.

In the end, she told no one. She wasn't sure of what she'd seen, and whatever it was, it was Naomi's secret. Since Naomi didn't come to ask why Ada's cake and not Ada herself had attended her birthday party, Ada knew the secret was a shameful one.

So Ada remained silent, and the next afternoon went about her regular work of tutoring Harold Smythe, Jr., and his sister Margaret. Thanks to Sybil's insistence on continued education during the summer, both Ada and Jon had finished high school a year early. When Ada graduated first in her class, Mrs. Smythe asked her to prepare her eldest children for the same honor. Harold Smythe, Sr., was joint owner of the Worden Meat-Packing Company, and his tithes paid for such items as the baptismal font. It was no hardship for the family to hire a tutor and music teacher, and Ada was glad to work a year before joining the convent. A donation was expected, if not required, when a novice took the veil.

Ada had plenty of experience in tutoring, as she'd taught Naomi since Naomi had been taken out of school at age fourteen to help care for her siblings.

The scene behind the bedroom door flashed through her head. She squeezed her eyes shut, lowered her chin, and rang the bell.

"Miss Will'ams!" Kathleen, the youngest Smythe child, answered the door. Her dark, curly hair clung to her flushed face. "Shall I get Meg and Harry for you?"

"Yes, thank you." She needed to think of something—anything—else. She unpacked her violin next to the finely carved spinet in the room Mrs. Smythe referred to as the "salon." Mrs. Smythe had been a professional singer before coming to Worden, and she occasionally indulged her friends with a house concert. She had never invited Ada to a performance, but Ada imagined how her warm voice would fill the spacious room.

Tentatively, Ada slid her bow against the bottom G string. She hadn't warmed up first thing in the morning as usual. In fact, nothing since last afternoon had gone as usual. Maybe things would never be usual again.

Kathleen's laugh echoed across the wooden flooring. With a sigh, Ada laid her violin back in the case and investigated the delay. Mrs. Smythe had told her they were attempting to tame Kathleen's exuberance, and Ada didn't want her to get into trouble.

Kathleen hadn't found her oldest siblings. Instead, she romped inside her brother Billy's room, whirling around a teddy bear. A blonde girl with her hair up sat at the foot of Billy's bed and massaged his leg.

There had always been something wrong with Billy's left leg. He moved with a hunched, jerky gait, and Ada knew he was in almost constant pain. It wasn't cerebral palsy or polio, but the doctors treated it similarly. At one point a specialist from Missoula put him in a set of iron braces that extended from his heel to the top of his spine. Ada had noted the pale violet bruises near his neck and was relieved when the specialist elected to remove the braces due to their inefficacy.

Now he was being helped by the town doctor's daughter. Ada put her hand to the pit of her stomach. "Dawn. I haven't seen you since graduation."

The blonde girl smiled. "Hello, Ada. I don't suppose Mrs. Smythe warned you I'd be here? She's out on a quick errand."

Ada shook her head. "Warned" was right. Dawn Graham was an unbeliever, although her family had attended church until ten years ago, when Dr. Graham's wife, Ianna, left Worden. When Ianna disappeared, so had the church organist, a handsome woman with muscular legs that pumped up and down the pedalboard. Ada didn't guess the significance of the double disappearance until several years later, when Dawn stated that her mother was of the Sapphic persuasion, and Ada, after research at the library, experienced a shock of discovery. The words of the Apostle Paul burned in her mind: "For this reason God gave them up to vile passions. For even their women exchanged the natural use for what is against nature." God had given up on Ianna, Ada supposed, and so Ianna's family had given up on God.

"I'll be working with Billy regularly," Dawn said, "as part of my father's treatment plan."

Kathleen hugged her bear, then walked it up the mattress to Dawn. "Dr. Graham is a pres—prest-ih-jus doctor. Just as good as the big city doctors. That's what Daddy says!"

Dawn gave the bear a pat. "He certainly is a good doctor, and he's teaching me everything he knows." She glanced at Ada with a rueful smile, as if guessing the gossip and judgments streaming through Ada's mind. "Don't let me keep you from your lessons. Your music will cheer us up."

Billy's face was white and drawn. His large, black eyes blinked at Ada in a mute expression of pain. Tears dampened her own eyes, and she pushed away her anxiety about Dawn. Returning to the salon, she found Margaret and Harry waiting for her. The rest of the afternoon, she distracted herself with music and algebra. She enjoyed the rules and processes of math and found it strange when her students confused or questioned them.

The ten-minute walk home from the Smythes' house, just outside town, afforded Ada too much time not to think of Naomi again. She recited a chapter of scripture, but the familiar words didn't captivate her thoughts. Just a quarter mile from the Smythes, Naomi would be helping her mother with household chores, making dinner, mending clothes, or sweeping the floor. Sometimes Ada stopped by after she finished her lessons. Not today.

She eased open the door of the white-and-brown house she had lived in all her life. Sybil was in the study; Ada could hear her talking on the telephone. Her father looked up from his favorite chair and smiled at her. He was reading a novel, his Monday vice.

Feeling its falseness on her face, she returned the smile, then went to her room and shut the door. She stored the violin case beneath her bed and lay across the mattress. She knew she should make up for her lack of practice but felt no motivation. Music was part of the reason she wanted to join the convent, and she hadn't discussed St. Cecilia's with anyone but Naomi for the last few years. She felt her plans unraveling like a slipknot she pulled on too hard.

When Ada was eight, Rev. Williams was asked to preach at a sister church halfway across the state, and they'd passed the convent, seen there was a concert scheduled, and gone inside. Ada remembered the warmth she'd felt inside the chapel and the deep fervor of the nuns as they sang, as if their music was God's fingers caressing the hearts of their listeners. Ada's whole body trembled, and Sybil looked at her with glistening eyes.

Afterward, Sybil had said, "Jonathon, I wish you could become a priest."

"You mean a pastor, surely," Rev. Williams said.

"If a pastor, then one like Paul, who didn't marry. I prayed so fervently for a child, like Hannah did for Samuel, and promised to dedicate him to God. A family takes one away from complete service to the Lord."

Even then, Jon had gone against the family grain. He picked at the upholstery of the car and kicked the seat in front of him. "I don't wanna be a pastor. I wanna be a pilot."

But Ada had said, "I'll do it, Mother. I'll be a nun and sing at St. Cecilia's."

They laughed, and Rev. Williams spent the rest of the car trip describing the heresies and excesses of the Roman Catholic Church. Nevertheless, for the next few months Ada talked about joining the convent with whoever would listen, and at one point Sybil conceded, "I think you'd be a very good nun, Alameda. I'm sure it pleases the Lord that you want to serve him so wholly."

Ada twisted the loose threads on her embroidered, pale blue coverlet. Things had changed so much. Now Jon hauled boxes from the factory to the railroad, and her aspiration for the convent felt like a childish toy she should throw away. Her future had always included Naomi, but Naomi was no longer pure. The fact that she hadn't come to Ada to explain indicated a guilty conscience.

But what if it didn't? Her mouth suddenly dry, Ada swallowed, then bit her lip. She winced and touched her mouth with her finger. A smear of blood. She picked up her hand mirror from the side table and examined her lip. The cut was superficial, and she set down the mirror, running her fingers across the ornate bronze frame. Handed down from her father's grandmother, it was her favorite possession, after her Bible of course.

It was selfish of her to obsess about her unfulfilled dreams when something serious was happening to her best friend. Exactly what, Ada didn't know, and what was worse, she didn't want to find out.

CHAPTER TWO

*A*voiding Naomi for the rest of the week was easy, but Ada saw more of Dawn than she had since they'd been in school. On Friday, Dawn surprised her by inviting her to tea on Sunday afternoon. Ada couldn't think of how to decline, and so she accepted. All the way home, she worried how her parents would react to the news. When she told them, her father looked pained, and Sybil raised an eyebrow and said she hoped Ada would be a good influence.

Friday was the day that Ada made extra batches of food and delivered them to elderly and ill members of the congregation. As usual, Michael Donner picked her up in his father's truck. It was Michael's day off from helping his father in the grocery store. He often wore a suit on their excursions, and today was no exception. With his tall, starkly thin form and black Homburg hat, he looked like a well-dressed scarecrow.

As they loaded the food into the truck, Ada told him about Dawn's work with Billy.

"I don't understand why Dr. Graham doesn't do it himself," Michael said, "or have Nurse Ellington assist instead of someone as young and … frivolous as Miss Graham."

"Dawn works with children in the Meatpacking District every week. She wants to be a children's doctor."

"Children should have a good example," he said.

"What do you mean by that?" Ada asked.

He opened the door for her, waited for her to get in, then shut it and walked to the other side. "For one, she doesn't go to church," he said as he climbed into the driver's seat. "For another, the whole town witnessed what happened with her mother. We believed Mrs. Graham and Miss Shoemaker were Christians, but that was a warning to us that 'they are not all Israel who are of Israel.'"

His comment stuck in her mind like a nettle in a stocking. "I don't think it's appropriate to repeat such things."

"It's not gossip, Alameda; it's truth. You would not be aware of it, but Miss Graham's character is hardly exemplary."

The truck jolted over a pothole, and Ada clutched the basket on her lap. "She has always been friendly to me. I'm afraid we won't agree, so let's not discuss her."

Michael was silent long enough for Ada to think the subject was closed. Then, as he parked at the first stop, he turned toward her. "We only need to discuss her if she desires to become friends with you. Remember, bad company corrupts good morals."

Ada thought of the tea invitation. "She was baptized in church like you and I were, so you can't consider her bad company. If I decide to visit her, I don't need your permission."

He looked as though he'd bitten into a crabapple. "Of course not. I merely thought that you, one of the most devout women in Worden, would be wise to consider how your actions reflect on your character and your family's name. You and I know your parents have enough to pray about already."

Flushing, she faced the window. He meant Jon, of course. Michael said such horrid things, but he always had a Bible verse to support his opinion. She was only friends with him because they'd grown up in the same church. Even as she thought it, guilt rushed into her heart. She didn't relent, however, and spoke to him no more than was necessary until they delivered the meals and returned to the Williams' driveway. Then she said, "Perhaps you shouldn't stay for supper tonight."

"Really? Are you unwell?"

"No." She hesitated. "I just don't feel up to company."

"I am sorry to hear that, but may I remind you that our Christian duty, not our emotions, must guide our actions?"

"Please let me out." She looked at the door handle.

He got out of the truck, came around the front without haste, and opened the door for her. "Give my regrets to your parents. I will see you Sunday."

"Yes, good night."

She hurried inside. Roasting chicken and thyme scented the warm air. Sybil emerged from the kitchen before Ada could go to her room.

"Where's Michael?" Sybil demanded.

"I asked him not to eat with us tonight."

"Why? That was ungrateful! He spent all afternoon escorting you around town, and inviting him to supper is the least you can do."

"Is it?" Ada breathed deeply. Here, in the short hallway, facing a photograph of her parents holding her and Jon in their arms after their baptism, she felt at a disadvantage. "What is the most I can do?"

Sybil brushed her hands on her flour-dusted apron. "You know the answer to that. What other prospects has the Lord laid before you in Worden?"

"Do you mean marriage prospects? Remember, I intend to join St. Cecilia's Convent."

"Join St. Cecilia's!" She threw up her hands. "That is a child's fantasy. I thought you'd given that up long ago when you learned about the heresy of the Mass."

Feeling the convent slip from her reach made her want it more. "I've talked with Father O'Connor and studied the matter. I could get past it."

"Could you 'get past' veneration of the Saints, Mary idolatry, superstition, the Pope?"

Ada looked down at the floor. The hardwood would need another mop and wax soon, as Sybil would no doubt point out. "I didn't realize you felt so strongly about it."

"Look at me when you speak, Alameda. I am the minister's wife, and you are the minister's daughter. People look up to us for a reason. To whom much is given, much will be required." Sybil's dark gray eyes filled with icy conviction.

The door to Jon's room opened. Freshly shaven and oozing cologne, Jon saluted them with his pork pie as he passed. His entrance relieved some of the tension, but Ada still felt like a child in her Sunday best caught playing in a mud puddle.

"Jonathon, aren't you staying for dinner?" Sybil asked.

"No, Mother, I'm going out."

"To the Meatpacking District?"

He turned and walked backward as he answered, smoothing his straight, dark brown hair. He and Ada had inherited the rich color from their father, the finer texture from their mother. "Where else? It's closing time at the factory, and Pete and I are meeting our friends there."

"Be careful," Sybil called after him. "'Be not deceived: evil communications corrupt good manners.' 1 Corinthians 15:33."

Ada wondered if Michael and her mother had been talking recently. Maybe it was a coincidence, but Ada felt uneasy that she had received the same sermon as her brother. *She* was supposed to be the good twin.

Taking advantage of her mother's distraction, she strode to her room and shut the door. In a few minutes she would go out again and apologize for leaving so abruptly and asking Michael not to stay. At first the isolation of the room calmed her. Then she noticed a wrinkle in the bedding and had to straighten it. The desk against the wall reminded her of unfinished tasks. She needed to write out invitations to the church's upcoming spring festival. Next to the stack of envelopes, her prayer journal was slightly out of place. She picked it up and flipped to a recent entry.

Dear Heavenly Father, I worry about my brother, for he is surrounded by evil influences at his workplace. I am blessed to spend all my time with those of the church. Yet sometimes I wonder, is the world this small? When I am a nun, I will be safe.

She and Naomi could have been safe together. Perhaps, after all, it was not too late. At St. Cecilia's, Naomi could escape whatever trap she had fallen into. If only Ada's parents were not opposed to the idea. If only God's commandment to honor them included exceptions.

As she put the journal away, resentment pinched her abdomen. She bent forward, pressing her hands to her belly. Her knuckles turned white as her grip tightened. It was a trick she'd developed as a young girl, a way to keep from sinning. Squeeze the flesh and remember that's where Satan tempted.

Formulating an apology, she opened the door and went to find her mother.

♪

After she washed up from supper, Ada practiced past her customary bedtime until her fingers hurt and her neck ached. She felt guilty for not talking to Naomi. The whole week she had tried to suppress her thoughts about her friend, and the effort exhausted her. Now, defeated by her conversation with her mother and the stupid, stupid idea of joining a convent, she had no will to fight the torrent of speculation and self-blame washing over her.

The moon was full, and white light streamed into the room, haunting the walls and furniture with grotesque shadow plays. Ada stared at the ceiling, then shut her eyes, helpless to stop the scenes from unfolding. The alarming buttocks flashed over and over in her head. As sleep seized her with paralyzing fingers, her memory warped into a nightmare.

"It's my birthday," Naomi said as she painted a sensuous line with her finger down the man's face. Exaggerating her movements, she swayed to the bed and sat, then drew her legs onto the mattress.

The man unfastened his tie and wound it in his hands as he approached. His black shoes gleamed with polish.

"Happy birthday." The man dropped his pants and planted his right foot on the bed. His manhood poised above Naomi like an eagle's beak. He circled her neck with his tie and drew her toward him.

Naomi's face purpled. She clawed at the necktie. Tears and spittle ran down her chin. She gurgled, then looked straight into Ada's eyes.

Biting back a scream, Ada lurched awake. Her heart pounded a jagged rhythm. She had imagined Naomi had found a lover, but the dream was so real, she simply knew her friend was unwilling. Even more, she recognized the gleaming black shoes. She had seen them at the entrance to the house, lined neatly next to Naomi's scuffed boots.

They were Dennis Gentle's.

Of course she considered that Naomi's uncle might have been outside at the calving. For that, he would have worn boots and left his shoes inside. And she wondered, uselessly, why would he do such a thing to Naomi when he was courting Edith Templeton? It made no sense, and it made her sick, but it could be no one else.

The nightmare distressed Ada so much that she left her room and sat shivering in the front room as her head throbbed. Not tomorrow—she needed more time to figure out what to say—but Sunday, she would confront Naomi and correct this disturbing situation.

CHAPTER THREE

*M*ichael waited for her outside the church. As he offered his arm to escort her to her pew, she glanced at him. He didn't seem upset, but his small eyes made his face hard to read.

Before she took his arm, she peered down the street at St. Dominic's. The Catholic church was already on its second mass of the day. One of Jon's friends, who worked for the railroad, waved from the tall steps. She looked back—yes, the wave was meant for her brother, who slouched outside the entrance. He returned Pete's greeting with a few gestures she didn't recognize yet felt were improper, especially on the threshold of the house of God.

Without a word, Michael led her to the front pew. He must be displeased with her, Ada decided as she sat next to her mother, although sometimes he made a show of silence before the service.

After Michael joined his family several rows behind, Ada opened her Bible, but she was conscious of his gaze on the back of her head. When she focused her attention on the book in her lap, she blushed. The Song of Songs.

Let him kiss me with the kisses of his mouth.

That was symbolic of Christ's love for the church, Ada reminded herself. Yet she turned quickly to Psalms. Dropping a bulletin to the floor and bending to retrieve it, she sneaked a look at Naomi's family in the back. Naomi's eyes were downcast. She ignored the younger sister tugging on her arm.

Jon snaked into their pew as the organ swelled to life and the congregation rose for the first hymn. Rev. Williams took his place at the pulpit. After the hymn, he read passages from the Old and New Testaments, led them in the Apostles Creed, and expounded on the central verse.

"Jacob I have loved," he said, "but Esau I have hated."

Ada straightened and fixed her gaze on the lectern as she listened to the tale of twins, one elect and one damned, which she had always disliked. Despite her sentiments, she admitted that double predestination was according to God's plan, and his purposes were beyond man's reproach.

She had long ago trained herself complete immobility. Her thighs and feet burned and tingled from her stillness. The urge to move grew from irritation to obsession, but somehow she turned her attention away from the itches and the discomfort of her tailbone against the hard pew. No one else could guess at the internal war she fought with her body. Ada knew only that it was important for her to win, and that as long as she remained motionless, Satan had no hold over her.

Standing for the doxology, her legs spiked with pins and needles. On the final chord, the organist tried and failed to add a bass note on the pedalboard. Gail Keller was not nearly as gifted as her predecessor, but definitely more upright, Ada reminded herself. The stops Gail chose on the organ were always the same. Sometimes Ada wished she could accompany the singing on her violin for a little variety, but that would draw attention away from the text and toward its musical trappings.

Rev. Williams lifted his arms and pronounced the benediction. Before the organist launched into the postlude, he added, "It gives me great pleasure to announce the engagement of Dennis Gentle and Edith Templeton. I would like to invite them to the back of the church so the congregation can congratulate them as they leave."

Ada's stomach turned. She would sooner stick her hand into a fresh cow pie than shake Dennis's hand. "I need some air," she said to Sybil, and fled through the side exit. Leaning against the building, she exhaled noisily and pushed her hair back from her eyes. The slight breeze, though cool, had lost its bitterness. Winter was ending, but Ada felt none of the optimism spring usually brought.

She stood there until cigarette smoke told her the meatpacking group had made it outside and lit up. She walked down the side lawn to the front yard. Young boys dashed around with their coats open while the girls strolled daintily, hanging onto each other's arms and whispering secrets.

Ada's gaze swept past the hard metal courting benches, in easy view of a chaperon. There was Naomi, handing homemade candy to a cluster of children.

No, after all, Ada couldn't confront her. Naomi would have to make the first move. Even as she berated herself for being a coward, she decided to walk home. She saw Jon flirting with Katherine Heath in the center of the meatpacking group. Ada would tell him she was leaving, and he could pass the message to their parents.

As Ada hurried across the lawn, Naomi broke free from the children and hailed her. It was too late to change her path. Ada awkwardly met her friend's eyes and smiled.

Not returning the smile, Naomi grabbed her by the elbow and dragged her down the street. Ada was too surprised to resist.

"What are you doing, Naomi? I have to tell someone I'm leaving."

If anything, Naomi's steps quickened. "Why didn't you come to my birthday party?"

"What?" Further words froze on Ada's tongue. She had never been able to lie.

"You brought a cake, but you didn't leave a note. Why didn't you stay?"

"I ... I had to go home."

"Yesterday I waited almost an hour at the Cow's Head." Naomi stopped. Her eyes were numb and red. Most Saturdays they walked through the Smythes' fields to Cow Lake, named after its vaguely bovine shape and the fact that cattle watered there. The southern end, the "head," had a long dock the local youth liked to swim and fish from.

"I'm sorry," Ada said. "Saturday was—I mean, I was upset on Saturday, and I'm sorry you waited. Your family doesn't have a telephone, so I couldn't call." She blushed. It wasn't a lie, but its implication, that she would have called if she were able, wasn't necessarily true.

"What did I do?" Naomi asked. "Are you angry with me?"

"Should I be?" Ada's voice was rough, and the words scraped her throat as they escaped. "If you were ever in trouble, you should tell me."

"Oh," Naomi whispered. "You saw."

"I don't know what I saw." She gripped Naomi's arm. Naomi flinched, and Ada let go quickly. "Tell me what's going on."

"We can't talk about it here."

"St. Dominic's isn't out yet. Let's go over there." Ada crossed the street. Naomi followed so closely she bumped into Ada when she halted.

Ada hated acting like an examiner, but Naomi stared at her silently, eyes welling up. She wouldn't speak unless Ada forced her. Ada sighed and asked, "Was it your uncle Dennis?"

Naomi covered her face with her hands. When she spoke her voice was tiny, like an orphaned bird calling for its mother. "Yes. He thought he heard something; I think it must have been when you came into the house. I made an excuse for you at dinner so no one would suspect, and lied about the cake ..."

"Has he done it before?"

A nod.

Pressure banded Ada's chest. "Have you told anyone?"

Naomi's hands slipped down so Ada could see her eyes, hazy from pain. "I can't say anything. My family needs his money to survive."

Dennis's arrival had helped the Gentles rise above their financial pinch. Naomi had told her that. But Ada shook her head violently. "No, you don't. The church will help your family."

"You know Pa doesn't take charity. It's different when it's his brother helping out, since we're feeding and lodging him."

"We have to tell someone." She squeezed her friend's bony hands. "We're both witnesses now. They'll have to believe us, and they'll keep him from hurting you."

"Who would? Everyone loves Uncle Dennis. He's the church deacon, and he goes shooting with the sheriff." She clamped Ada's wrists. "My family thinks he's a godsend, and now he's in with the Templetons too."

"I'll tell my father, and he'll talk to the deputy. They'll believe us."

"No!" Naomi's voice climbed half an octave. "If I tell anyone, he'll kill me. He said if I even threaten to tell anyone, he'll kill me."

"Naomi, please." Ada disentangled her fingers from Naomi's. "He doesn't know that I know, correct? I'll go back to church right now and talk to my father."

"No. No! I can't bear for anyone else to know. If it gets out, I can't go to St. Cecilia's."

She took a step back. "You still want to go to the convent?"

"With you! Yes. I need to leave this place."

Ada bit her lip. She wasn't sure their dream could be put together again.

Naomi must have sensed her hesitance. "You still want to go, right?"

"Of course I want to, but I'm not sure it's God's will. My mother reacted badly when I brought it up again." She glanced down the street. "Look, I have to leave. Dawn Graham invited me to tea, and I was going to change first."

Naomi shivered. "Can't I go with you?"

"I don't know. It's not really my decision."

"Please? He and Edith will be over for lunch, and I don't want to be part of their *celebration*." She said the word with bitterness.

The tightness in Ada's chest increased, and she struggled for breath. "I'll call Dawn when I get home and ask."

Naomi hugged her wordlessly. Ada pulled away as soon as she could and hastened down the street. She waved as she passed Jon, not even pausing to see him signal that he understood she was leaving.

When she reached her house, she burst into her room as if surfacing from a deep dive. The feeling of breathlessness didn't leave her as she picked up the phone from its cradle, holding it like an injured animal. Dawn answered and sounded nervous when Ada introduced herself, as if afraid Ada was canceling.

"Of course your friend can come as well," Dawn said when Ada explained her request. "I bought scones and made plenty of sandwiches."

Ada changed from her dress to a long, brown skirt, cream-colored blouse, and dark cardigan, then shrugged on her jacket. She found Naomi waiting outside the front door.

"You should have come in," Ada said.

"I didn't want to bother you. What did she say?"

"You're more than welcome to tea."

Naomi smiled. Her eyes were tired and reminded Ada of faded corn-flowers. They walked in silence. Ada noticed that her friend's pace lagged a little, and she adjusted her own. Ten minutes to the church, fifteen more to the hospital on the edge of the Meatpacking District.

When Naomi spoke, her voice was quiet and emotionless. "Why did you agree to tea with Dawn?"

"I like her. I think it's a shame that people gossip about her family."

"It's not just gossip about what happened with her ma, it's talk about her too. And some of it's true. It's only your good reputation that keeps you from being smeared by association."

"Is that why you don't want to tell anyone about Dennis? Because of your reputation?"

Naomi shook her head. "I told you, he threatened me."

"What did he say, exactly?"

"That he'd kill me. He'd do it, Ada. I know he would. I've seen how much he likes wringing a chicken's neck for supper. Sometimes he just pops the head off."

Ada shivered and rubbed her hands together. She'd recently lost her gloves and hadn't gotten around to knitting another pair. "But something like this can't be hidden. 'For whosoever shall commit any of these abomi-nations, even the souls that commit them shall be cut off from among their people.' Leviticus 18:29. He needs to be punished."

"God will judge him. He will make things right in the afterlife."

"I don't want him to hurt you anymore in this life! We have to tell someone."

"Please promise not to." She spoke rapidly. "Don't tell, not yet. I'll be okay. I've figured out how to avoid him mostly. He's only gotten to me a few times."

Ada stared at her friend.

"Please? Just for now?" Desperation pinched Naomi's face, and Ada's resistance caved.

"Okay, I promise. For now." She clenched her hands together. She wished she could force out the guilt that flooded her over what she had just vowed.

"Oh, thank you." The lines around Naomi's eyes flattened out. Her step gained new vigor. "Look, there's the hospital."

The red brick hospital was one of the oldest buildings in town, although no one remarked on why it had been important to have a hospital before the meatpacking factory went into production. In the West, dangerous occupations were something to be proud of.

The Grahams' house was an adjoining building. Tall above the dark, ice-hard earth, rosebushes rimmed the walkway to the front door. Naomi shrank from an overgrown cane bristling with thorns.

"Come in," Dawn said, opening the door before they were halfway up the walk. "I've already laid out the tea." She grabbed their coats and ushered them into the small living room. The shades were drawn, and the main light was from a brass and crystal chandelier.

Devoid of the knick-knacks and ornaments a wife usually provided, the room yet possessed a feminine fussiness. Its most imposing feature was a tall, gilded mirror next to the fireplace. The carpet looked dingy, although a vacuum was pushed against one of the bookcases.

Dawn seated Naomi and Ada in upholstered chairs and handed them steaming tea in what must have been her mother's china. Pink roses, blue forget-me-nots, and golden ribbons of vines climbed across the bone-white curves of the cups and saucers.

"This is the first time in years I've had girls my age over," Dawn said. "Thank you for coming."

Naomi murmured something polite, but Ada's attention was transfixed by the black-and-white photographs on the mantel. The closest to her showed two young men in uniform, one with the cross of a medic on his helmet and arm. Their resemblance was striking, and Ada guessed they were brothers. The medic was in another, larger photograph, recognizable by his kind expression, despite a full beard. A stretch of beach unrolled behind him as he rested his hands on the shoulders of a small girl in a dress with a muddy hem. A woman posed next to them, looking out to sea as if distracted, but holding a plump starfish up to the camera. The starfish had only four rays. Where the fifth ray should have been, a stump with a clean, straight edge protruded.

"They grow back their arms." Dawn offered a tray of scones and miniature sandwiches to Ada. "Starfish do. I sometimes imagine my mother cut it off, just to see how long it would take to regenerate. She liked to prune things, said it made them grow better."

"She cut it off?" Naomi asked. She held the teacup uneasily.

Dawn chuckled. "Gee, I don't know! I haven't asked my dad because I'm afraid he'll ruin my fantasy. Have you been to the seaside, Ada?"

Ada shook her head and bit into the sandwich. The bread was slightly soggy, the cucumber almost bitter. She set her plate on the coffee table, noting a messy pile of medical texts and papers half hidden between the table legs.

"Dad and I try to go every few years. The ocean is unforgettable. There's so much mystery and power to it, it feels like God." Dawn sank into the chair as Naomi and Ada exchanged looks.

"You mean it reflects God's power?" Ada asked.

"More than that. It's full of ... energy, I guess, the energy of the earth's life. It's a larger reflection of us, if you think of our bodies as miniature oceans. It's no wonder that people use water to symbolize their major beliefs—baptism, destruction, the creation of the world. The earliest story ever written, the Epic of Gilgamesh, was all about a man who is magically able to breathe underwater."

"I don't remember that from the Bible," Naomi said.

"It's not from there! Not everything worth reading is in the Good Book. And not everything in the Good Book is worth reading." She laughed.

"You shouldn't joke about that," Ada said, putting down the sandwich.

"I'm sorry. It's something my dad says, and he's an atheist. He only went to church for my mom. You don't suppose God would strike him down for that, do you?"

The lights went out. Naomi screamed.

CHAPTER FOUR

*T*he room brightened as the central chandelier switched on and a hundred sparkling points lanced across the polished rock crystals.

"Forgive me. I didn't mean to startle you so much." Dr. Graham stood in the doorway, his hand on the light switch. "Dawn knows this is my home examination room, so to speak, and she might have warned you."

"Dad loves playing that trick when I have people over," Dawn said. "He hopes to catch me misbehaving, but he never succeeds."

"Not because you don't misbehave," Dr. Graham said.

Naomi moaned and clutched her stomach. Dr. Graham crossed the room in three strides. He placed a hand on her back.

"Take it easy, honey. Lean forward—there, like that—with your head on your knees." He positioned two fingers at her wrist and looked at his watch. "Tell me what hurts."

Ada hadn't seen Dr. Graham so close since she was a child, as Nurse Ellington had administered her school vaccinations. The beard from the photograph was gone, and his face might have been classed as boyish if not for the dark circles beneath his eyes. He wore glasses, and his short, brown hair thinned at the crown of his head. His build was sturdy and his movements energetic. He had strong legs and a slight belly that rolled down from his firm chest and wide shoulders.

Studying him, Ada couldn't help remembering the scandal of his wife. What must it be like, to love someone who couldn't love you back, at least not in the way you wanted?

"I'm ... fine," Naomi panted. "Just a littly dizzy."

"Take deep, steady breaths," Dr. Graham said. He swung a stethoscope from his neck and listened to Naomi's back as she breathed. He glanced at her untouched plate. "When was the last time you ate?"

"I don't remember."

"Do you know?" he asked, looking at Ada.

25

"No, I'm sorry," she said, her words coming out in a tumble. "I wish I did."

He addressed Naomi again. "Do you mind if I take you to the front and ask you a few questions? Nurse Ellington just came back on shift, and she can be with us the entire time."

"Or I can be," Dawn said. She had come behind Naomi's chair to help steady her. "Would you like that, Naomi?"

"Not this time," Dr. Graham said before Naomi could reply. "Miss Williams, would you please help your friend up? Dawn, perhaps you should get the wheelchair."

"Please don't. I'm fine," Naomi said as Ada took Dawn's place and supported Naomi's arms. Naomi swayed as she stood, and Dr. Graham put a hand to her shoulder. Cringing, she drooped against Ada.

Ada followed Dr. Graham's instructions and guided Naomi down a short corridor to the entrance of the hospital. Dr. Graham led them to an exam room, and Ada helped her friend onto the raised pallet. A minute later, the rail-thin Nurse Ellington joined them. The room was crowded and stifling, and itchy perspiration beaded Ada's forehead.

"Out now, everyone but Sara," Dr. Graham said. "Miss Williams, would you wait with Dawn until I determine whether Miss Gentle should return home?"

"How long will the exam take?" Ada asked. Sybil expected her home within the hour.

"Fifteen minutes if she cooperates." His tone of voice was kindly. Ada couldn't imagine anyone being uncooperative when encouraged by that voice. "If that's a problem, Dawn could see her home, but I think she might prefer a close friend."

"It's not a problem. I can stay."

"Thank you." He winked at her before turning to Naomi.

Ada's stomach contracted, and her heartbeat sounded loud in her ears. She rejoined Dawn in the sitting room but couldn't concentrate on their conversation. Her imagination invented a thousand scenarios where Dennis hurt Naomi … inside. She shut her eyes, but the images only grew more disturbing.

She checked the time again and apologized to Dawn for her inattention.

"Don't worry about it," Dawn said, "or about her. My dad is the best. Well, except for his shocking entrances, which I doubt he'll repeat."

Twenty minutes later, Nurse Ellington opened the door and ushered Naomi into the room.

"It's time she went home, girls," Sara said, then turned on her heel.

Naomi kept her eyes down. Dawn exchanged a look with Ada before disappearing into the kitchen. A moment later she was back with a paper bag, which she handed to Ada. "It's the leftover sandwiches," she said. "For

Naomi, in case her dizziness was from lack of nutrition."

Ada thanked her, took the bag, and turned to her friend. "Are you ready?"

Naomi tipped her chin up and clasped Ada's free hand. Her palm was cold and moist.

"Thank you for the tea," Ada told Dawn. "Please thank Dr. Graham for his help."

"I hope you'll come again," Dawn said. "Perhaps when Naomi is feeling better."

Ada said nothing as they walked back, and Naomi maintained the silence. Naomi's steps grew slower and slower as they approached the Gentles' house. When they reached the poplar and pine trees lining the drive, she stopped altogether. She dropped to her knees and clenched the bottom of Ada's brown skirt. Her spine rose and fell with silent sobs.

"I'm pregnant." Her voice was tight and high. "Dr. Graham thinks I'm a couple of months along. He wants me to tell my parents."

Ada stared. The bag of food thumped on the ground. At last a thought crystallized. "We have to tell your family now. There will be no hiding it."

"There is, there is! The doctor told me about a place—Haven House— where I can go when the time gets close."

Ada swallowed. Her thoughts spun. "What about the baby?"

"I'm giving it up. I don't want to keep it. It's like poison spreading inside me. I wish ... I wish I could get rid of it now."

"That would be murder!"

She wiped her face on her sleeve and looked up. "Please don't hate me. I know it's wrong, but God would forgive me. If I were such a child, I wouldn't want to be born. At St. Cecilia's I would pray for its soul every day."

"You mustn't think like that." She searched for something else to say. "If God doesn't want it to be born, he will take it early."

"I wish he would, before I start to show. I can't bear my parents knowing. They will be so ashamed. My life is over."

Ada bent to pick up the sandwiches. Her muscles felt wooden, her body numb. "How early can Dr. Graham arrange for you to go to the House?"

Naomi stood. Her shoulders stooped. "Not until closer to the end, in four or five months. You'll be eighteen by then."

"Four months." The timing would be tight. Many women looked unmistakably pregnant at six months. Since it was Naomi's first, however, it might not be too obvious.

"You won't go to the convent without me, will you?"

Ada shook her head.

"Then nothing's changed. There's just this ... thing," she said as she touched her belly, "but it will be over soon."

Ada's stomach coiled further. It remained knotted and sour as she said goodbye to Naomi and headed home. Her steps dragged, even though she knew she ought to hurry, and she rested her head against the door before she went inside.

"Alameda, is that you?" Sybil called from the kitchen. "You're later than you said you'd be."

"Naomi had a dizzy spell," Ada said, going to her. "I walked her home after we left the Grahams."

Sybil lifted a small bag of red potatoes and plopped them into the sink. "She has not looked well to me for some time. I wonder if there is some secret sin she has left unconfessed. Physical afflictions are often born of a spiritual malady."

The taste of iron and salt filled Ada's mouth, and she realized she had bitten her tongue. "Shall I peel the potatoes?"

"Yes, thank you, my angel."

Ada scrubbed the ruddy, rough skin of the potatoes. The anxiety in her belly deepened into dread. Her hands shook as she worked, and the knife slipped and cut into the middle flesh of her finger. A channel of scarlet flowed down her palm and onto the pale surface of the skinned tuber. She dropped the potato and knife and turned on the faucet to clean the cut. The water turned red and then pink. As Ada watched the blood flow from her finger, the knot in her stomach eased.

She kept thinking of Dr. Graham. His wink disturbed her in a strange way. She wasn't sure why, but she wanted to see him again. She knew Naomi hadn't told him everything he needed to know. Pushing aside her misgivings, she planned how to see him tomorrow.

♬

If the hospital waiting room hadn't been empty, Ada would have turned around and left. Even so, she hesitated before ringing the bell. Half a minute later Nurse Ellington appeared behind the desk.

"What can I do for you?"

"I need to speak with Dr. Graham, please."

The nurse checked her book and frowned. "You aren't on the schedule, but I can get you started on your paperwork while you wait."

"You don't have to do that," Ada said quickly. "I didn't come about myself. I just need to tell the doctor something in private."

Nurse Ellington gave her a studied look, and Ada tried not to blush. "He's with a patient right now, but if you're willing to wait, I will tell him you're here. Come with me." She led Ada to an examination room and shut the door.

Remembering that the doctor had chosen the stool as his seat when he'd helped Naomi, Ada perched on the edge of the examination table. An eye chart was pasted to the door, and jars with large labels were organized on the counter.

What was she doing here? He wouldn't want to talk about Naomi. He probably wasn't allowed to. Ada put her hand over her heart. It throbbed like a bird about to take flight.

The door swung open. Ada caught her breath and gripped the pallet.

With a smile, Dr. Graham held out his hand. "Miss Williams, what a pleasant surprise to see you."

Ada shook his hand. His fingers were warm and strong, and their heat lingered. She felt the light hair on the back of his knuckles as the shake ended and their fingers slipped apart. "Good afternoon."

"Did Miss Gentle make it back to her house yesterday without a problem?"

She nodded, waited a beat, and said, "She told me what's wrong with her, and that there's a place you can send her to soon."

He sat on the stool and sighed. "You have to realize something. The real danger to your friend is malnutrition. If she doesn't start taking better care of herself, she and the fetus won't make it to Haven House."

"You can't be serious."

Behind the dark frames of his glasses his blue-gray eyes were tired but insistent. "I am serious. She needs to tell her parents. Then I can work with them to keep her safe and healthy."

"She'll never tell them." A thought struck her. "You can't say anything to them, can you?"

"She's eighteen and has a right to privacy that I cannot breach. But if you truly are her friend, persuade her to change her mind."

"I wish she would tell someone," she said, "someone else, everything."

"Everything?" He bent forward.

Heat prickled Ada's neck, and she reminded herself he was a doctor, used to talking freely about such subjects. "I don't know what she told you, but it's important you send her to Haven House soon." She fingered the bills in her jacket pocket that she'd been saving for St. Cecilia's. "If it would help, I have some money."

He shook his head. "It wouldn't help. Unfortunately, your friend isn't the only young lady in trouble. I called Haven House, and Naomi is on their waiting list, but it is unlikely they can admit her early."

"But this is … a special circumstance." Ada's mouth dried.

"Explain."

"It's not her fault that she's in the family way. She was unwilling."

"I feared as much." He looked into her eyes, but she glanced away. "She wouldn't confirm it or tell me who the man was. Do you know?"

29

She twisted her fingers in her lap. The secret stuck like a piece of food in her throat. "I can't say."

"Do you want him to be free to hurt other young women?"

Ada thought of Naomi's younger sisters and then of Miss Templeton, who just a few months ago was considered a spinster because no one in town was good enough for her, and now she was to be married this summer. "Do you think he'll hurt someone else?"

"From what I know of similar cases, I believe he will, especially if he gets away with what he did to Naomi. If you know anything, you should tell me. Officer Reynolds is a good friend of mine."

Any hope she had slipped away like a penny from frozen fingers. Dennis went shooting with the sheriff. "I can't. I promised not to say anything. Please trust me—the sooner she can go to Haven House, the better."

"Of course I will do my best to get her in as soon as a room becomes available, but that shouldn't be our goal. If she were a minor, I would be required to report this to the police. I wish I could now."

"I wish you could too," she said, and allowed herself to meet his gaze. Her heart hammered. "I'll try to get her to see sense."

"Thank you."

She wanted to say more, tell him that it wasn't just embarrassment that kept Naomi from revealing her secret. Her throat constricted, and she licked her lips.

Seeming to sense her indecision, he moved the stool closer. It scraped against the floor. "Whatever you or she tells me, I will believe you, and I will do my best to bring whoever it is to justice."

She had to leave before her resolve broke. What was it about the doctor that made her feel so powerless? She slid to her feet and made her farewell. Her upper leg and groin muscles ached as if they'd been tensed too long. She felt vaguely ashamed of the sensation.

At home, she replayed her interaction with the doctor as she prepared supper. Was he right—would Dennis hurt someone else? She wished there were someone else she could ask, someone who wasn't an atheist, someone who knew Dennis Gentle.

Jon.

She cornered him after the meal, knocked at his door before he had a chance to go out with his friends. Comb in hand, he let her in.

"What is it, Ada? Do you want to go out with us tonight?"

"No. I need to know something, and please don't laugh at me."

"I won't." He worked the comb at the back of his head to create a central part. "What's the matter?"

She clasped her hands behind her. "What drives a man to hurt someone else? And do you think, once he has a means to express whatever it was that caused him to do so, he would hurt anyone else?"

"You're going to have to repeat that more clearly, unless you're talking about original sin, in which case either of our parents would be a better conversational partner."

"I'll try," she said. She watched him apply gel to his hair, puffing the front of his hair and accentuating the back ducktail. "You know after marriage a man has certain … privileges with his wife."

"You mean sex."

She flushed. "And I've heard it's sometimes hard for people, before they're married, not to desire those privileges."

"It's hard for everyone on the planet, except for you it seems."

"What if a person in that situation," she persevered, "say a man, even a Christian, did something about his desires with someone who couldn't really say no—"

Jon flung the comb onto his desk. "Has he done something to you? I'll kill him if he has. I'll drop that hypocrite right in his father's shop."

She was unprepared for his sudden snap to attention, the anger that bolted through his eyes. "What are you talking about?"

"Michael, the bastard. Has he hurt you?"

His oily hands were on her shoulders, and he didn't let go until she shook her head. "I wasn't talking about Michael. For goodness' sake, Jon! He'd never do that."

"I don't know about that. Wolves are safer in sheep's clothing than anything else."

His statement troubled her. Wouldn't God protect his flock? Yet somehow Dennis had been elected deacon after being in Worden a slim six months. "This is a hypothetical situation. Since you brought up Michael, say he and I were engaged to be married, and he couldn't wait until we were married to … you know. Would he have the same type of trouble after we were married too?"

"Are you thinking of marrying him?"

"No! That's not what I'm talking about at all."

"Good, because he's a wimp. Counts money all day, maybe throws around a few sacks of bread. If you were interested in men, I could introduce you to a few who are worth several of him."

"Well, I'm not." The words took her by surprise, and she wondered if she had just lied. If she wasn't interested in men, then why did the doctor intrigue her so much? "Thank you for your lack of help." Trying to hide her confusion, she headed for the door.

"Wait a minute." His tone changed. She looked over her shoulder at him. "If you're asking me why some men fornicate, as it's known in this house, it's because it feels good and it's part of human nature, which God created. If you're asking why they commit adultery, it's either because they aren't getting enough at home or they've fallen for someone else. But don't assume that because someone isn't a virgin that they're a sexual monster. You can ask your friend Dawn about that one."

Ada reached for the knob and missed.

In her room, she couldn't calm the thoughts and images that washed over her. Gasping in their constant flow, she focused on taking deep, regular breaths. Jon hadn't answered her question, but he had sparked a mental storm in her head. She knew she should think about Naomi's situation, try to discover a way to help her, but she couldn't help replaying her time with Dawn, and then, inexorably, with the doctor.

She recalled Dr. Graham's kind eyes, his steady manner, his handshake. Sitting on the bed, she shrugged off her shirt and slip. The low light sallowed the curve of her belly. Slowly she lay back until her head sank into the pillow.

She closed her eyes and remembered how warm Dr. Graham's hand had been. As she imagined his vibrant fingers skimming up her arm, her heartbeat jumped. She unfolded her fingers as if to touch him and teased them across her other arm, from her soft palm to her armpit, then across her chest.

Thy two breasts are like two young roes that are twins of a gazelle. The verse came unbidden to her head. She reached for the lamp and clicked off the light. Dr. Graham—George—wouldn't quote scripture. He would touch her breasts, perhaps even kiss them. Then his hands would move down, across the waves of her ribs, the crest of her hips. Her breath caught as her fingers slid under the elastic band of her skirt.

She circled the inside of her thighs, not daring to go farther. But she would let him touch her wherever he wanted. She imagined his weight on her body, his breath on her neck. His hands sliding up her leg, into her groin. Her back arched against the bed, and she bent her legs.

She groaned as a delicate feeling of pleasure blossomed in her center. Her feet curled into the blanket. Even as the sensation grew, other emotions flooded her and dulled the swell of pleasure. This wasn't good enough. She wasn't good enough. Her hand fell away, empty and wet.

As the throbbing faded, disappointment and guilt took over. She sat upright and turned on the light again. She felt cold. This was wrong. Didn't Jesus say, "Whoever looks at a woman to lust after her has already committed adultery with her in his heart"? The verse certainly applied to looking at a man.

She wiped her hand on a pair of dirty stockings, dressed, and opened the Bible on her desk. She flipped to Matthew and found instead, "If your right hand causes you to sin, cut it off and cast it from you, for it is more profitable for you that one of your members perish, than for your whole body to be cast into Hell."

She couldn't cut off her hand, but she remembered the potato's pale flesh stippled with pink from the watered-down blood of her finger. Pain deepened into action, and she dressed and crept to the kitchen. She opened the silverware drawer and took out a fillet knife. Almost as an afterthought, she carefully unfolded a clean, dark rag from the cabinet as well.

Light leaked from the bottom of the door to her father's study, but Ada knew it was Sybil there who labored on the sermon. A horrible, dead feeling curled her stomach as she went into her room. She turned on her bedside lamp and placed the knife and rag on the table. Again, she removed her shirt and slip. Spreading the rag on her lap, she poised the knife above her belly. She exhaled and held her body still.

The first cut was shallow, experimental. A thin slit of red stained the metal blade. She gritted her teeth and tried again.

She drew the sharp edge of the knife along her flesh and see-sawed it in the opposite direction when the blade ran out, like she was playing the violin. Bright notes of blood dropped on her abdomen. Absorbed by the smooth rocking motion of the knife, she hardly felt pain, and she stopped only when the blood threatened to spill onto her comforter. She wiped it away with the rag. She had thought she would feel cleaner, holier, but she did not. Tears rose in her eyes. She rubbed down the knife blade and hid it beneath the underclothes in her wardrobe.

CHAPTER FIVE

On Saturday she met Naomi, and they walked to the Cow's Head together. The sloping brown mountains revealed fresh green below their foggy sides. Frost glittered like broken glass in the shade at the edge of the meadow, but soft, new leaves unfurled from the willow branches that dipped into the lake.

Inching alongside the shore in a rowboat, Old Man Keller and his grandson cast fishing lines into the water. Ada imagined the spring sun waking the sluggish bass from their murky hiding places. Naomi peered down the long dock.

"When are you going to learn to swim, Ada?"

She tugged the edges of her coat together. "Never. The water's freezing, and it's dirty."

Naomi bent down and rippled the water with her fingertips. "It's not that cold. We could wade at least."

"No, thank you." Ada looked pointedly at three brown cattle milling near the water. One lifted its tail to release grassy feces.

Naomi shrugged, a subtle gesture beneath her oversize coat. "Maybe it's the last time I'll get to enjoy the water. If I'm still here in the summer, I won't be able to swim."

Ada swallowed. By the time the weather warmed up, Naomi would really be showing. She needed to get out of here, and soon.

Naomi unlaced her boots. "I've been thinking, what happens after I go?"

"You'll give up the baby and join St. Cecilia's."

"You really think the convent would take me?"

"Of course. I'll ask Father O'Connor to make sure—discreetly."

Naomi tugged the boot from her right foot. "So we'll meet each other there, and become novices together?"

"Don't put your foot in there, Naomi! It's too cold. I want to go; you know that."

Holding the boot, Naomi balanced on one foot. "I won't come back to Worden," she said. "Not while *he's* still here. And I won't go to the convent without you."

"You might have to," Ada said. "Besides, he'll probably leave after he marries Miss Templeton. The railroad is always moving him."

"Not likely. He said he intends to be the mayor of Worden, soon as Mr. Templeton's term is up."

Ada grabbed the boot and squatted beside Naomi. Her hands shook as she forced Naomi's foot into the woolly interior. "You have to take care of yourself. And your baby."

"Why?" Naomi jerked her leg away. "I know why you want me to go. You can't stand to think about what my uncle does to me. You want me far away, where you'll never have to see me again!"

"You know that's not true." Ada kept her eyes on the ground. Blades of grass had erupted from the soil like miniature emerald spears. She wished she could snatch a handful and jab them into her heart, just to stop the guilty pounding.

"If it's not true, then say you'll go with me. You have to. We have to go to the convent together because Dennis knows."

"He knows?" Ada's vision snapped to Naomi, and she stood. "He knows what?"

Naomi stepped back, splashing into the shallows. "He knows you know. He guessed somehow, and I was afraid to lie about it."

"What did you tell him? How could you?" Panic took her over. She shook Naomi by her shoulders until Naomi's lank, blond hair whipped back and forth like jump rope.

"Please, stop! Ada!" Tears softened Naomi's dry, red eyes.

Ada let her go. Stricken, she sank to her knees. Wet soil patched her dress and bled through to her stockings. "Forgive me, Naomi. I'm so sorry. I didn't mean to hurt you. Please, please say you forgive me."

Naomi wiped her eyes with her arm. "If you're sorry, then don't tell anyone."

Ada stood and brushed flakes of mud from her dress. Her belly ached from her still-healing cuts. "I—I don't know." The secret was too heavy. She couldn't breathe beneath it.

"If you don't," Naomi said, "he said he'd find you. He'll find something to persuade you. That's what he said. Promise me, Ada."

"I already promised for now. Once we go to the convent, though, I have to say something."

Naomi grasped her shoulders, and even through her jacket Ada felt her fingers dig in. "You can't. I already said he'll find us. Besides that, I can't bear to think how people would laugh that I ran away to a nunnery!"

Ada looked past her to the lake. The rowboat was past earshot, but she could still distinguish the two figures. "But he might try to hurt someone else. I've been thinking, what about Miss Templeton?"

Naomi's wind-chapped cheeks tightened, and she dropped her arms. "What about her?"

"Shouldn't we warn her about him?"

"She never cared to listen to me," Naomi said, "because I don't wear the latest fashions. Seems like all she ever wanted was a husband with ambition and money. She's got one at last."

"I could tell her."

"Tell her what?" Naomi's tone turned fierce. "Anything you come up with she'd ask how you know. She might even say you want him for yourself. Girls like them don't listen. We learned that years ago."

"But ..." Ada smeared a tuft of grass into the mud with her shoe.

"But nothing. You can't say nothing. He'll ask if I made you promise. If you don't, he'll kill us. He said he'd find a way even if he got arrested."

Reluctantly, Ada nodded. She didn't dare correct Naomi's grammar, which occasionally slipped into vernacular. The subject was too serious.

"You have to say it out loud," Naomi insisted.

"I promise."

"Good! I know you can't lie, so there's an end to it." Her eyes dulled, losing their fire, and she brushed her hand across Ada's shoulder. "Thank you."

Ada wished she didn't feel like running away screaming.

"I'm tired," Naomi said. "Will you help me home?"

Ada took her arm. Naomi leaned against her as they labored toward the Gentles' property. Her breaths rasped in Ada's ear.

"I'm sorry," Naomi said after a few minutes. "I feel so weak. Dr. Graham said I might."

Just hearing his name made Ada's pulse quicken. "Are you going to see him again?"

"He wants me to, said I don't have to pay, but I better not. My ma's worried about me. She's already watching me too close."

Not closely enough, if she hadn't spotted her brother-in-law's abuse. Ada frowned.

"Frankly, I don't want to see him," Naomi continued. "He kept asking me questions, like he was the police or something. The only time I want to hear from him is if it's about the House. I told him to call you about it, and you'd let me know."

"Oh." Her face heated as she pictured the ringing phone, Sybil's puzzled questions about why the doctor was calling, her scattered explanation. She imagined his voice, intimate through the phone line, directed solely at her.

"It only makes sense," Naomi said. "We don't have a phone, and you're helping me with everything anyway. I thought maybe you could tell my parents after I left, so they don't try to stop me."

"You want *me* to tell them?"

"I can't bear to." She lowered her head. "They'll be so ashamed to know even part of the truth. Maybe you could think of something else to say, so they wouldn't have to find out. Maybe someone your mom's relatives know needs a nanny all of a sudden."

"I can't lie. Didn't you just say that?"

"Yes, I know, but you could work around it." Her hands trembled. "I hope someday they'll forgive me."

Even though it probably wouldn't come for months, Ada thought about the doctor's phone call. Every time the telephone rang, she jumped up and listened in case Sybil summoned her. She wanted to see the doctor again, or simply hear his voice. She did not repeat her fantasy of him. Jon said that lust was part of human nature, but they'd been taught that human nature was broken. Still, there was nothing wrong with asking the doctor when he thought the House would be ready, to save her nerves the anxiety of waiting for his call.

As she finished scripting the invitations for the church's spring festival, she thought of the perfect excuse to visit him. Although her interactions with Dawn were regular, they were brief, as both concentrated on their tasks at hand. Dawn finished before Ada, so there was usually little time for chitchat. Ada had been planning to return Dawn's invitation to tea with an invitation to the spring festival. She could have passed it to Dawn at the Smythes, but now she thought of a better opportunity.

On Friday, she convinced Michael to drop her by the hospital. She soothed his mood and stopped potential questions by making sure he knew he would be welcome at dinner afterward.

She marched toward the hospital with confident steps but trailed to a halt as soon as she passed through the door. No one was at the desk, but Ada merely looked at the bell without ringing it. The clock behind the counter ticked loudly. She hadn't noticed how loud it was last time. She shifted her basket to one arm and put two fingers to her throat to check her pulse. It was much faster than the clock.

"Miss Williams, have you been waiting long? Did you ring the bell?"

He came through the doorway, drying his hands with a towel that he discarded into a bin behind the desk.

She dropped her arm to her side. "No, I've just arrived. I brought you— and Dawn—some dinner, as thanks for helping Naomi."

"I wish she'd come in for a checkup. Is she taking better care of herself?"

"I hope so. I talked with her about it." She set the basket on a chair to hide her face. Now that she was here, she didn't want to discuss Naomi or Haven House. "I brought chicken and biscuits and a salad and apple cake for dessert. I hope you like it."

The smile that spread across his face made all her work and secrecy worthwhile. "I'm not the most deserving recipient of such kindness, but I'm certainly one of the most grateful. Dawn and I eat a lot of sandwiches." He rubbed his belly. "It smells heavenly."

"I like cooking," she said. She envisioned him sitting down to a supper of scraps. It was too sad.

"Yes, I've heard about your Friday trips to the elderly and infirm." He came around the desk. "You're a regular visiting angel. Dawn is attempting to follow your example for the Meatpacking District, but instead of cooking she visits Donner's Grocery."

"It's nothing."

"It's not nothing. We need more people like you in Worden, Miss Williams."

"We need far better people than I," she said. Her face reddened under his praise. "Is Dawn home?"

"She's visiting a patient down the street. She shouldn't be long. Would you like to wait for her at the house?"

"Oh no, I couldn't." The idea of herself in his living room, serving him dinner on a tray, smashed in the awkwardness of reality. "I'd better go." She picked up the basket, then thrust it into his hands. "There's one more thing in here. For Dawn, but you're welcome to come as well of course."

"What is it?"

"An invitation to the church spring festival. It's held at the Town Hall. I do hope," her mouth quivered as she realized how old-fashioned she sounded, like a stuffy character from the books her mother allowed her to read, "I mean, I hope you'll come."

"Whether I do or not, thank you for asking."

His look was so kind, it hurt.

CHAPTER SIX

*M*ichael found her at the Baked Goods table. "Are there any waltzes scheduled for tonight?" he asked, sliding a program across the wooden surface and highlighting a word with his finger.

"No, only jigs, mixers, and reels," Ada replied. "My father took your concerns about indecent dancing seriously. I'll miss playing my favorite waltz."

His finger drooped. "My letter recommended that waltzes be reserved for courting or engaged couples, not that they be excluded. I was hoping you would be free to dance this year."

She blinked. "I'm playing with Mrs. Keller, as usual."

"Then I'm sorry to lose you as a partner." He pocketed the program. "If you baked that cake, I'll buy a slice."

As Ada served it to him, she watched the door. No one had entered the Town Hall in the last fifteen minutes. Rev. Williams had given the speech Sybil had written and blessed the evening's activities. In another ten minutes Mrs. Smythe and Gail Keller would start the recital with a song. Would Dawn arrive before then? Would she come at all? Would her father? Ada felt sick from anticipation, but she thought she would go crazy if the doctor didn't attend.

On one side of the hall, tables were topped with handcrafts, preserves, and pies. In the midst of judging, Mrs. Donner and Sybil consulted over the entries. On the opposite side Naomi served punch and tended the refreshments. She no longer tried to meet Ada's eyes. Ada had smiled and waved to her earlier, but that was all. She hated the guilty feelings slithering inside her stomach whenever she looked at Naomi.

Jon was outside, smoking. Ada knew because Michael had told her Jon was buying packs from the store again. Michael had probably told Sybil as well, although Ada hadn't cared to find out. For once her brother's irregular vice didn't bother her. She had too many other things weighing on her mind …

… Like the fair-haired man who propped himself against the upright piano. Next to him, Edith Templeton laughed and teased the ribbons of her new hat. He curled a finger in her dark hair. How could he act so charming when the girl he had wronged glared at him across the room? Even Mayor Templeton, one of the sternest people Ada knew, smiled and clapped him on the shoulder.

A familiar laugh drew her attention. Dawn danced into the room and deposited a plate of cookies onto Ada's table.

"I baked them myself," she said with a wink.

"If you believe that, then believe that I helped her," Dr. Graham said as he came up behind his daughter.

A wide grin spread across Ada's flushed face as she met his eyes for an instant. "Did you?"

"No," Dawn said. "I bought them from Donner's Grocery. But at least I took them out of the tin."

Rev. Williams joined the group and shook Dr. Graham's hand. "I haven't seen you at a church function in many years, George. Welcome."

His look was wry. "Thank you, Silas. Don't worry; it's only a temporary lapse in my judgment."

Dawn grabbed her father's arm. "You can chastise him later, Reverend," she said, then led Dr. Graham toward the chairs set up in front of the make-shift stage. They lingered by the piano to say hello to the mayor. Ada's skin prickled as she watched the doctor shake Dennis's hand and flash his genuine, caring smile.

As Mrs. Smythe and Gail took their places for the first number, Ada sat in the back row. She divided her attention between the performers and the doctor, who sat restlessly at the edge of the crowd. Had he come to the spring festival because she asked him or as a thank you to her for the basket of food? Perhaps he wanted to check on Naomi. Ada hoped he would catch the rift of tension between her and her uncle. Dennis had patted Naomi's head once in passing, and she remained glued to her chair as if his touch anesthetized her.

Dr. Graham was an easy diversion to that situation. Ada allowed herself to stare, drinking him in like the special mead the Kellers sometimes shared for the holidays. His ears were rather large, although they fit the leonine proportions of his head and body. His suit fit him well, but it needed a better pressing. She imagined ironing his shirt, washed clean of his scent but still redolent of his presence. Doing chores for him would be an honor, not an obligation. Suddenly his eyes met hers, jolting her from the daydream. She glanced away in embarrassment.

When she had gathered herself enough to look about again, she realized that the doctor was observing the audience as minutely as she observed him. His eyes flicked from Naomi, hedged about by her sisters, to the other rows of chairs.

Had he sniffed out Naomi's uncle? Ada's stomach twisted, and she couldn't help but turn toward Dennis. Eyes closed, he leaned back to enjoy the music. His eyes opened wide, however, when it was Edith's turn to sing. Edith had a pleasant, high voice, trained under the careful tutelage of Mrs. Smythe. She beamed at Dennis as she sang "I'm Looking Over a Four-Leaf Clover," and Ada was struck by fresh guilt. Dennis was not a four-leaf clover, and no matter what Naomi said, it was Ada's Christian duty to warn Edith about him. But first she had to perform onstage.

As the audience clapped, Ada went to the Baked Goods table and took her violin out of its case beneath her chair. She checked her tuning and skated a lump of resin across her bow. Only one more presentation, and then it was her turn to end the show.

Jim Reeves read from a slim book of poetry. Jim was the only meat-packer to attend the festival, and he was the only one of the group that Ada thought was not a dangerous influence on her brother. Volunteering to read Keats for the evening's entertainment showed how unusual he was, as many of the factory workers couldn't even read.

Halfway through the poem, his narration stumbled. He wiped his fore-head, which was peppered with perspiration, and read on. He mixed up his words. After another botched sentence, he hurried to his seat. Ada hadn't thought he would have trouble with nerves. Was he not feeling well? No time to analyze; it was her turn.

She walked to the front. Once she was onstage, she didn't look anyone in the eye. Instead, she breathed a prayer to calm herself. Then she positioned the violin at her chin and began. She had practiced the Franko cadenza from Mozart's third violin concerto hundreds of times. It was the last com-position Miss Passerini had taught her before she died.

Miss Passerini, Jewish-Italian, was a self-proclaimed gypsy who had come to town, laid out her hat on Main Street, and performed. When Ada heard her playing, she begged her parents to let her learn the violin. Miss Passerini had agreed to teach one lesson, but after that lesson, she stayed for eight years. She joked that Worden was the perfect place to die; all she had to do was follow the slaughtered cattle to their maker.

Remembering her teacher, Ada faltered. She blinked away tears, at last experiencing the ranging emotions Miss Passerini had encouraged her to channel. Ada preferred her music like mathematics, with clear tonality, precise dynamic changes, and logical musical phrasing. Miss Passerini had worked hard to bring out Ada's passion and spontaneity, what she called her Dionysian side.

Although Ada was careful not to look at Dr. Graham, her body knew where he was. She faced her instrument in his direction and steadied herself, regaining her confidence. As she played, she felt strangely released from musical strictures. She darkened the cheerful tones of the cadenza. She dug deep into the dissonances and daringly changed a few of the harmonies to suit her mood. Allowing the sound to resonate in the hall, she stretched out the silences. Her focus and breathing intensified as she neared the end of the piece. She sped her fingers and bow in arpeggios with double stops and settled into the trills with frantic energy that climaxed at the G major resolution.

The applause caught her off guard. She smiled and curtseyed and quickly left the stage. As she took her seat, she noticed Jim rush from the room and Dr. Graham follow him out. Sadness replaced her exhilaration as she wondered if he had even paid attention to her performance.

From the stage, Sybil encouraged everyone to buy goodies and prepare for contest winners to be announced. Ada estimated she had half an hour before she was needed for the dance music. Pushing aside her disappointment in the doctor, she concentrated on her other goal for the evening. Catching Edith alone proved harder than she had anticipated, but strangely enough, it wasn't because Edith was so popular. Instead, Ada couldn't escape her duties at the Baked Goods table.

"You played so well!" Dawn said as she paid for a wedge of carrot cake. "I bet you could play professionally in a symphony or something."

She appreciated Dawn's compliment and would have said so, but Mrs. Lamm quickly sidelined the conversation.

"A Christian would be sorely tested as a performer," she said, "especially a Christian woman. Homemaking should be your focus, Alameda." She ordered the last of Mrs. Donner's petits fours.

"Ada doesn't want to be a homemaker," Jon said, briefly resting his hand on Ada's shoulder and capturing a few sweets by sleight of hand. "She wants to sing chants at St. Cecilia's Convent."

"You're not converting to Catholicism, now, are you, Missy?" Old Mrs. Keller asked with a sniff. "'Twould be a scandal for a good Protestant girl, especially when she's the minister's daughter." She handed Ada a five-dollar bill. "I'll take some of the toffee."

Ada stacked the candy on a plate, wrapped it in cellophane, and presented it to her. "If there were a Lutheran convent nearby, Mrs. Keller, I assure you I would join it instead."

"Even the Lutherans don't have a proper understanding of the Lord's Supper," Michael said, edging into line. "Consubstantiation seems a compromise between the Catholic error and truth."

Jon made a face at him that only Ada could see. She noted the cookies her twin hadn't quite concealed in his napkin.

"Jon, dear brother, would you please watch the booth for a moment? Then you will have a chance to sit down and enjoy your dessert." Not giving him a chance to argue, she bolted toward the powder room, where Edith Templeton had just disappeared.

She walked to the mirror and pretended to smooth her hair, peeking at Edith's reflection next to her. Edith powdered her nose, touched up her lipstick, and checked the seam on her stockings.

Assured no one else was in the room, Ada gave a half-hearted smile. "I never congratulated you on your engagement, did I, Edith?"

"No," Edith said flatly, "you didn't."

She blushed but refused to lose her nerve. "That's because I worry your fiancé isn't the gentleman he claims to be. I only bring it up because—and please forgive me for interfering, but I want the best for you—I have seen him mistreat people. And once he … he kicked Ham, the Gentles' dog." Naomi had told her that last bit.

Edith stopped primping and turned to Ada. "You want the best for me? What a virtuous girl you are. What else do you feel compelled to tell me?"

"I—I've heard that he acts inappropriately with other girls, even since you've been courting."

"You've seen? You've heard?" Edith tossed her head, bouncing the ribbons on her hat. "You've imagined, more like! I've always thought you were naïve, but now it's clear you're just stupid. I think I'll tell Dennis what you said, and perhaps he will see fit to talk with the elders. You should certainly know what bearing false witness means." She strode to the door, but Ada flung herself in front of it.

"Please don't tell him! I only wanted to warn you. Even though we're not close friends, you deserve to know what kind of a man—"

"Let me out, you meddling ninny."

"I'm sorry," Ada babbled, moving aside. "Please don't tell him. Just … be careful."

"Oh, I'll tell him," Edith said, opening the door. "You can be sure of that, Alameda Williams."

When she was gone, Ada sank to the floor. Knees to her chest, she pinched her calves and thighs, but it was like trying to scratch an itch with a feather. And any second someone else might enter the room.

She stood and locked herself inside a stall.

She had hoped Dr. Graham would come to the festival, and she had prepared herself for that possibility. With unsteady hands she extracted a small bundle from her purse. She unwrapped the cloth she had sheathed around a paring knife and set it aside.

Her shirt was a delicate ivory edged with lace, and she didn't want to mar it, so she hitched up her skirt and pulled down her tights. A just-closed path of red showed her where to cut. The paring knife was a little dull, and she hated how she had to press it into her skin to draw blood. Her stomach knotted at the pain.

She drew another line of life, then another, and at last felt some relief. She hated the failure of good in herself and the world. At least this gave her a sense of pain expressed and justice served. A feeling of calm and inner alertness enveloped her. If Dennis did approach the elders, she would tell them the truth about Naomi, no matter what it cost. She couldn't lie to God's shepherds. But if Dennis came to her instead …

"Ada, are you in there?"

She nearly dropped the knife. "Mother?"

"I've been looking for you. Gail is preparing for the dance."

"I'll be ready soon." She pressed the cloth to her cuts. She heard her mother move toward the stall. Her steps were hesitant.

"Are you feeling well, my angel?"

"I'll be out in a minute," she said. She tied the cloth around her leg and pulled up her tights. They would hold the bandage in place. "You don't have to wait for me."

"Lana Jonson won the preserves category again," Sybil said, "but you won the pie. I don't know what Lana puts in her peaches, but all you would have to do is taste it, and you could duplicate it. Make it better even."

Ada flushed the toilet. "I'm happy she won it." She studied her blood-stained hands. How to make it to the sink without her mother noticing? Wash in the toilet? The idea of flushing the toilet a second time was mortifying.

"Well, I'll tell Gail you're coming." She heard her mother's high heels tack toward the entrance. Again a pause, and then the door opened and shut.

At the sink, Ada washed her hands slowly, although her mind screamed for speed. She would have to be more careful. She couldn't afford to attract Sybil's attention any more than she already had. Something dark and contagious, like ink or tar, vined around her heart.

By the time she retrieved and retuned her violin and took her place next to Gail, whose brother called the dances, couples were lining up on the makeshift dance floor. Head down, Naomi remained by the refreshments; her younger sister Christabella was on the floor with Michael. Dr. Graham practiced a dance move with Dawn. He looked just clumsy enough to make Ada want to laugh and show him where his steps were going wrong.

Swallowing her feelings, Ada played and played, switching tunes as the dancing required. Right before the final mixer, Mrs. Smythe and Margaret came up to her.

"It sounds lovely as usual, Alameda," Mrs. Smythe said. "I know we've been discussing when Margaret will be ready to play for events like this. She's been practicing the last piece you gave her diligently. Do you think she could play for this dance?"

"Of course," Ada said, rising from her chair. "Would that be all right with you, Gail?"

Gail nodded. Mrs. Smythe nudged Margaret.

"Thank you, Miss Williams, Mrs. Keller," Margaret said.

Ada pointed to the sheet of music on the stand. "Play eight times through the A section, eight times through the B section, do it all again, then look at Mrs. Keller to see when to end." When Meg nodded, Ada put away her violin. She was exhausted and hungry, and for a change, all she wanted was to talk with Naomi. But Michael intercepted her en route to the refreshments.

"How lucky that you're free. May I have the honor of this dance?"

She glanced at Naomi, but her friend provided no assistance. Her eyes held no expression; she seemed lost to her surroundings. With a gesture of assent, Ada allowed Michael to lead her to the dance floor.

For this dance, the men stood in a ring while the ladies moved clockwise, passing from partner to partner. Normally a lady would make a full circuit before the dance ended. Only now did Ada comprehend what saying yes to Michael meant. Hope surged through her as she realized she might be partnered with Dr. Graham. Fear quickly followed as she worried she would be forced to dance with Dennis.

Gail's husband, Ben Keller, called the dances. "Five, six, seven, eight!" he shouted, and the music began. It was too late to excuse herself. She trembled.

"Congratulations on winning the pie category," Michael said as they stepped together, then apart.

"Thank you." The angle of her chin felt unnatural when she tried to meet his eyes, so she stared at his chest.

"Old Man Keller won the wood carving competition again."

"Was it the pod of dolphins? That was my favorite."

"Yes, it was." They do-si-doed, and Michael brushed her shoulder. "Sometimes it overwhelms me how richly God has blessed Worden. He has given such talents to his people. You he has anointed with hospitality and a teachable spirit, and I believe he has given me the gifts of leadership and ministry." His grip tightened as they turned side by side and walked clockwise for eight counts. She wanted to shake off his hard fingers. "Imagine what God could do through us if we combined our talents."

Worden isn't as wonderful as you make it out to be, Ada almost said, but she kept silent. She had spoken out earlier, and it had been a mistake. Silence seemed to be what was required of her.

Michael turned her under his arm and passed her to the next man. Her new partner spoke only to ask if she were enjoying herself. She moved from him to the next, her student Harry Smythe. Her feet and arms followed the dance movements haltingly as she strained to look down the line and see who her subsequent partners would be. Too many dancers in the way; too many movements she had to perform that required her attention. Her stomach roiled in anxiety.

"Meg's playing well," Harry said.

Ada obliged him with a smile.

"She's been assaulting our ears for hours every day to prepare," he added. "Billy says next year he's going to out-dance me."

"He's been working so hard with Miss Graham. I can't wait to see." As she spoke, she recalled she wouldn't be able to see him if she and Naomi joined the convent. Father O'Connor had been clear. Dedication to God meant renunciation of other loyalties. She wouldn't be allowed to leave for just any reason—probably only to attend her parents on their deathbeds.

She passed to the next man. She wanted the dance to be over but could tell from the music that it was only half finished.

Suddenly she found herself facing Dr. Graham. When he took her hand, her entire arm tingled, and a jolt of intense focus, greater than she'd achieved in her cutting sessions, arrowed from her wrist to her scalp.

"How are you enjoying yourself, Miss Williams?"

She glanced down. Step in, step out. "Very well, thank you. And you?"

"Quite well. Thank you for the invitation. It's a chance to study my patients in their natural habitat." Just as she gained enough courage to look up, he winked at her. She stumbled, and he caught her. Her body shivered and erupted in gooseflesh as she felt the heat of his skin through his shirt.

"I'm sorry," she said. She grasped his shoulder to right herself, then quickly let go. They were out of step with the other dancers, and she rushed to do-si-do.

"It's not your fault," he said. "I'm not as graceful as you are. I must have tripped you."

She didn't dare meet his eyes. He was probably just being gallant. She was afraid to imagine what he really thought of her. Struggling through her confusion, she cast about for a topic to distract them both.

"I noticed you went after Jim Reeves. Was he ill?"

He cleared his throat. "Yes. He and a few others from the Meatpacking District have developed flu-like symptoms. I told him to go home and said he shouldn't work until he felt better, but I doubt he'll listen."

"Why not?"

"He can't afford to lose the money. One of the problems of factory work is that the workers are expendable."

"Surely Mr. Smythe would understand and let them keep their jobs."
Already they were walking clockwise. After her stumble she should have
been relieved, but it was as if a hand squeezed her heart.

"Mr. Smythe might be co-owner of the factory, but he leaves the difficult
decisions to Mr. Stone." Dr. Graham said.

Ada wanted to sweeten the moment before he passed her on, but she
couldn't think of anything to say. And then the moment had gone.

She danced with Jon, who had noticed and now made fun of her fall,
then with Mayor Templeton, then, unexpectedly, Dennis Gentle. Dancing
with Dr. Graham had made her forget to watch out for him. Her breath
caught, and she clamped her lips together.

"Edith told me you warned her away from me," he said. His hands were
cold and firm. No chance of slipping away. "Good thing she's a girl of sense."

Ada looked around, but everyone else was caught up in the rhythm of
the dance. She was the only one who felt caged by it.

"You, on the other hand, don't seem to have any sense," he said. "No
sense of propriety, no sense of danger."

"You have to leave her alone," Ada whispered. "Don't you fear God?"

"Oh, God. Yes, of course. But not as much as you should fear me." He
turned his fingernails into her hand, clawing her skin. "What's this?"

She followed his gaze down. A bloodstain on her wrist. She had washed
her hands so thoroughly, but there was a small smear just below her sleeve.

"Did you cut yourself?" A smile curved up his cheek.

She wanted to lie, but she faltered. She jerked away from him. The
music was slowing, and no one noticed her break from the line. She ran
to the back wall and pressed herself against it. Her chest heaved against a
mosaic of tiles, and their smooth surface cooled her cheek. Afraid someone
was watching, she turned around. The room looked the same. But she knew,
beneath the bandage, that her cuts had begun to bleed.

CHAPTER SEVEN

On Sunday, none of the meatpackers attended church. They were not regular attendees, but Ada was concerned about their absence. She hoped they hadn't caught whatever was going around the factory.

Naomi seemed unusually cheerful as she extracted a promise from Ada to walk to the Cow's Head that afternoon, since the spring festival had preempted their usual walking time.

Before she returned home from church, Ada walked down the street to St. Dominic's. The second mass had just finished, and Father O'Connor stood outside the doorway, blessing parishioners as they left. She held back, waiting for the crowd to clear.

"Did Jon send you?" someone next to her asked.

Ada's attention fastened on Pete O'Connor, her brother's friend and the priest's nephew. He was tall, with reddish blond hair and a face marred by acne scars and chicken pox. His immense build was the result of years of loading railcars. He puffed on a cigarette and exhaled, then smiled, showing stained, irregular teeth.

"No," she said. "I've come to ask Father O'Connor a question."

"I'm glad you're here. I'm always asking Jon to bring you along on our jaunts."

"Really?" She wondered why Jon had never mentioned it.

"Oh yes. Jon has the prettiest sister in town."

Her face heated. She was grateful for her brother's protective impulse.

"But I forgot," Pete said, "that you want to join a convent. You probably don't appreciate compliments."

Unsure of what to say, she looked down.

"Obviously I have no problems with you converting," he said, "but are you sure you want to become a nun?"

She glanced at Father O'Connor. Only a few parishioners were left in line. "I'm considering it. I can think of no better way to serve God."

Talking with him about it soiled her dream, as if he were a dirty finger stirring fresh cream.

Pete ground the cigarette beneath his heel and stepped closer. "I have an idea. Why don't you ask me whatever it was you were going to ask my uncle? I can tell you anything you want to know about the Roman Catholic Church, and I'll do it over dinner."

She met his dark eyes. Was he joking?

"I have a car," he said. "I could pick you up tomorrow. Say around six? From what Jon says, you're pretty much the household servant, and you deserve a night off."

"No, thank you."

"C'mon. Just one date with me, and if you don't like it, I'll drive you to the convent myself."

She shook her head and moved past him, hurriedly climbing the church steps to the priest. He smiled at her. In his sunlit robe, he looked other-worldly, a luminescent saint. He was older than her father, and his white hair stuck up like a crown.

"Alameda, welcome," he said in what was still a distinct Irish brogue. "What can I do for you?"

"When you have a moment, Father, I'd like to ask you something."

"That moment is now. Come in."

She followed him into the church, overwhelmed as usual by the gigantic, tortured Christ on the cross, which was the first thing one saw in the nave. Two stained glass windows on either side of the Christ filtered jeweled light onto the altar. Father O'Connor led her to the side chapel, where several candles burned at the feet of a statue of Mary. A woman knelt before it, praying. She rose and bent her head for a blessing from Father O'Connor before she left.

"Now, what is on your heart?" he asked Ada, lowering himself onto a bench. She sat a few feet away from him.

"I've talked to you before about joining St. Cecilia's, and about what conversion would entail."

He nodded.

"Only now, however, do I realize what a blow that decision would be to my parents."

"You must do as God guides you, without fear of man's opinion."

"What about honoring my parents?"

"While you are living with them, of course you must obey them. You will be eighteen soon—"

"On Friday," she said.

"And then you will be independent in the State's eyes. In the Church's eyes, you have already reached the age of accountability, and it is your conscience you must follow, not another's. If you come to your decision through prayer, fasting, and godly counsel, then God will bless it."

"And what if," she hesitated, "I have done something, or allowed something evil to be done to me? Would I still be able to become a novice?"

"You must confess and make penance, of course, but often it is that evil thing that drives us into God's arms, for he will always forgive us."

She had meant to keep the conversation about Naomi, but his answer convicted her. She had touched herself, imagining that it was Dr. Graham. She pushed away the thought and blurted out the rest of her question, which she had been formulating for days. "Father, what if someone who desired to become a novice were to have a child out of wedlock? Would her duty to the child prevent her from joining? Would giving up the child end her parental responsibility, or would God rather she took care of it?"

Father O'Connor waited several moments before he replied, and his words were slow. "If a woman has a child, she must raise him or her to eighteen before taking vows, for her vows to God supersede all other responsibilities. Giving up the child for adoption would indeed allow her to join the convent. But I would strongly urge her to consider why that child came to be in the first place. Perhaps a lifelong vow of chastity is not God's plan for her."

Although Ada couldn't read anything from Father O'Connor's mild expression, his words were ice chips in her stomach. They were supposed to be talking about Naomi, not her. "If it wasn't her fault … If she were taken against her will …"

Now she could read his expression. Concern, questioning. "Has something happened to you, Alameda? Sometimes keeping silent is a sin."

She rose, hastily, guiltily. "No, not to me. Not to me. Thank you for your help, Father."

"I already offered to be your character reference, and you have never been less than honest about your questions. Have doubts or certain feelings been plaguing you? The devil often seeks to tempt the purest souls."

"Another time we can discuss it. I'm sorry, but I have to leave."

"Very well." He made the sign of the cross. "May Christ and the Saints guard and keep you."

Trying to forget his words, she rushed home, prepared lunch for her family, and then walked to the Gentles. Still, the words cycled in her mind. *Perhaps a lifelong vow of chastity is not God's plan.* She had cut herself, hadn't she? She would continue to cut out her yearning for the doctor. The priest was right; Satan was tempting her.

Once on the Gentles' property, she hung back from the house. She didn't want to run into Dennis. She waited until she saw Naomi leave the house, then waved. Naomi waved back.

"Are you sure you won't be cold?" Ada asked. All Naomi wore was a navy cardigan over her dress. "Look at the clouds—there might be rain later."

"I'm fine," Naomi said. Her pale hair was pulled back in a messy braid, but for a change it looked lustrous, not dull. Pregnancy suited her, Ada thought, then felt like a traitor.

"I brought a loaf of bread and some cookies for you. Why don't you take them inside and get a coat?"

Naomi peered at the basket Ada offered. "You know, Ada, you don't have to cook for us. We're not so poor we don't get enough to eat."

"They're molasses cookies—Mattie's favorite. And your mother told me Hezekiah and Priscilla are growing like weeds."

"I'll take it to them." Naomi ran up the walk, opened the door, and set the basket inside. She didn't grab a coat, but Ada decided not to press the issue.

As they hiked up the hill, their favorite shortcut to the Cow's Head, Ada shielded her eyes from the bright sun. *Sometimes keeping silent is a sin.* But sometimes it was necessary too.

"And you thought I'd be cold!" Naomi said.

Ada tripped over a tuft of grass and landed on her knees. She felt the skin on her left thigh stretch, and she hoped the scab hadn't torn apart. Her leg hurt, but she was glad for the distraction. She worried that Dennis had told Naomi about her confrontation with Edith and that Naomi would be angry with her.

"Are you all right?" Naomi asked, helping her up.

"Fine, thank you."

"I saw you trip at the festival when you were dancing with Dr. Graham."

Why would Naomi bring that up? Did she suspect something? Ada crossed her arms. "I suppose I need practice. I usually play, not dance."

"Did you talk to him about me? Did he say when Haven House would have an opening?"

"I didn't ask."

"Why not?" Naomi stopped at the top of the hill. The wind whipped her bangs across her face. "I'm going to start to show soon." She pressed her dress against her belly.

Ada swallowed. She didn't want to reveal her inner chaos and admit that dancing with the doctor had driven rational thought from her mind. "I'm sure a place will open soon. I did talk to Father O'Connor about having a child, though. If you give it up for adoption, there won't be a problem. But you'd have to tell the nuns and do a proper penance."

Naomi nodded. "I'm just sorry that *this*," she put a hand to her stomach, "is delaying our plans. Otherwise we could leave the day after your birthday."

"Maybe it's good that we have more time."

"Why would you say that? You can't back out now!"

"What happens," Ada asked, and her voice rose, only partially to be heard over the wind, "if I decide to? What would you do if I told the truth about your pregnancy?"

"I would die of shame," she said. "Why do you have to say anything? It's my secret, so it's my decision."

Ada couldn't answer. What Naomi said seemed logical, but her heart knew it was wrong.

"Besides, there's nothing in Worden for me," Naomi said. "I have no choice. But I guess you do. Maybe you want me to rot in the convent so you can marry Michael instead."

"I don't want to marry Michael."

"If it's not the convent God wants for you, then it's him. Anyone can tell he's the only one in this town self-righteous enough to be paired with you!" She ran across the summit, then arrowed down the incline toward the lake.

"Thinking about him makes me sick," Ada protested as she ran after her friend. She wasn't sure Naomi heard her, and she would have repeated herself, but she saw they weren't alone. A group of boys played in a grove of willows farther down the shoreline.

Naomi flung herself down on a flat rock within throwing distance of the dock. Ada sat next to her. "I don't want to make life miserable for you," she said.

"It's already miserable," Naomi said.

Ada linked arms with her and squeezed. Dennis couldn't have told her. Maybe, just maybe, he was afraid Naomi would follow Ada's example and speak up to somebody. "I'm sorry I scared you. I don't know why I'm having difficulty committing to this. I've been planning it since I was eight."

"I know." She disengaged her arm from Ada's. "What's changed?"

"I suppose ... *I* have. I still think that to be as the Apostle Paul is the best thing, but my father has been choosing pointed verses to read after dinner—'Be fruitful and multiply'—to emphasize his wishes. I realize my parents never took my desire to join seriously, and that's why they haven't challenged it until now. And there's another problem."

"What is it?"

"I'm not sure a life of chastity is for me." She blushed and cupped her chin in one hand to conceal her face. "I've been having feelings and thoughts I've never had before."

"Really? For who?"

"For whom." Ada glanced up with an apologetic smile. Naomi's eyes were round with curiosity. Only a thin line of brown circled her overly large pupils.

"For whom, then."

Ada groaned. "I can't say!"

"Then I'll guess. Is it Michael?"

She stuck out her tongue and made a face.

Naomi ran through the short list of eligible men in the church, then began to branch out. "Is it Pete O'Connor?"

"Please!" She hoped she looked sufficiently mortified.

"Is it someone else from St. Dominic's?"

She shook her head.

"A meatpacker?"

"No."

Naomi was very quiet. Then she took Ada's hand in her own. "Is it ... Dawn?"

Ada's gasp was so loud it shocked herself. "Naomi!"

"Well, it's not as if that doesn't go through people's minds when they look at her, and she's become your friend lately, maybe more than I have, and ..."

She didn't want to hear it. "It's Dr. Graham." Afraid to see Naomi's reaction, she shut her eyes.

"Oh." Then a moment later, "Is he even divorced?"

"I don't know. I didn't say I was proud of it." She looked up at last, to see Naomi's mouth pinched in judgment. "Of course it's wrong. But now you know my secret, just as I know yours." She hunched her shoulders and turned away.

"Isn't he rather ... well, old for you?"

"I don't care how old he is."

Naomi pressed Ada's hand. "What are you going to do?"

"I don't know." A raindrop spattered her forehead as clouds grayed the valley. "Nothing. We'd better go back."

"I don't care about a little rain."

Ada realized she was irritated, and felt ashamed of it, but no less angry. "You have to take care of yourself, Naomi. Start eating properly and wear a coat, for goodness' sake!"

"I don't have to, not if I don't want to." Naomi stood and surged toward the dock. A long roll of thunder drowned out her footsteps on the wooden planks.

The wind carried the boys' shouts of disappointment to Ada. She peered at them, making sure they wouldn't wait out the change in weather under the willows. The trees were too close to the water. But as rain plummeted from thick, dark clouds, the boys scattered.

Reassured that they would be safe, she turned to her friend. "What are you doing?" she yelled, but the wind tore the words from her mouth. Gusts transformed raindrops into needles, spearing her face and hands. She pulled up her hood and sprinted to the dock.

"It'll never happen," Naomi shouted over the wind. "You'll never marry Dr. Graham. He's too old, and he doesn't believe in God. Do you want to go to Hell?"

"Of course not. Where are you going?"

Naomi picked her way to the end of the dock. Waves sloshing her shoes, she stared across Cow Lake. She didn't even hold onto the pylons for support as the dock bobbed up and down.

"Maybe this is the answer," Naomi said. Ada could barely hear her. "We put ourselves in God's hands."

"What do you mean?" Ada bent her knees for better balance on the wet slats. She put out her arms and gripped the widely spaced pylons for support. Broken cobwebs wrapped around the dirty poles, and she ground her teeth at the crumbly, sticky sensation. She was acutely aware that if she fell into the water she couldn't swim to shore.

Resisting the urge to crawl, she reached Naomi. She felt her friend's cardigan. It was soaked through. Struggling against the wind, she removed her jacket and wrapped it around Naomi's shoulders.

"Come on, let's go before we get struck by lightning," she urged.

Naomi's eyes reflected the turbulent water. "That would make it easier," she said. "Tell me right now, do you want to stay here and be seduced by the devil, or do you want to go to St. Cecilia's with me?"

"I don't know what God wants," she said. Her teeth chattered.

"Honestly!" Naomi tore off the jacket and thrust it at her. A red spot flamed in each cheek. "How do you know what God wants? If he's in control of all that happens, then he wanted this to happen to me."

"His decretive will and preceptive will are different—" Lightning sizzled the sky. Ada was speechless. Apparently it was God's will that she skip the sermon.

Naomi yelled into the face of the storm as thunder throbbed through the air. She sobbed loudly and urgently. Ada backed away. Naomi's pain was so raw, it seemed an element of its own, like the wind and water skidding around her.

Lightning flashed again. Ada swallowed, stepped forward, and grabbed Naomi's arm. "We have to go. Now! The lightning ..."

"Ada, you have to come with me." Naomi's fingers threaded through Ada's hair, caressing her neck. She clutched Ada's elbow with her other hand and drew her toward her. "Promise me now. Please." Her pale lips quivered. "I love you."

Ada jerked away. Naomi's hand caught in her hair, and as Ada pulled free, she lost her balance. Ada tumbled to the dock, her stomach heaving in fear. The wooden surface tilted perilously. Her left foot slipped into the water, and a frigid wave doused her leg. Her fingernails scrabbled for purchase on the slimy, pitted wood.

"I'm sorry. Forgive me. I'm sorry." Naomi dragged Ada away from the edge of the dock. Ada got to her knees and lunged against a pylon, hugging it as the dock creaked from side to side.

Veins of light crackled from the lake to the sky. Thunder boomed. Naomi shouted in Ada's ear that they had to leave. She peeled Ada's fingers from the pylon. Ada was too afraid to resist as Naomi pulled her down the dock. Rain slicked the wooden slats, and Ada prayed not to slip again.

At last they reached the muddy ground. Naomi lifted her wet, sad eyes to Ada. "I didn't mean to make you lose your balance. Will you forgive me?"

"Yes." Ada tried to catch her breath. She was thankful Naomi didn't say anything about what had happened right before that. "Come on."

Only when they'd reached the cover of pines did Ada's trembling lessen. Ada gave her jacket to Naomi again, and her friend put it on without complaint. They waited under the trees, speechless and not looking at each other, until the worst of the storm was over.

CHAPTER EIGHT

$\mathcal{N}$aomi's words haunted Ada in her sleep. When she awoke to gray light seeping through her window shade, she didn't get up immediately as she had been taught to do. Her troubled dreams and the day's obligations weighed on her.

Naomi had always been her best friend, and Ada loved her—as a friend. The way Naomi said she loved Ada, while touching her hair, surpassed what Ada judged to be friendly. Ada was suddenly afraid that Dennis's abuse had ruined Naomi for the convent. Or were Ada's interactions with Dawn warping her mind, making her see sin in innocence? The thought that she was being polluted and perverted made her bones ache. She wanted to cut, but there wasn't time before Sybil would expect her at breakfast.

In the bathroom, she glanced in the mirror to see dark patches under her eyes and a face she hardly recognized. She turned away in disgust. In a haze she breakfasted, accomplished her tasks for the morning, walked to the Smythes, and began their lessons. Halfway through, she heard Dawn arrive and start her exercises with Billy. She checked her watch. Dawn had never arrived this late. She remembered Dr. Graham's concern for Jim and the rest of the meatpackers, and the fact that they hadn't been at church.

She told Meg and Harry to keep working and went to Billy's room. Dawn looked up as she helped Billy stretch his leg.

"I'm sorry to interrupt," Ada said, "but I was wondering about the meatpackers. Is anyone else sick?"

Before Dawn could answer, Mrs. Smythe walked into the room. Rose-scented perfume wafted from her, and her chestnut hair was perfectly curled. "You're late today, Miss Graham," she said. "I almost telephoned the hospital to see what the emergency was."

"Mrs. Smythe, I'm happy to explain." Dawn finished Billy's stretch and patted his leg. "Let's talk in the other room. Ada too."

Ada followed them to the front room. Mrs. Smythe poised on an armchair and folded her hands. Dawn didn't sit down, and Ada hovered uncertainly next to her.

"I'm planning to take a couple of weeks off, starting tomorrow," Dawn said. "Billy is doing well, but it's important to keep up the exercises I've shown you."

Mrs. Smythe's blue eyes widened. "I heard there was a bug going around in the Meatpacking District. Is that why you need a break?"

Dawn nodded. "I have to help my father. He and the nurses are out making so many calls that we're understaffed at the hospital."

"It's that bad, is it?"

"I'm afraid so. I've been very careful not to come into contact with any patients myself, but if the infection continues to spread, I won't be able to avoid it. Just to be safe, I won't be back until it's passed."

"That's very thoughtful of you." Mrs. Smythe stood. "Actually, if you're that worried, you might as well go now. I will tell Billy."

"Are you sure? I've barely started with him."

"No, it's fine. And you know, Ada," she flashed a concerned frown, "you look a little peaked. Why don't you take off the afternoon as well? I'll call you when I want you."

Ada exchanged looks with Dawn. She hadn't expected such an extreme reaction. Did Dawn think it was extreme too? "Whatever you think is best, Mrs. Smythe." She gathered her things from the salon and followed Dawn out.

Dawn's bicycle leaned against the front fence. Dawn headed for it but didn't hop on. She threw her leather bag, a smaller version of her father's, into the basket and wheeled the bike beside her. As she matched Ada's hurried strides, her knee-length skirt swished against her thighs. "I didn't want to frighten Mrs. Smythe, but I'm not sure I succeeded," she said.

"It's serious, isn't it?" Ada asked.

"Yes, and if it spreads out of the Meatpacking District ... Well, it's already bad enough, but that would make it an epidemic."

"Do you think anyone will die?"

In the sunlight, Dawn's eyes were very green. Her mother's eyes, certainly. "There's no question. We should be more worried about how many will die, not if they do. I just hope my dad doesn't catch it."

Ada twisted her lip with her teeth. She couldn't think about Dr. Graham's vitality being dulled with sickness. "What caused it?"

"We don't know yet. Meatpackers are mostly the ones infected, so perhaps some slip in hygiene at the plant." She shuddered. "I'm glad I've never eaten that meat."

"That's awful. I will pray about it."

"Praying is fine and all," Dawn said, "but keep yourself safe too. If you can help it, don't go to the Meatpacking District. You should warn your brother to take a few days off, too, at least until we know what we're dealing with."

"Of course!" Fear giving her unexpected energy, Ada surged forward into a jog. Dawn mounted the bike to keep pace.

"Please don't panic," Dawn said. "It will be okay."

"We're in God's hands. His will be done."

When she reached home, she burst into the study. Rev. Williams dropped his book, and Sybil jumped up.

"Alameda, how many times have I told you a lady doesn't run!"

Ada hadn't heard that reproof for years. "I'm sorry, Mother. I just talked with Dawn Graham, and there's something going round the Meatpacking District. She recommended we call Jon home for a few days."

"Come here." Rev. Williams beckoned to her. Ada advanced with stilted steps. He took her hand and held it between his palms. "What is your only comfort in life and death?"

She glanced down. The last thing on her mind was the Heidelberg Catechism. He squeezed her hand. She knew she must recite it before he would let her go. She took a deep breath and rushed through the answer.

"'That I, with body and soul, both in life and death, am not my own, but belong unto my faithful savior Jesus Christ, who with his precious blood has fully satisfied for all my sins, and delivered me from all the power of the devil; and so preserves me that without the will of my Heavenly Father not a hair can fall from my head—'"

"Not a hair," he repeated. "That is Jon's comfort as well. There is no need to call your brother home early. Let him finish the work he contracted to do. He serves a higher master than illness or fear."

"Yes, Father." Subdued, Ada turned around and went to the kitchen. She heard her mother's voice as she left.

"Silas, it does sound rather serious. If the doctor's daughter has recommended it ..."

Ada imagined her father's response as she busied herself making bread. Her parents would pray over the matter, calling down protection for their son.

She should pray as well, but the words jumbled in her mind. She was probably overreacting, but fear and guilt clogged her thoughts. Whatever was happening, she sensed, was a symptom of another illness, the corruption of the church, the secrets she had bottled inside. She kneaded the dough methodically, counting the rotations and folds to calm herself.

By the time Jon's shift ended, she had placed four loaves of bread in the oven. When he was due home, she armed herself with clothing to be mended and sat guard in a chair facing the door.

He was late. She waited twenty agonizing minutes before he came in.

"Jon, how are you feeling?" she asked. The cloth she was working on dropped to the floor.

He scooped it up and tossed it into her lap. "Tired. A few guys were home sick today, so I had extra work."

"Dawn told me there's something going around."

"She did, huh?" He perked up. "I heard Stone wasn't in today. Nobody mentioned anything at the railroad or factory, though. What else did Dawn say?"

Mr. Stone, Ada knew, was the foreman of the meatpacking factory. If he was experiencing symptoms as well, perhaps he would have mercy on the other sick workers. "She said you might want to stay home for a few days."

"Suits me. I doubt our parents would agree though." He yawned, then sniffed. "Do I smell bread?" He wandered into the kitchen.

As he cut himself several generous slices and dressed them with butter and honey, Ada finished mending the cloth. Jon acted so casual, and her parents had pooh-poohed her fears so thoroughly, that she reassessed her own reaction. Perhaps it was only her anxiety and indecision about the convent that made her fear the worst. Her father was right. Christ was her comfort.

♫

The next morning, Ada awoke with a start. Her stomach knotted. She listened, not knowing why. Her room was still dark, but she sensed sunrise was near.

The phone rang. She heard it through the walls, and it pulsed through her temples like a sore tooth. She threw on a robe and ran to the office.

Sybil fumbled to place the phone on its cradle. She sighed.

"What is it, Mother?"

"That was Janet Lamm," she said. "Her mother is seriously ill, and she thinks your father's services might be required shortly."

Ada swallowed back the urge to say she had been right to worry. Because of the secrets she kept, she felt she'd been given special insight into the situation.

"Old Mrs. Keller—Alice—is ill as well. And the youngest Stone child died this morning. I must wake Silas."

"I'm so sorry. I'll make soup," Ada said.

As she chopped vegetables and simmered broth, her stomach coiled nearly into her throat. The infection had spread beyond the Meatpacking District. According to Dawn, it was now an epidemic. Ada thought a better word might be plague. Like the ten plagues of Egypt.

God was judging Worden. What were the sins that offended him? He hated liars and hypocrites. Would he cease his punishment if she repented? She could speak up about Dennis and Naomi, about herself committing adultery in her heart and punishing her flesh, which was the temple of the

Holy Spirit. She had already beseeched God for forgiveness a hundred times. Must she say it out loud? To a priest even? Perhaps it was already too late. King David had repented after sleeping with Bathsheba, but God had still killed his son. The onions that stung her eyes did nothing to relieve her need for pain.

"I called Donner's Grocery," Sybil said, standing at the kitchen entrance. "Michael will be here soon to help you deliver the food. Be sure you don't go inside the houses; wait for someone to answer the door. Just tell them you're in a hurry."

"Do you know where Jim Reeves lives?" Ada asked. "I want to take him some broth."

Sybil shook her head. "Don't go to the Meatpacking District. I told Michael not to drive you there. There's plenty of our own to serve."

"But surely they would appreciate—"

"No. I don't want you so close to where it started. They can take care of their own."

Ada bit her lip to keep from pointing out that her mother used to work at the factory and that the group of meatpackers that attended services were certainly the church's responsibility. She knew her mother would brook no argument.

As Michael drove her along their route, he speculated on the cause of the epidemic. "I wonder if this is God's judgment on Worden for something, or whether it's simply a case of our Heavenly Father not intervening in a natural event."

"Do you think this is a natural event?" Ada frowned, then rubbed her forehead to hide her expression. "Because I don't think it would occur naturally. We created the situation by the way we raise and slaughter animals."

"Not this again," Michael said. "The factory is a good and necessary part of this town. I agree that 'a wise man is kind to his animals,' but animals were put under our dominion. Man's fallen nature means that he is imperfect in following God's commandments. So it *is* natural, at least until the earth is remade."

"I know. I didn't mean it that way." She crossed her legs. "I just wish it could have been prevented."

"Well, if your mother is correct in thinking it is a judgment, then quick repentance might stay God's sentence." He shrugged. "But I wouldn't hold my breath. It was usually *after* the pestilence, plague, or famine that Israel called on the Lord to save them."

She glanced at his hands on the steering wheel. His double-jointed fingers flexed across the crested vinyl. "How can you be so flippant about it? A lot of people could die."

"Alameda, are you afraid of death?" His tone was mildly disappointed. "With Christ, 'to die is gain.'"

She faced the window. "Not everyone who dies will be a Christian."

"Oh, I see why you're bothered. You're too sympathetic. I got caught up thinking about the raptures of Heaven." He exhaled noisily. "I feel sorry for the lost souls of the wicked too, but I just remind myself that they rejected Christ."

She touched her reflection in the glass. "They couldn't choose Christ because he passed them over."

"Yes. Thank the Lord for electing us! Otherwise, all of us would go to Hell and be deserving of eternal punishment."

The seatbelt pressed against her chest, and she tugged at it, gulping a little for breath. "Is—is that our first stop?"

He parked. She unclipped the seat belt and reached for the door.

"Wait. I'll get it," he said. He maneuvered around the car and opened it for her. But once she'd selected a jar of soup and a paper bag of bread from the back of the van, he took the items from her. "Allow me." He went up the sidewalk and rang the doorbell.

Feeling useless, Ada waited by the van as he handed the food to Mr. Hautman, a widower who had returned to Worden to care for his mother and small child. Michael spoke with him and bobbed his head a few times. They closed their eyes in prayer, and it was several minutes before Michael returned. Ada had already climbed into the van and shut the door.

"Next time I would like to deliver the food myself," she said, trying to sound pleasant. Besides offering comfort, she wanted to ask questions about the sickness.

"You don't have to prove me wrong." He smiled and touched her shoulder. "I know you're brave and you trust God to protect you. I am doing this more for myself than for you. I couldn't stand if anything happened to you."

"Let's take turns then," she suggested, folding her arms. "I'm sure your parents wouldn't appreciate that you're taking all the risks."

"You're just like your mother," he said, "a wise counselor. Your father is truly blessed to have such a helpmeet. She is very knowledgeable about the rarest doctrines. Why, the other day she mentioned something to me about supralapsarianism …"

Letting him drone on without interruption, Ada looked outside. The idea that the epidemic was somehow her fault, whether for sins of commission or omission, haunted her. And yet, her main fear was that Dr. Graham would fall ill and die. Then she would truly know God's punishment on her.

CHAPTER NINE

*O*ver the next few days, the sickness infected more and more people. The phone kept ringing as church members requested prayer and visitation. Rev. Williams buried four bodies before he developed a cough and fever and Sybil forbade him to go out again.

"But they need God's comfort," he said as Sybil and Ada put him to bed.

"After you are better." Sybil touched his forehead.

Before the death toll rose to six, the doctor officially ordered isolation. All unnecessary socialization was to cease, even between unaffected households. No vigils for the dead were to be kept, and burials were to be simple, speedy, and sparsely attended. A more elaborate ceremony might be held later. The epidemic struck the young, old, and vulnerable of every sect and circle.

Jon brought a basin of cold water into the sick room. "I just got off the phone with Pete," he told Ada. "Father O'Connor is ill too."

Sybil looked heavenward. "'All ye shall be offended because of me this night: for it is written, I will smite the shepherd, and the sheep of the flock shall be scattered abroad.' Matthew 26:31. We must repent. Jonathon, you must repent."

He stiffened and banged down the basin. "This illness isn't my fault."

"Not yours alone," she said. "We all have fallen short, and each has gone his own way."

"When you call up everyone to tell them that, give them some good news too. Dr. Graham contacted a friend, Dr. Jerome Lansky, to help him identify the sickness."

"What is it?" Ada asked. She wondered how he'd found out, and felt oddly jealous. It was a strange emotion to mix with guilt, and it fed her hopelessness.

"They don't know yet. Dawn said they're still running tests." He brushed the back of his hand against his forehead. Ada noticed a sheen of sweat.

"How are you feeling?" she asked, trying to hide her anxiety.

"Really useful," he said, "sitting around playing nursemaid."

"You can make some calls for me then," Sybil said. "Alameda, get some broth."

Ada took turns with her mother watching over Rev. Williams. He vomited twice and released foul gas that made her gag. Sybil helped him to the bathroom, but when he grew too weak, he used a bedpan. Ada felt strangely numb as she emptied and sanitized it. Her mother insisted she wear gloves and a rag over her mouth; otherwise she wouldn't have bothered.

As she returned to the room, she realized how old her father looked. Often she forgot how much older he was than Sybil. His dark eyes roved the room without fastening on anything.

"Romans," he moaned.

Ada knew what he wanted. She opened the Bible on his bedside table and read, "'Who shall separate us from the love of Christ? Shall tribulation, or distress, or persecution, or famine, or nakedness, or peril, or sword? As it is written, for thy sake we are killed all the day long; we are accounted as sheep for the slaughter. Nay, in all these things we are more than conquerors through him that loved us. For I am persuaded, that neither death, nor life, nor angels, nor principalities, nor powers, nor things present, nor things to come, nor height, nor depth, nor any other creature, shall be able to separate us from the love of God, which is in Christ Jesus our Lord.'"

He quieted, and his eyes closed. Ada ran her finger down the smooth paper of the Bible. She touched her father's cheek. Gray stubble scratched her fingers. Why had he found peace in the passage she had just read, and she found only condemnation?

As the night grayed into dawn, she gave in to exhaustion, stumbled to her room, and fell asleep. What seemed like a few minutes later, several sharp knocks roused her. "Ada! I think you'd better come out."

"What is it?" Her voice slurred with sleep.

"I called the doctor," Jon said. "Father's getting worse, and I need your help."

Ada struggled to her feet. The door to her parents' bedroom was open, but not wide. Jon slouched against the doorjamb, staring in. Ada stepped beside him. Hands clasped in prayer, Sybil knelt at Rev. Williams' bedside. Her lips moved in furious, incomprehensible petition.

"She's been like that since I checked on her," Jon said. It was the tone of his voice, more than his words, that frightened her. His Adam's apple bobbed like a tightly wound spring as he swallowed.

"Is the doctor coming?"

"The nurse said he's at the Stones. She was going to call there to tell him to come as soon as he could. What should we do, Ada?"

"Get her a shawl," she said. "She looks chilled." She advanced into the room and touched Sybil's shoulder. "Mother, why don't you lie down and rest? Dr. Graham is on his way."

Sybil only hunched closer to the bed and moaned her prayers into the coverlet. Ada examined her as Jon draped a red shawl over her. The flush of her cheeks might have been caused by zeal, but also by fever. She turned to her father. His lips were cracked and bloody. She felt his face. Cold. Only his wheezing breath alerted her that he was still alive. She should never have left him.

"Fill the kettle, and when the water's hot, bring it here," she told Jon. She fetched a clean cloth and dipped it in cold water. She wrung out the drops onto his tongue and moistened his lips. He moved slightly under her administrations, and his eyes opened briefly. They were glassy and bloodshot.

The thought surfaced again. Her father's illness, and the whole plague, was God's judgment on her hypocrisy and secrecy. God must hate her for questioning her calling, for being tempted by the lusts of the flesh, for protecting a rapist. She sank to her knees beside her mother and added her prayers to the offering. She must put to death her desire for Dr. Graham by increasing her love for God. Love for the one must replace her lust for the other. She would join the convent with Naomi. She would be celibate, joined only to Christ.

Unexpectedly, Sybil fastened her gaze on Ada. "'Is any sick among you? Let him call for the elders of the church; and let them pray over him, anointing him with oil in the name of the Lord.' James 5:14. We must summon the elders."

"The doctor said no one is supposed to leave their house."

"Call Michael Donner. Have him pray over the line."

Ada's head ached. "You mean Eric Donner. He's the elder."

"Yes. Call him!"

Ada lurched to the office. She raised the receiver and spun the numbers on the dial. Charlotte Donner answered after a single ring. "Mrs. Donner, this is Alameda. Is your husband available?" Ada heard her mother shout Jon's name. She covered her free ear, struggling to hear the voice on the line. It changed to a masculine timbre. "Mr. Donner, I'm so glad you're there. My father is very ill, and I think my mother is as well. She covets your prayers."

Now both Sybil and Jon shouted at each other. With a hurried apology, Ada placed the handle in its cradle. She ran to the bedroom.

Sybil heaved the bottom of the bed toward the door. Jon pushed against her from the other side.

"Don't move it!" Jon said.

"He needs to be near the prayer. He needs to hear it."

"You're going to kill him!"

Ada frowned at Jon, then walked to her mother and put her hand on her arm. "I called Mr. Donner. He's praying right now."

Sybil snapped to attention. "Wait here." She rushed from the room and returned a moment later with a jar of vegetable oil.

"I think she's feverish," Jon whispered to Ada. His cheeks were ashen and clammy. "She needs to rest."

"Let her do it. The doctor isn't here, so what else is there?"

"I don't know." He sat abruptly on the chair by the bed.

Sybil dipped her fingers in the oil and brushed her husband's forehead. "You need prayer too, my son." She anointed his head, then Ada's, then her own. She clasped her hands and faced the heavens. "Oh Lord, we beseech thee, have mercy!"

The phone rang. Ada raced for it and answered breathlessly. The base nearly scooted off the table when she picked up the receiver.

"Ada, this is Dawn. I'm sorry, but my dad won't be able to make it to your house today. There are too many cases here, and frankly, there's not much he can do anyway. The best thing is to keep everyone hydrated and cool. And don't give up hope; we're working on an antibiotic."

"But he's going to die! There must be something else—"

"I'm sorry. I have to make other calls. Someone will be there as soon as the antibiotic is ready."

The line went dead. Ada hung up the phone. From the bedroom, her mother's prayers continued, rising in pitch. Jon tottered into the office and slumped against the wall.

"Ada, I feel terrible."

"Let me help you to bed." She slung his arm across her shoulders and supported him down the hallway. He groaned.

"I think I'm going to faint. Was that the doctor?"

She shook her head. "He won't be here for a while. Lie down. I'll get you something to drink."

He fell across the bed and vomited. Ada brought him a glass of water and helped him sip it, then cleaned up the mess. This time the smell hardly reached her. Afterward, she dipped a cloth in cool water and laid it across his forehead.

"Thanks." He smiled feebly. "I hope you don't get sick."

She dragged a chair down the hallway to his room and began her vigil. She felt like dead wood that could snap at any minute. The rods on the back of the chair dug into her skin, but she stiffened her spine. She wouldn't move for her comfort, only for her brother's.

As Sybil watched Silas, Ada watched Jon. He shivered beneath blankets one moment, then flung them off, soaked with sweat. He vomited again, and often Ada helped him to the toilet. Several times he didn't make it in time or collapsed on the way, and so Ada was also busy with laundry.

"Damn the angels," he muttered as she wiped his forehead. "I can see them, dancing on a pin."

"Shh." She tilted a cup to his lips. "The doctor will be here soon." If she said it enough times, he would come.

"It's my fault," he said. "My fault. My—"

"No, it's not, Jonathon. You must rest."

His eyes roved as he tossed and turned. "She said it was. I have to repent."

"It's not your fault," she repeated. She longed to tell him why. She wished she'd told him her first secret when she'd staggered home on Naomi's birthday. If there was any chance God would have mercy on her father, mother, and brother, she had to confess. Only now, losing her sanity in a household of sick people, did she have the recklessness to break her vow.

"There's something I need to tell you." Working her way around the bed, she smoothed the sheets. "In case I catch this plague and die, which would be my just punishment. It's the reason for the plague—or at least part of the reason."

Jon groaned and rolled away. She wrung out the washcloth and stretched across the mattress to dab his brow.

"For the last few months, Naomi hasn't been well. Someone took her innocence. He forced himself on her, and now she is in trouble." Bitter tears flooded her eyes, nose, and throat. "I saw ... something, but she made me promise not to tell. He said he'd kill us, and I believe him, but maybe death is what I deserve for keeping this a secret, and for other things. I'm not a saint, Jon! I only wish God would help me become one." Sinking to the side of the bed, she smeared her tears against the sheets. She felt Jon's hand hit her as he repositioned himself. What would he say?

"Ada." He sat up and fumbled with his fingers as if searching for something. "I'm so cold."

He had dumped the blankets on the other side of the bed. She sniffed and rubbed her eyes. "Didn't you hear me? Naomi was raped—by her uncle Dennis."

"A dentist?" He shuddered. "So many teeth."

She clambered to the other side and grabbed the covers. As she tucked them across his quivering limbs, anger hardened her body into granite. He was feverish. God, or the devil, wasn't allowing her to communicate the secret that weighed on her conscience. She closed her lips, determined not to be weak again.

Over the next hour, Jon's fever climbed. He raved about hellfire and threw off his blankets. When she tried to get him to drink, he struck away the cup. In desperation, Ada scattered ice over him. It melted quickly into the mattress.

Panic deadened her mind. What should she do? She lurched to her parents' room. Sybil was reading from the Bible. Some chapter of chronology. The cadence of names rolled over her like a wave of dizziness.

The meatpacking stench. She inhaled again, then retched. The room smelled of feces, blood, death. Her father lay so still.

With a cry of pain, Ada reeled from the room. She made it to the office chair and picked up the telephone. The letters on the rotary dial stared at her. They might have been pictographs or hieroglyphics. How did they go together again? Her hand shook as she dialed.

"Worden Hospital, this is Jan. How may I help you?"

The line echoed, making Ada feel she was lost in a cave with no means of egress. She didn't recognize the voice or the name either. "Who is this?"

"Jan, from the hospital. I'm helping with phone calls because the doctors and nurses are busy. Can I take a message?"

"Tell Dr. Graham that it's Ada Williams. My father and brother are dying, and my mother is ill also. Please hurry. Please hurry, Dr. Graham!"

"My name is Jan," the voice said. "Dr. Graham is out, but I'll pass along the message."

Something stuck in Ada's mind, a mental friction that made her wince. "Doctors. You said doctors."

"The veterinarians are helping out, mostly in the Meatpacking District."

"All right." She started to lower the telephone handle.

"Wait, don't hang up. Are you well enough to drive to the hospital?"

"I can't leave them," she said. "I told you, they're dying." *They're dying,* the phone echo repeated.

"That's not what I meant," Jan said. "Dr. Lansky is scheduled to arrive with an antibiotic by the first train tomorrow morning. Anyone who can is to come to the hospital to get a shot, but I'll make a note to send someone over with it for your household. How many are there?"

"Four." Her mouth tasted sour. She hated Jan's carefree tone.

"Thank you. In the meantime, try to keep their temperatures down with compresses or ice baths. And push fluids!"

Ada hung up. She tried not to think how many long hours lay between now and the first train. "'Weeping may endure for a night,'" she quoted as she crossed the hall to her brother's room, "'but joy cometh in the morning.'" It sounded like a lie.

Jon was quieter now, and some time later his breathing steadied. He must be sleeping. Her own head nodded and snapped as she struggled to stay awake in the chair. If she kept watch, he wouldn't die. She tapped her heels, then her toes against the carpet, counting each tap. She matched groupings of taps to Jon's breaths.

The clock struck midnight, and a scant minute later, there was a frantic pounding on the front door. She surged to her feet. Was the doctor here early? She emerged into the hallway just behind her mother.

The pounding continued. "Open up!" a young male voice called. "Please, is Ada there?"

"Who is it?" Ada reached for the lock, but Sybil struck her arm away.

"Do not open that door," she said with the voice of an apocalyptic angel. Sweat glistened on her cheeks and dampened her collar.

"We need to," Ada said. "It could be the antibiotic shot."

"Ada, is that you?" the boy shouted. "It's Hezekiah. Naomi is so bad— she wants to see you."

Again Ada moved toward the door, but Sybil planted herself in front of it. "You will not go. Your responsibility is to our household."

"Please, Mother," Ada pleaded. "My best friend needs to see me. What if it's for the last time?"

"You have to come," Hezekiah said through the door. "She's saying your name."

"Go away!" Sybil shouted. She spoke nearly as forcefully to Ada. "They have the plague there. I cannot bear for you to catch it too."

Ada's stomach contracted painfully. "But I've already been exposed."

"I have anointed the house. No more spirits of sickness can pass through."

"Mother, you're feverish!"

Sybil seized her arm with fingers like talons. "'The lot is cast into the lap, but its every decision is from the Lord.' Proverbs 16:33. This house is holy now, clean from sin. If you leave it, you give up God's protection."

"But I must see her!" Angry tears burned her eyes. She reached for the knob again.

"If you go, you can never come back."

Ada stared at her. Her mother's cheekbones stood out like soldiers on guard. With a cry, Ada tore herself from Sybil's grasp and stumbled to her room. She shut the door and dragged her wardrobe in front of it with frenzied strength. Then she grabbed the knife from its bottom-drawer coffin.

A holy house, free from sin? It was no freer of sin than it was of sickness!

The scar on her upper thigh reopened in drops of dark, thick blood. For once her cutting gave her no pain, and she took advantage of the numbness with grim purpose. She imagined Naomi burning with fever, perhaps morbidly triumphant that her illness must cost the infant inside her its life, perhaps hysterically repentant of ever wishing the babe would die. Perhaps still deciding whether she should give it up.

Worse than that, somehow, was the image of Naomi crying for Ada, babbling that she loved her. Because of Dr. Graham, Ada knew the pain of perverse love, and she felt for her friend. If God would save the lives of her family and Naomi, Ada swore that she would enter the convent. She and Naomi would both give up their lusts and devote themselves to Christ. No more deliberation, no more doubt. This was God's test.

Blood streaked down her body and dripped onto an old towel between her feet and the cold floor. She drew words and symbols on herself, dipping the pen of her finger into the ink of her wounds, and applying the knife when the fountain ran low.

A spinning weakness dropped her to her knees. She examined the cut she'd just made. It was deeper than any before, and seeing her flesh cover the metal blade sickened her. Fear forced itself up her throat, and she gagged. What if she fainted and were discovered, naked and bloody as a stillborn?

She threw down the knife and washed the rag in her cold washbasin. The icy water burned her. Gooseflesh pimpled as she waited for her last cuts to clot. She slipped on her oldest flannel nightgown and lay carefully on the bed. She felt like she would never rise again. Visions of Jon and Naomi haunted her. She had left her post at Jon's bedside. Would God punish her by killing him?

Ada sat up, shortened breaths clenching her chest. She had fallen asleep. She ached inwardly and outwardly, and when she splashed cold water on her cheeks, her face felt like a puffy mask beneath her fingers. Her head was foggy, but she knew she had to check on her brother. She had to check the time.

She threw on her robe and hefted her shoulder against the wardrobe. It seemed heavier than before, and she could barely unblock the door.

Voices in the living room. Was the doctor here? She limped down the hallway.

"Mrs. Williams." The voice was familiar, a woman's voice. "I'm here with a treatment. Would you bend over, please?"

Ada turned into the front room. Her mother stood before Dawn. Sybil's eyes burned as if she were in the presence of God. "Dr. Graham," she said to Dawn, "your services are not required in this house. The Lord has decreed this suffering to purify the souls of his sheep. Those who please him will be saved."

Dawn moved forward to feel Sybil's forehead. "She's delirious. Ada, can you help me?"

Ada stared at her, willing her mental stupor to pass. She flung her head from side to side like a dog shaking off water, then grabbed her mother by the arms. Dawn moved behind Sybil and lifted her skirt. Embarrassed, Ada looked away as she realized where Dawn intended to inject the needle.

"What are you doing?" Sybil demanded. "Although the serpent bites, I will crush his head. Genesis, Genesis …" She yowled as Dawn's needle pushed into her buttocks.

Dawn patted her back. "I'm sorry that hurt, Mrs. Williams. Ada, who's next?"

Ada led her to Jon's room. She helped Dawn roll Jon onto his side and then glanced away as Dawn swabbed the area and guided the needle into his rump. When she heard Dawn tug up his pants, she looked again. Jon's eyes watered from the pain. Dawn put her hand on his cheek. "Now your father," she said.

"Here." Ada opened the door.

The stench was as malignant as ever. Dawn didn't react to the smell. She walked to Silas, but instead of prepping the shot, she placed her fingers on his wrist and leaned close to his face, watching his chest.

"What are you doing?" Ada asked.

Dawn straightened. "I'm sorry," she said as she turned. "I'm afraid there's nothing I can do."

"You can give him the shot! Help him!"

"He's cold. Ada, he's been dead for hours."

"No, no, he's not! My mother has been watching him. He's not dead!"

"I'm sorry," Dawn said again.

Ada's knees buckled. The floor pulled her down.

"Ada, it's going to be okay."

Dawn's arms around her were snakes, twining and compressing.

"What about Naomi?" Ada asked, fighting her panic. "Have you been to the Gentles?"

Dawn hesitated. "My dad dropped me off here. He's gone on to give the rest of them shots."

The rest of them? Ada struggled against Dawn's embrace. Her eyes blurred, but she spotted the needle in Dawn's fingers. "Wait. Don't."

"We have to treat everyone who was exposed." Her voice was firm.

"I'm not ill. Let go of me."

"No. Stay still, Ada!"

"Let go. Let go of me." She was weak from cutting, or else Dawn was absurdly strong. "Get your hands off me, you bitch!"

Her robe peeled off in Dawn's hands, and Ada jumped free of her. She didn't wait to apologize or answer her mother's tremulous call. She sprinted from the room, then the house. Her slippers squelched in the mud, and her feet bruised against the stones.

CHAPTER TEN

Ada's nightgown was no defense against the early morning chill. The bitter air burned her throat, and her fingers and toes quickly lost sensation. Once she reached the street, she checked if Dawn had followed her outside. She hadn't. Ada's breaths were so heavy she hardly noticed she was sobbing until she was another block down. Here the city road pitted and pooled, transitioning into a stubble path through the Smythes' field. Half-tripping, she ran through the field until she reached the creek and crossed the bridge. She kicked off her remaining slipper. The pain in her side forced her to slow.

The doctor's car was parked beside the Smythes' Corsair. Had he already gone to the Gentles, or had he stopped at the Smythes first? An empty, hollow sensation knifed through her chest, and she increased her pace. She was almost there. She raced up the Gentles' drive.

Ham barked as Ada fumbled with the front gate. She saw movement through the windows and marched through the yard before her nerves failed. She knocked so aggressively she skinned her knuckles on the wood.

The bolt drew back. The door creaked open.

"Alameda. What are you doing here?" Mrs. Gentle's eyes were huge in her desolate face.

"Hezekiah said I was to come see Naomi."

"You're too late. Please, just go." She swung the door closed, but Ada stuck her foot in the doorjamb to stop it. She grimaced as it pinched her instep.

"I need to see her, Mrs. Gentle. I am so sorry I couldn't come sooner."

Mrs. Gentle stood back. "Your shoes ..."

Ada peeled off her muddy socks and stepped inside. Sweet and coppery, the smell hit her. The smell of slaughter—urine and blood, diarrhea and vomit. No lights were on, and the dim sunlight shadowed the room. Ada's legs trembled as she walked toward Naomi's bedroom. She hadn't been there since that day.

When she opened the door she heard a cough, and her heart throbbed in her chest. But it was only little Mattie stirring on her bed. On the other side of the room, Mr. Gentle sat beside Naomi's mattress. He looked up when Ada entered. The grief and confusion in his demeanor made her feel worse than ever.

"I should have been with her," he said. "One of the cows had an emergency. I wasn't even here when she passed."

He had never been there. Some nights he hadn't even made it to supper. Ada understood he worked so hard because the Gentles were poor, not because he didn't love his family. But just now, that excuse was meaningless.

"Henry," Mrs. Gentle said from the doorway. "Let Ada say goodbye. The undertaker will be here in half an hour."

Mattie cooed as her father rose. He scooped her up, blankets and all, and left the room. Ada touched the hard back of the chair before the bed but didn't sit. Naomi's face was the color of putty. The gray blanket pulled up to her chin outlined one arm forever bent upon her belly. More tears dripped down Ada's face.

"I'm sorry," Ada whispered.

"I'm sorry too," Dennis said behind her.

She whirled around, but he'd already closed the door, swiftly and noiselessly. She hadn't noticed his car in the drive, had somehow missed it in her panicked flight. She wasn't prepared for this.

"I'm sorry she's dead," he continued, "although she was getting a bit old for me anyway."

Bile and panic climbed her throat. She couldn't speak, only cower in front of her friend, arms out in a final attempt to protect Naomi.

"You're nearly as old as she is, but you're more innocent." He stepped toward her. "At least more than she was in the end. The things I got her to do, that she *wanted* to do ..."

Ada opened her mouth to scream, but nothing came out but strangled air. She must be in a nightmare.

"She got sly, too, avoiding me. It made it a game. I knew she enjoyed it because she never screamed. I don't think you will either."

Ada shrank against the bed. Any minute she would wake up, or Mrs. Gentle would come back, or Hezekiah would find her and yell at her for not going to Naomi last night before it was too late. All she needed to do was cry out. But her throat clenched, blocking off sound.

"You like to hurt, don't you, Ada?" he asked. "I've seen the way you hold yourself. You act like such a nice nelly, but underneath you're a little whore, just like she was. Why else would you come here in your nightgown?"

His words mirrored the dark voices that accused her. She gritted her teeth and at last found her voice. "She was with child. *Your* child. Everyone was going to see what you'd done to her."

His expression didn't change. Ada realized with a shock that he didn't care. The news that he might have been a father didn't register on any emotional level.

"Well, she and the brat inside her are dead, so that saved me some trouble," he said in a matter-of-fact voice. "Now that you're the only one who knows, I'm going to make sure you won't tell anyone. No one will want you when I'm through with you, not even God. And you're going to like it."

He hit her, and it was like a horse's kick between her ribs. Her breath whooshed out, and she slammed against Naomi's body. The corpse was stiff and light, a dried-out corn husk she might crush.

With pinching fingers, Dennis hauled her to her feet. He held her wrists in one hand, her neck in the other. "You won't say anything." His words were slow. Saliva sprayed her cheek. "Go home, Alameda Williams, and pray. Pray you will be so good I won't carry out my threat."

The center of her ribs ached with each breath. When he released her, she weaved for the door. Still she didn't have strength or air to scream. She noticed no one as she ran through the house. Ham yipped at her and jumped into the bushes when she burst out the front door.

Sunshine blinded her. Chirping birds disoriented her. The sun must have rattled free of the clouds while she had been inside. How could the world be so bright and brassy when nothing about it was right?

Instead of crossing the footbridge, she dashed into a clump of trees. She could see the Smythes' house and Dr. Graham's car still parked in front. She pressed her forehead into the rough bark of a pine and wept. It was her fault Naomi was dead. Ada had avoided her, and at the end she'd even been afraid of her, if she was honest with herself. Naomi hadn't wanted to fight the fever, and Ada didn't want to fight it either. She felt powerless. Dennis would never pay for his sins. He would only choose another victim.

Fear, rage, and hatred swirled through her like a lightning storm. She ripped a chunk of bark from the tree. She broke a nail before the bark came free, and sap stained her fingers. She lifted her nightgown and dragged the edge of the bark against her leg. An angry white line appeared, then small drops of red. Not enough. She scraped herself again. Slivers slid beneath her skin. Her lower thigh flamed with pain, and the sensation shot down to her toes and up through her buttocks. It wasn't enough—she needed a knife. She dropped the bark and wiped her hands on the hem of her gown.

As she crossed the bridge, the Smythes' front door opened and Dr. Graham walked to his car. She stopped, but it was too late. He'd seen her—dirty and disarrayed. She clenched her fists and strode on. It helped to focus on the crystal of anger growing against him. He hadn't tried hard enough to save Naomi. Had he even seen her, or given the household shots? How long had he been at the Smythes, one of the richest families in Worden?

He raised his hand, but she turned away, pretending she hadn't seen him. Her foot caught on a root, and she lurched forward. She landed on her forearms in a slick of mud. The front of her gown smeared with brown. Her head swam.

"Ada, are you all right?"

She pulled her nightgown down past her knees as he reached her. He panted slightly from the run and reached out his hand. Ignoring his offer of help, she scrambled up from the puddle and crossed her arms. "I'm fine."

"Are you sure? I think you cut your leg." He crouched and put his hand on her thigh.

"Don't!" She leaped backwards, lost her balance, and sat down hard on the grass. "I said I was fine!"

"Forgive me." Red scorched his face, and he tipped down the brim of his tweed hat. "I wanted to examine the cut. It might get infected."

"I don't care if it does," she said. She despised his medical stare that saw only what was wrong. His profession could never survive if people were whole; perhaps doctors wanted people to stay sick.

His eyes were darker and larger than ever. "You don't mean that. Did you just come from the Gentles?"

Of course she had. His question was inane. Worse—artificially tactful. "You didn't save her," she said, "or her baby. You chose to save the rich Smythes instead."

"I'm not God. I didn't choose one life over the other." His quick reply showed she'd stung his pride. "Naomi was more vulnerable to the bacteria because she was pregnant and malnourished, and she had little will to fight. Billy and the other children had hope."

Hearing that he'd struggled to save Billy made her feel stupid. Nevertheless, the crystal of anger grew, restructuring itself in harder, if more splintered lines. "Naomi had hope! Maybe if you had found her a place at Haven House sooner so she didn't decided to starve herself to keep from showing, she'd be alive. She'd be out of Worden!"

"I wish a place had opened earlier, I really do." He cleared his throat. "My pressing concern now, however, is your dying of exposure as we debate who was to blame. I'm going to drive you home."

"I'll walk."

"No. Come along." He grabbed her arms. His rough woolen coat was wet from a light rain, and his warm, large hands heated her entire body. "You're ice cold. Here." He shook off his coat and wrapped it around her.

"Is that a bruise on your neck?"

She hunched her shoulders. "I don't know." She walked rapidly toward the car. The coat smelled like him. She hadn't realized he had a smell until now. Antiseptic soap, something like mothballs, and a deep, slightly spicy musk. How could he do this to her? She wanted to stay angry with him. For God's sake, and in Naomi's memory, she determined never to see him again. Just as soon as he drove her home.

In the cab, she stared at the dashboard. Her body shook beneath the coat, and she hoped he didn't notice. She refused to look at him.

"Promise me you'll wash out that cut," he said.

"I'll wash it."

"Did Dawn give you the antibiotic shot?"

Ada hesitated, then twinged with shame. She had almost lied. And it would have been a useless lie, for Dawn would tell him how she'd fled. "No."

"I have some with me. I'll administer it when we stop."

"No, thank you, Dr. Graham."

The car bumped to a halt. Ada broke her resolution and glanced at him. He looked pale. Nearly sick himself.

"What did you say?" he asked.

"I said I won't take your silly shot. If God wants me to fall ill, I shouldn't resist. I shouldn't have any help that Naomi didn't. Besides, it's inappropriate."

"Miss Williams, frankly I don't believe you are in a condition to make such a determination. I'm going to give you that shot whether you consent or not. You're not eighteen yet, and I will appeal to your parents—"

"Yes, I *am* eighteen," she said. "Goodbye." She opened the car door and jumped out. Her house was in sight. She threw his coat onto the seat and ran up the walk.

"I've got you!" Dawn shouted as Ada passed through the door. Ada's breath whooshed from her as Dawn tackled her and pinned her to the ground with her knees. Ada struggled weakly as Dawn maneuvered her nightgown past her buttocks. She managed not to scream but bit her lip until it bled at the aching pain of the needle.

As soon as Dawn released her, Ada rolled away and leaped to her feet. Through tears of fury, she staggered down the hall.

"Ada, I'm sorry—" Dawn's voice trailed after her.

"Go away." She slammed the door to emphasize her point. Trembling with rage and helplessness, she dragged her desk chair to the door to serve as a barricade.

At the moment, she hated Dawn for taking away the possibility of oblivion. She wanted badly never to forgive her, even if God demanded she do so. Her teeth chattered as she pulled off her nightgown. It was so muddy, she might as well throw it away. Her skin felt like frozen stone. Her legs were hardly bloody. She would fix that.

The blood was warm as it trickled down her skin. She spread it out with her fingers so she could examine the cuts she made. As she carved deeper, the pain and anger receded, and a rush of exhilaration heated her. Each cutting session had left her vaguely dissatisfied. One more cut, a little more blood—it was never enough. Now the only thing that stopped her was the brown-spotted rag blooming red like a sea sponge. A stray drop stained her comforter, resounding like an archangel's trumpet in the brimming well of her psyche.

With a whimper of anger, she stopped and began the sticky waiting period before bandaging. She felt spent and wanted nothing more than sleep. A knock, uncharacteristically tentative, shattered that possibility. She wrapped her thickest robe around her and moved the chair from the door.

"Ada," Jon asked as she opened the door, "are you all right?"

He looked so much better, she nearly forgave Dawn. Still, he sagged against the side of the door, and his breathing was labored.

"No," she said. "Why aren't you sleeping?"

A pause. "The mortician is on his way, and I need your help telling him what to do. I'm letting Mother sleep."

Her world spun. Somehow, Dennis's threats and her cutting had made her forget that her father was dead. There were practicalities that must be dealt with, coffins to choose, financial changes to effect. Moreover, there was a good man and father to mourn. He had always been a calming influence in the house, and she could have set her watch to his habits. Another day, her anguish at losing him would have overpowered her, but now her emotions were used up. Later, she would weep.

"I need time to get ready. You might have to start without me."

"Please hurry." His voice cracked.

"I will." She closed the door. She walked to the washbasin and dipped in a washcloth. The cold water smarted on her cuts. She remembered something else. "Are you still there, Jon?" she called.

He tapped the door. "What is it?"

"Happy birthday."

A pause. "You too."

CHAPTER ELEVEN

*N*aomi Gentle, Alice Keller, Victoria Hautman, and James Hill were buried in a single ceremony that Mr. Smythe, one of the church elders, read from the liturgy at the back of the hymnal. Ada wondered how many graves had been opened in the Catholic churchyard, or in the town graveyard in the Meatpacking District.

For her father's funeral a few hours later, however, Eric Donner stood at the burial plot without a word. At one point he tried to speak but gave only a garbled cry. Ada watched as Michael marched to the front of the crowd. Eric gave the hymnal to him, covered his face with his hands, and rushed to the back of the gathering.

No one objected, and Michael calmly read through the service. During a special church board meeting afterward, Michael was elected as the temporary minister until a replacement was found. Ada thought he was too young for the honor, but no one else sought the position.

Sybil was well enough to stand stoically by the grave and say God's will be done, blessed be the name of the Lord, but Ada's stomach wrenched as if it were the vilest blasphemy. Her head felt fuzzy, and her neck, abdomen, and thighs were sore. She had washed her cuts as she had promised Dr. Graham, and only then noticed that an older one was not healing as the others did. It was raised and streaked red and white, and the skin around it was hot and dry.

As she watched her father's plain coffin being lowered into the dank hole of earth, she felt incurably fatigued. Even though nearly everyone had been given the antibiotic shot, the doctor had warned against a reception. His caveat disappointed Sybil but relieved Ada, whose body felt as vacant as the nearby open grave awaiting the next service. Later, when she'd had some sleep and her mother was fully recovered, they might host a memorial. Do something for all the dead, not just for her father.

Following the funeral, Ada retired to her room and lay on the bed. Already the house felt different, as if someone had rearranged everything in her absence. Her stockings were sticky and sweaty as she rolled them off. She knew she should be with her mother and brother to see if they needed anything, but she was too exhausted. The same thoughts looped and tangled in her mind. She would never see Naomi again. She would never hug her father. Perhaps in the heavenly realm, some day—but the hope was slim comfort.

She awoke an hour later. Her head ached, and her jaw felt constricted. Pain spiked beneath her ears as if she'd tasted something exceedingly sour. Her teeth knocked together.

A sensation rose in her belly and lower back, building up to her head. As the wave reached her eyes, she panicked. Her entire body jerked. She opened her mouth—it took some effort, and it was only an inch—and screamed.

The door scraped open. "What's the matter?" Sybil asked in a rough, urgent voice.

"I am … I feel—" She put her hand to her neck. Dennis hadn't squeezed her so very hard, had he? She swallowed back the choking sensation as her tongue rose in her throat. She felt her belly twitch of its own accord. Then the spasm took her. Her back arched, and her head snapped backward.

"My angel!" Sybil tried to settle her back onto the bed. Her arms seemed weak, like a bird's broken wings, and the wan afternoon sunlight highlighted the gray in her hair. A crease ran down her forehead, a crucifix of worry. "I'm going to call Dr. Graham. You'll be okay. You're God's special child."

"No!" The word tore from her like a sob. "Don't!" Her stomach muscles clenched, and she cried out. Her jaw felt like someone had taken a hammer to it and nailed it partially closed. She knew in her bones that she would die. This was God's punishment for abandoning Naomi and lusting after Dr. Graham. *Whoever looks at a woman to lust for her has already committed adultery in his heart.* And she hadn't just looked, she had imagined him touching her. If she died now, perhaps God would forgive her, for she knew how vile she was, and she repented absolutely.

Her agony was so intense she noticed nothing outside herself until someone turned her on her back and she looked into Dr. Graham's face. She reacted as if she'd seen the devil.

"No," she slurred, striking at him with her arms, "go away!"

Strong hands held her down, forced her arms to her sides. The face was replaced by Sara Ellington's. She heard the word "hospital," and she cried out again, "No!" Her body spasmed again and again, sometimes so forcefully she thought her bones would break. She struggled for breath as her ribs crushed against her lungs. During a moment of relief, she saw Jon's face in her pain-narrowed field of vision. His cheeks streamed with tears. She wanted to brush them off. Of course she forgave him. What was he sorry for? When he picked her up, her body shook so violently she lost consciousness.

All sense of time slipped away. In her mind she prayed repeatedly, obsessively, repenting of all she had ever done, thought about doing, or yet might do. Breaking her promise to Naomi again, she confessed what Dennis Gentle had done, but the words sounded like gibberish even to her. Demons in her sheets touched her with burning fingers, igniting more spasms. Several times she felt a sharp pain in her upper arm. Then came a hideous nightmare when the demons peeled her clothes from her and probed her naked flesh. She screamed and fought them, over and over, but they always won.

"Father!" she shouted. Somehow she felt he was near. She sensed his presence, cool and bright as the moon above her face. She struggled toward him, but something kept her from him.

Faceless voices ranted at her. The demons grabbed her. They strapped her down and carried her away, back to her pain, back to the darkness.

Ada awoke. She was on a small, hard bed, and white curtains walled her in. She wore a loose nightgown she didn't remember putting on. Her fingers explored her rigid belly and her upper thighs, found that bandages covered her cuts. A tube was taped to her arm, and when she moved her arm, something beeped.

The curtains shifted, and a short woman with blotchy red skin entered. She grabbed Ada's arm and readjusted the tube, smoothing out its snaky length all the way to the wheeled machine it was attached to. A half-full bag of translucent liquid swung from the machine.

"Alameda, don't try to talk," the woman said. "You've been feverish for three days, and you're lucky to be alive."

With her free hand, Ada investigated the pressure in her jaw. She moved gingerly, afraid of sparking another paroxysm. Her mouth was firmly shut. Panic welled as she tried and failed to part her lips.

"Since you're awake, I'm going to help you eat something." The woman walked to a side table. Ada strained to watch. Her neck felt stiff and weak, barely capable of moving her skull, much less supporting it.

The woman used a large syringe to extract a puce-colored substance from a bag. Ada frowned. She didn't like the needle, and she wasn't sure she liked the woman. Who was she? This had to be the hospital, but where were Jon and Sybil?

"Thankfully your jaw didn't fracture," the woman said. "It might not feel like it to you, but there's actually a small opening I can use to feed you. Mostly you've been using it to drool and jabber through. If your pillow starts to stink, I'll change it for you. Dawn did it yesterday though, so it's probably okay for a while."

Had Dawn been taking care of her? Had she seen her cuts? Had the doctor? Where was he? Ada gurgled furiously, struggling to form questions. The infuriating woman wouldn't stop blathering to listen.

Ada's failed words morphed into a cry of pain. Her chest rose into the air, and her head jolted back as her body seized. Her monitors beeped.

The curtain swished apart, and Dr. Graham rushed into the room. "For pity's sake, Jan, I said to call me when she regained consciousness!" He stabbed a needle into Ada's IV bag. "This should help you relax," he told her. "It will make you tired too. When you wake up again, your mother will be here."

Her body lowered back to the bed. Only then did she feel his firm hands on her shoulders, easing her into position. She wrestled against his efforts.

"I told her not to talk," Jan said. "I was trying to orient her, but she didn't pay attention."

Ada wished she could say something in her defense, but consciousness slipped from her like thread from a needle.

♫

"We're going to take you home," Sybil said, squeezing Ada's fingers. "The doctor said it's safe."

Sara Ellington harrumphed. "Not quite. Dr. Graham said there's less risk associated with moving her than there was, not that there's no risk."

"She needs to be somewhere she's loved," Sybil said.

"She needs to be somewhere she's cared for properly," Sara replied. "Watch; this is how you'll have to feed her."

No one had asked her where she'd rather be, Ada thought as Sara lifted a cup toward her and expertly passed a straw through her lips. The familiar feeling of powerlessness suffocated Ada more than the coaxed, difficult process of swallowing did. At least Sara no longer had to use a syringe, and she didn't try to converse with Ada, unlike the nursing assistant, Jan. Or at least, Jan had been a nursing assistant fifteen years ago. During the epidemic, anyone with training, experience, or an expired license had been called in to help. Now Jan was considering returning to the field she had dabbled in as a young adult. Even if Ada had been able to talk, she doubted she could get a word in edgewise to tell her what a bad idea that was.

"Her jaw is starting to open more," Sara said. "Soon she can start eating soft foods, like yogurt and bananas."

"Can you wheel her out yet?" Sybil asked.

"The doctor wanted to check on her one more time before she's discharged. Why don't you take a seat in the waiting room."

"I don't see why I can't stay here."

Sara set the cup on the table with more firmness than usual. "It's for Alameda's privacy. We have to follow the law."

"I follow the law," Sybil said with a frown. "God's law. And nothing should be going on with my daughter that I can't hear about."

"The doctor was quite clear that Alameda is not in a position to sign a privacy release right now. Your presence here will only make the checkout process longer."

"Very well." Sybil touched Ada's cheek. "I'll see you soon."

Ada was so exhausted her limbs felt pressed against the thin mattress. She closed her eyes. She didn't want to see the doctor. When he was in the room, she tensed, and she had learned that tension led to spasms.

"Just as I thought," Sara said. "She leaves the room, and your muscles relax. If it were up to me, you wouldn't be going home yet. But it's not; it's up to Dr. Graham. And your mother has been wheedling him for days to let you go home."

Ada's eyes flicked open. She didn't want to be drowsy when he came in. He hadn't made a full examination of her, at least not when she was conscious. As far as she knew, only Sara and Nurse Brandt had dressed her cuts. They hadn't talked to her about them, but they must have told the doctor. What would he make of the scars and slashes? It was too much to hope he hadn't recognized they were self-inflicted, but Ada clung to the thin hope as tightly as a spider clings to its web on a gusty day.

"That's another puzzle," Sara said. "When I mention Dr. Graham or he's in the room, you tense up as well. Trust me, you're not the first to be nervous around doctors."

And probably not the first to fall in love with one. The thought came from nowhere. It wasn't true—she wasn't in love with him. What she felt was the basest of emotions.

"Miss Williams." Clipboard in hand, he came around the edge of the curtain. "How are you feeling today, honey?"

She swallowed. It was one of the few movements she could accomplish without disaster. She couldn't lie to herself as she looked at him, not after he called her honey. She breathed air into her lungs and tried to talk. "I don't … want you … here."

He exchanged looks with Nurse Ellington.

"I don't know what she said," Sara said. "Jan insists she can tell, but I think she's faking."

"I think I know what she said." He handed Sara the clipboard and stepped close to the bed. "She's said it before. Ada, do you want me to go away?"

No, she didn't want him to leave, but God would want her to tell him to leave. Or at least she thought God did. She nodded.

"That's a bit of a problem," he said, "as the other doctors in Worden specialize in animals. But if you continue your protest, perhaps the hospital board will advertise an opening."

"What is the problem?" Sara asked. Ada couldn't tell if the question was directed at Dr. Graham or her.

"She blames me for her friend's death," the doctor said. He turned his serious expression to Ada. "I explained this to your mother and told her how I handled the case. I even proposed she talk with the Gentles if she had doubts. She didn't."

Ada bit her lip.

"I am sorry you are unhappy with what I did," he said, "and I can't blame you. I wish I could have done more. I wish I didn't have to choose which sick person needed me most. This was an epidemic Worden wasn't prepared for. I've been trying to get another doctor installed at the hospital for years. I think at last it will happen, but not in time for him—or her—to attend your case."

She rolled her eyes toward the wall. A rusty sensation filled her, as if her bones had turned to iron. What if she should fall, further than she had already? For her soul's sake she didn't want him here, but she was wrong to take out her anger on him. It was unfair to blame Dr. Graham when God was the one not helping her.

"The point is," Sara said, "the doctor needs to examine you before you can go home. Are you going to cooperate with us?"

Ada inched up the coverlet.

"May I?" Dr. Graham asked.

She shut her eyes and nodded.

"Thank you," he said. "Also, I don't want Sara's comments to mislead you. If we discharge you from the hospital, I will be making house calls to ensure you heal properly."

Sara folded back the blankets so a single sheet hid Ada's nightgown from view and then helped her slowly turn onto her side. Dr. Graham placed his stethoscope against her back and told her to breathe as the nurse took her wrist and counted her pulse.

"Your breathing sounds good," he said.

"Her heart rate is ninety," Sara said.

Ada kept very still. Sara helped her roll onto her back again and then pulled down the single sheet. Ada snatched it back so forcefully her stomach muscles contracted again. Her back arched, and a moan forced itself from her stiff jaw. She wheezed after the spasm passed. Sweat prickled her brow.

"You need to let the doctor examine the infection site," Sara said. She put her hands on her hips so her bony elbows stuck out like the handles of a teacup.

"No!" Another wave of heat surged from her stomach to the roots of her hair.

"It's all right, Sara." Dr. Graham put his hand on the nurse's shoulder. "Let me talk to her."

Ada was mortified. She imagined how her cuts would disgust him. He would try to hide his feelings of course—she gave him that much credit—but she would be able to tell by the twitch of his lips or the slant of his eyebrows. Absurdly, she was proud of her wounds, each one a testament written in blood.

"I don't know if the nurses told you," Dr. Graham said, "but you have tetanus, or lockjaw."

"I don't know how," Sara murmured. "She should have gotten her booster shot about six years ago."

Ada thought she remembered being stuck with a needle, but it didn't surprise her that a vaccination had failed to protect her from God's will. By whatever means, God had ordained for her to contract the illness.

"Skin is the body's first defense against germs," Dr. Graham said as if he were teaching a class on hygiene. "When the skin's integrity is compromised by a scrape, a burn, or a cut, the body is open to attack. Several bacterial strains, including *clostridium tetani*, which causes tetanus, colonized an opening in your body. Tetanus induces muscle rigidity and severe spasms that can break bones and interfere with your breathing, potentially leading to death." He said the word gently, perhaps in deference to her recent loss. "I treated you with antibiotics, the tetanus antitoxin, and muscle relaxants. You're doing quite well. Judging by the opening of your jaw, your case is mild to moderate. Over the next few weeks, your jaw will loosen, and the tetany—that's the technical term for the spasms—will reduce in number, duration, and intensity. You could be fully recovered in a few months."

Mild to moderate? Her muscles twitched.

"You're lucky," he said. "No bones broken, not even your jaw. It's vital that you maintain your fluid intake and avoid excess stimulation as your nerve endings regrow. Also, we want your wounds to heal properly. What I need to check now is whether they're healed enough for you to leave. Sara."

As Sara approached and they uncovered Ada's belly, Ada closed her eyes and tried to think of anything else.

"The color's good," Dr. Graham said. Ada heard a pen scrawl across the clipboard. She shivered as she felt a finger against her skin. Whose was it? "The swelling has gone down. The skin is still slightly warm to the touch."

"You haven't had a patient conference about the nature of the cuts," Sara said. She lowered her voice, but Ada had no difficulty understanding her. She went cold.

"I'll do it during a house call. Her mobility is limited, so that's not a major concern right now."

Tears squeezed from her eyelids. She didn't understand why they talked about her as if she weren't there. She would never have chosen for Dr. Graham to see her like this, with her belly open to the world. It was God's cruel way of making sure the doctor never shared the feelings she possessed for him.

"She'll be fine," Dr. Graham said. "Call one of the orderlies and move her to a gurney."

She was going home.

CHAPTER TWELVE

The window shade was down, but she could hear a sparrow singing on the other side of the wall. Ada felt as muted as the bird's song. She was in her room, but nothing felt familiar. Her father's death had changed the tone of the house, and her illness only added to its strangeness.

"Mother?" The word came out in a garbled whisper, and Ada felt her neck twinge as she said it.

"My angel, you're awake." Sybil spoke from the corner of the room. A Bible lay open on her lap. "I am so sorry you have to face this trial. But be of good courage; God does not give us anything that is too great for us. And he must judge your strength to be great, to give you this so soon after the plague." She closed the book and walked to the washbasin.

"Your illness seems to have chastened Jonathon," she said as she filled a glass. She plopped a tablet into the water and stirred it with a straw. "Perhaps his repentance is one reason God brought the plague and now this upon us. It has caused us all to reexamine ourselves. Even you, my darling daughter, might be brought under conviction." She inserted the straw between Ada's lips. "Here. You're supposed to drink as much as you can when you're awake. It should help you sleep as well."

The drink made her drowsy. She had nearly dropped off when Sybil said, "I've put a bell on your nightstand. If you need something and Jon and I aren't here, just ring it." Sybil's lips brushed against her cheek.

Ada awoke some time later and shifted her position. The bedclothes drew across her stomach, prompting a spasm. She gasped as her muscles contracted. After they relaxed, she gathered her breath and held very still.

The house was quiet, and she felt alone. She looked at the bell. Who would come if she rang it? Would they still come if they knew what she'd done, why she'd gotten sick? She had to go to the bathroom, and her stomach rumbled with aching hunger, but she closed her eyes and ignored everything. Sometime later, a knock startled her awake.

"Hey, Sis, I've brought you some soup." Balancing a tray, Jon entered the room. "First let's get you sitting upright." He set down the tray and bolstered her up with pillows. Then he handed her a spoon. "Dawn said to make sure you do as much by yourself as you can."

She glanced at him. Dawn, not the doctor?

"I brought you lots of napkins," he said, "so you don't have to worry about spilling or drooling."

"Thanksh." She shifted uncomfortably. She was afraid that her bladder would empty if she had another spasm. Looking at the hot liquid of the soup was horrible, but she deserved to be in pain. She dipped the spoon into the bowl and tilted it to her lips. A stream of drops slopped onto the linen napkin on her lap.

"Work was slow tonight," Jon said.

Not as slow as her dinner looked to be. She tried another spoonful, with the same result.

"Try slurping," he suggested. "For once, don't worry about good manners."

She sipped vigorously, and the soup tasted so good she no longer felt like she was punishing herself. She put down the spoon.

"I can't believe how many people died," he said. He stared at the wall-paper behind the bed.

Ada was conscious only of the burning urge to void and her embarrassment at asking her brother to help her. It didn't matter that she'd done the same for him when he was ill; he'd been so feverish he probably hadn't been aware of it. She would force herself to manage alone.

"I can't believe Father is dead." He rubbed his hands through his hair. "Our family is going to fall apart without him, but maybe that needs to happen. Maybe we need this change."

More of Dawn's philosophy? She pressed her hands against the pillows and adjusted her seat. The noise returned his focus to her.

"What's the matter? What do you need?"

"To get uhh," Ada slurred. "'Athroom."

"Oh. Okay." His brow creased. "Maybe I should get Mother."

She shook her head and tried to move her legs over the side of the bed. As a warning sensation of tightness welled up, she paused, but Jon had caught the idea and pulled her legs so her feet touched the floor.

"Wait a second and make sure you're not too dizzy," he said.

She did, and she was able to walk, although not without awakening each sore muscle to a new intensity. He refused to leave her side, and after a moment she recognized her false pride and allowed him to help. Leaning on his shoulder, she made it across the hall. In the bathroom, she was on her own. She stooped, contracting to a quasi-fetal position on the toilet, and sat there for a long time, willing herself to get up.

Jon knocked on the door. "Ada, are you okay?"

"Yesh," she answered. She lurched to her feet, then nearly fell as the room went black. She caught herself on the counter and laid her head in the sink until the dizziness passed. Hardly noticing the wetness of the water or the texture of the towel, she washed and dried her hands.

This was humiliation. God had made Nebuchadnezzar like a beast of the field, and he had eaten grass and gone around on all fours, but God had shown mercy and taken his sanity too for those seven years. He hadn't been stuck, as she was, in her mind, experiencing every sensation and thought viciously and repetitively.

Hearing Jon speak about their father deepened her feelings of guilt. If her secrets had come to light before his death, how he would have grieved. And it was wrong, absolutely evil, that she felt relief, even though it was minuscule, that at least now he would never learn what kind of a daughter he had, or what members of his flock had done.

With Jon's assistance, she made it back to her bed and ate her soup. She didn't try to talk again.

♫

Nurse Ellington made several house calls, mainly to change Ada's bandages and give unwanted advice to Sybil, but Dr. Graham didn't come until Ada's jaw had loosened enough for her to carry on a short, if somewhat salivary, conversation.

She had just finished dinner—more soup, as chewing was painful and minimally effective—and was sitting upright in bed trying to concentrate on her devotional when she heard Dr. Graham at the front door. With a stab of panic, she picked up her hand mirror. She brushed her fingers through her tangled hair, trying not to cry. The mirror's swirling border deserved to frame more beauty than she saw reflected.

She set aside the mirror and grabbed her devotional as Dr. Graham knocked and entered her room.

"I'm glad to see you looking so well," he said. "Sara has been giving me reports, but I had to see for myself. I'm sorry I haven't visited sooner."

Her hands tightened on the book's spine. "I'm in the middle of my lesson."

"You're speaking very well too." He sat next to the bed. "That's good, because I want to talk with you. I asked for some time alone, so no one will disturb us."

Unbidden, a frisson of delight frisked up her back. She straightened her shoulders and closed the book. She held it like a shield against his presence.

"I'm pleased with how well your cuts are healing," he said.

So the patient conference had come at last. She wished now her posture wasn't so erect; she wanted to hide against the pillows. She bobbed her head nervously.

"My concern," he said, "is that more of them will appear. Tell me about the cuts on your abdomen and legs. Did you do them yourself?"

She looked at the door, which he'd left ajar. They were speaking quietly, but if the wrong phrase carried, and her mother heard ... "I don't want to talk about it."

"Honey." His voice was sad. At the word, emotion swelled through her. "Please, talk to me. I don't think you'll be able to heal until you start talking about what's bothering you."

"You know what's bothering me—Naomi." That was the easiest explanation for her behavior, although much more was behind it. She couldn't tell him that her feelings for him made her feel so guilty, so out of control, so desperate. It was impossible to identify the root of her guilt anymore; it had spread so far into her being.

"You started this when you found out that Naomi was being abused?"
She nodded.

"Before then, did you do anything similar?"

She thought of pinching herself when the devil tempted her, of the sermons she had paralyzed herself through, of the time she'd gotten a splinter and didn't dig it out until it festered and her mother spotted it. The few times she'd been spanked for being naughty, her mother had ended the discipline with a prayer and a verse, Proverbs 20:30. *The blueness of a wound cleanseth away evil: so do stripes the inward parts of the belly.* After an unusually painful beating for an outburst of temper when she was eleven, Ada had truly taken the scripture to heart. She promised herself she would never face the shame of corporal punishment from her mother again. She learned to discipline herself as soon as she had the evil thoughts, before they were incarnated into action. Since that day, her mother had become Sybil in her head, and Ada had become her equal in the rites of discipline.

"I don't know," she said. And then again, "I don't want to talk about it."

He waited a little, and when she kept silent, said, "I wish you could talk with a psychiatrist, but since Worden doesn't have one, you'll have to make do with me."

"A psychiatrist?" she repeated. Those were doctors for crazy people, not people like her. They were doctors who put you away in an asylum.

He shifted in the chair. "Would you rather talk with someone else? A nurse perhaps?"

She met his eyes. Blue as the sky, they hid his emotion like rain in a cloud. God would want her to say yes. If she said yes, she would sever their bond, which she valued despite its perversity. She would be forced to talk with someone, but she thought she would be able to control what she said. With the doctor, she wanted to do anything he might ask.

"No," she said, surprising herself. She set the devotional on the bedside table. Dr. Graham's right hand rested on his knee, but his left lay on the edge of the bedspread. Under the covers, her leg inched toward his hand.

"Thank you for trusting me," he said. "You are very brave."

"No, I'm not." If she were brave, she would tell him the truth about Naomi and then never see him again. She was a coward, and that was why she cut herself—to keep the cowardice from claiming her.

"You don't think it takes bravery to withstand pain?"

She dropped her gaze, not wanting to admit he was right. She was worse than a coward; she was as prideful as Uzziah, and God had smitten her as he had the king, not with leprosy but with tetanus.

"Why do you want to hurt yourself?"

She willed her leg to be still, but for once her self-paralysis failed. A single fold in the blanket separated her from his fingers. "I don't know. It just … helps."

"Do you feel that you deserve to be punished?"

"We all deserve to be punished. 'There is none righteous; no, not one.' Romans 3:10."

He leaned back, crossing his arms. "But even in your religion, there's grace. What about Christ's atonement?"

"Limited to those who are chosen to believe." Despite her soreness, she drew her knees up to her chest. She was mortified that he might have drawn away because her leg had crept too close. Under the blankets, she pinched the sides of her thighs. "That leaves out a lot of people, no matter how one looks at it."

He smiled a little. "People like me."

She pinched harder. "You think I'm silly. That I'm stupid for believing the way I do when it makes me sad. Well, I believe it because it's true. I wish you'd stop judging me."

"I don't judge you. It hurts my heart that you feel this way." Looking away for a moment, he rested his chin on his palm. "Cutting yourself is dangerous. There are other ways to deal with feelings that trouble you."

The pain made her grimace and gasp for breath, and she let her hands relax before it became obvious. "What other ways?"

"Writing them down is good; so is talking with someone you trust. What about your mother or brother?"

"I can't tell them!" Especially not now, when the harmony of their home had been fatally disrupted. Besides, any telling would require Naomi's name to be disgraced. Now that her friend was dead, Ada couldn't stand for her memory to be tainted. It would be useless as well as cruel. Naomi would have been the main witness against Dennis. Without her, he stood no chance of conviction. At least if his attention was on Ada, he wouldn't victimize anyone else.

"Is there anyone you could tell?" he asked.

You, she thought. She said, "Maybe Father O'Connor."

His eyes shadowed, and he pressed out a wrinkle in his sleeve. "I'm so sorry, but Father O'Connor died in the epidemic."

Tears squeezed past her eyelids, trailed down her cheeks. She didn't bother to brush them away. "Is there anyone you *did* save?"

"Too few."

His words were broken, and she wanted to reach for him, to share his sorrow. Instead, she faced the wall and allowed her gaze to wander through the repetitive patterns of the wallpaper, like a child lost in a maze.

"I have to ask," he said after a moment, in a calmer voice, "what did you use to cut yourself?"

"A kitchen knife." Strange, now that she'd started to tell him, how difficult it was to hold anything back. "A fillet knife, mostly."

"Can I have it?"

"No. My mother might notice it was gone and ask about it."

He sighed. "Some of the cuts were quite deep. Did you know you could hit an artery?"

"I suppose not."

"Did you intend to kill yourself?"

"Suicide is a sin."

"Does that mean no?"

She twisted around and looked into his eyes. They were full of an emotion she'd never seen before and recognized dimly, as if from another life, reality, or instinct. "I didn't want to kill myself, only quiet myself."

"Explain."

"My head fills up with what everyone says. They're always telling me what to do, and what they and God would think of it. I'm so full of everyone else's opinions and emotions that I'm being … squeezed out of my head, or—or split apart at the seams. I need to do something extreme to stay together. Because sometimes I wish I could be like them, to be someone who influences instead of someone who's influenced, to act on a desire, even when I know that it's wrong, that it's part of the sinful nature I must fight, like I must fight my feelings—" She bit her lip to stop herself. She sounded pathetic. He probably thought she was hysterical, or worse, insane, since he talked about psychiatrists. If he ordered her another sedative, she would take it. She needed something, anything to blunt the stimuli of existence. Her face reddened as she blotted her mouth with a handkerchief in case drool had escaped during her tirade. Her jaw ached all the way through to her teeth.

"You're very empathetic," he said. "I'm empathetic too, and I think that's why we've had a special connection since the day we met."

She swallowed. She knew what he was talking about, but it stunned her that he felt it as well and admitted to it. It was the invisible force that pulled her even now toward him, that whispered it was safe to trust him. Finally she felt justified enough to gaze at him without glancing away when he returned the look. She traced the lines of his face with the appreciativeness and possessiveness of an artist. She wanted him to keep talking. "A connection?"

He took off his glasses and wiped them on his shirt. "I think, whether it's due to my training, personality, or experience, I can sense a creature in pain. So can you. That empathy is a strength if you recognize it for what it is—insight into another person that allows you to understand them. Although you participate in their pain in order to help them, you must separate it from yourself. You have to learn to let go of it before it overwhelms your senses and judgment."

"How did you learn to let go?"

"I'm not sure I have." His smile was feeble, a twisted thread. "Not completely. I work long hours and usually don't attend social events. I see people in a setting where I am mostly able to heal their pain, and so my own. But others sculpt, or paint, or write to draw out those emotions, to funnel them into something apart from themselves. Maybe that's why people who feel so keenly tend to be artists." He paused. "I heard you play at the church festival. That's when I knew my impression of you was correct."

"You liked my playing?"

"Very much."

She glanced down. "I saw you walk out right after I played. I thought you hadn't noticed."

"I noticed." He scooted closer and lowered his hand to the mattress again. "You have something special."

"I had a good teacher."

"Miss Passerini? I remember her. She smoked cigars all the time and refused to put them out, even in the hospital."

She stared at his hand, so close to her legs, which were still tucked to her chest. She stretched them out, feeling the cramped muscles ease. There was no sin in that, surely. "It feels like art or music when I cut myself."

"I noticed the symmetry and precision of your cuts. You want to express something, I understand, but your body is not the right canvas for that. Can you promise me that you'll stop?"

"I have to stop?" She closed her eyes, imagining the sharp slide of the blade against her skin, the warm blood that thickened so mysteriously, the vicious satisfaction that energized her afterward.

"Yes."

She shook her head.

"I would be negligent if I allowed you to continue to hurt yourself. Could you at least tell your mother, and make yourself accountable to her for your safety?"

"No! And you can't either." She searched his eyes. "Can you?"

"As your doctor, everything you tell me is in confidence, but you can't continue this behavior. There are places … unpleasant places I wouldn't want you to end up in. I'd be ethically bound to send you there if I thought you were going to hurt yourself."

"You'd send me to an insane asylum?" Her stomach clenched.

"No—a mental hospital. The people there could help you, like I'm trying to."

"If you want to help me, don't threaten me." She felt like crying again. "I can promise not to cut myself, at least until I see you again."

He blinked, clearly weighing her words. Would he spot her hypocrisy, that she was bargaining his presence for good behavior? "Okay," he said. "I'll see you in a few days. In the meantime, Nurse Ellington will report to me on your condition, so I'll know if you've kept your word." He moved his hand at last, and touched her lower arm. The contact was brief, but it invaded her entire body like a tetanus paroxysm. "I can see you're going to be my challenge."

Motionless, she watched him gather his bag and stand. A tear rolled down to her lips, but he was already gone.

CHAPTER THIRTEEN

There was a presence in her room. Dark. Menacing.

"Who's there?" she cried. The sheets coiled around her like bands.

"Did you think I'd forgotten about you?" His face was blurry, a smudge of yellow on top, and an indigo stain for eyes. "I've been waiting, hoping you'd die. Now that you haven't, I'm coming for you."

Ada tried to get up and dash out of the room, but someone clasped her around the neck. She struggled against the embrace, but the arms were rigid. She craned her neck to see who held her. It was Naomi's corpse. With bleached-out skin, nearly translucent eyelids shrunk across the eye sockets, and mouth a small black slash between colorless lips, Naomi's body was already a ghost. Then the mouth quivered, the eyes opened, and the face lunged at her.

Ada gasped and sat up. Her body shuddered with a small spasm. Her eyes were wet, and her heart pounded. In the blackness of the room, she needed light. She limped to the desk and lit the lamp. She sat on the chair and picked up her Bible, mouthing the familiar words as she read.

"'There hath no temptation taken you but such as is common to man; but God is faithful, who will not suffer you to be tempted above that ye are able; but will with the temptation also make a way to escape, that ye may be able to bear it.' 1 Corinthians 10:13."

Telling the doctor about her cutting hadn't helped. It hadn't disgusted him, had instead somehow brought them closer. Why wasn't God helping her? Where was her way of escape? *Escape.* Overwhelming sadness squeezed her insides. It had been two days, and she needed to cut.

He'd sent her a journal, a beautiful leather book with a frontispiece featuring gulls and seashells over a peaceful strand of beach. She had written nothing in it, had in fact hidden it beneath her pillow. It was a gift she ought to return, but she hadn't the fortitude.

On display, instead, was a card Michael had bought her. Tissue paper cut in delicate patterns adorned the front. He had written encouraging verses in it and signed, "Yours in Christ, Michael." She didn't want to think that he was hers. She didn't want that responsibility. But Sybil would notice if Ada took down the card.

The open card seemed to watch her as she struck her belly with her fist. Her abdomen was so sore, she doubled over and sucked in air. A tremor snapped her chest forward and her neck back. She dug her fingernails into her thighs. What was she doing? What was the matter with her? She couldn't stop herself. She didn't have even an animal's instinct for self-preservation. Blood tipped her nails. She felt the stitches on her deepest cut and clawed between the puckering edges of her skin. The pain made her weak. She gasped. She had grown too soft these past weeks.

The softest of knocks brushed the door. Ada hobbled back to the bed and flattened her expression. "Come in."

In the lamplight, Jonathon was a Caravaggian figure, full of shadows and strangely intense colors. He wore evening clothes, not pajamas.

"I heard you cry out," he said. "Are you all right?"

She glanced at the clock. Two a.m. "Did you just come in? Mother said you were reforming."

"I'm trying not to go out when she'd notice. She has enough to worry about."

Beneath the covers, she pressed down on her thigh to staunch the bleeding. "Were you with Katherine Heath?"

"No. That's been over for a while. I was with Pete. He said he has something for you from Father O'Connor."

Fresh agony washed over her. "Did he give it to you?"

"Naw. He wants to put it in your hands personally."

"Oh." She scanned her room. "That won't happen for a while."

"That's what I told him." He tugged off his coat and hitched it on his arm. "Are you sure you don't need anything?"

Her palm felt warm and wet. She hoped she wasn't ruining her sheets. "Jon, how do you think things are going ... without Father?"

Tucking the coat under his elbow, he looked away. "The table is empty," he said. "Mother is different too. And church—well, the sermon I heard was roughly the same as always, since Michael met with Mother to go over things, but I don't think I can stand to attend for much longer."

"Do you think God brought the plague upon us to draw us closer to him?"

"If he did, it's not working for me. Is it working for you?"

She was too tired to blush. She knew Jon wouldn't mock her struggles, but she didn't want to harm whatever faith he possessed by sharing them. "God's ways are not our ways," she said, but it sounded trite and false even to her ears.

"Sure. Well, let me know if I can get you anything." He closed the door quietly behind him.

As soon as he left, she flipped up the sheets. She hadn't mutilated the stitches as much as she'd thought, but a few carmine drops had leaked into her bedding. She dipped a cloth in her water glass and tried to work out the blood. How would she explain the newly broken skin to Sara? If only this cut had tingled, like the ones on her stomach, and she could say she had but scratched an itch. There was no getting around it; Sara would tell Dr. Graham.

Technically, she had kept her word to the doctor. She hadn't cut herself. Comforting herself with that thought, she closed her eyes.

♫

In a light, fitful sleep, Ada half-heard the door open and click shut and two voices converse, but she didn't come to full consciousness until a painful spasm squeezed her abdomen. Her back no longer arched with the tetany, but her body still tightened with aftershocks. She rubbed the sleep from her eyes and sat up.

"Alameda, the doctor's here to check on you," Sybil said. "Dr. Graham, can I get you anything? A cup of tea?"

Ada hastily drew the covers over her shoulders and smoothed her hair.

"No, thank you," Dr. Graham said. "All I require is twenty or so minutes of Miss Williams' time."

Sybil's lips tightened. "I'll be in the office if you need me."

When she was gone, Dr. Graham said, "I don't think she likes leaving me alone with you."

"It's on the border of being improper," Ada said, willing her heart to beat more slowly. "Even Michael hasn't been allowed to see me in my bedroom. You're a doctor, so short visits are acceptable, but only until I've recovered."

"I could tell her I'm giving you counseling."

"Counseling is done by pastors and possibly elders. Any mental problem a person has can be traced to a spiritual fault in his relationship with Christ."

"You speak so flippantly," he said as he scooted the chair closer to the bed and sat. "Do you really believe it?"

"Yes." It didn't matter that she didn't want to believe it. Her doubt stemmed from her tainted nature.

He grabbed her arm, and she exclaimed, pulling back.

"What's wrong?" he asked.

"I'm sorry." She swallowed. "You startled me."

"I should have warned you I need to take your pulse. Your mother will expect some medical readings." He grinned conspiratorially.

She extended her arm, and his warm, strong fingers settled into the groove of her wrist. She felt sick to her stomach.

"Have you kept your promise?" he asked.

She thought about a few nights ago, when Jon had interrupted her clawing herself. But she hadn't cut. "Yes."

He let go of her arm and wrote something in his notebook. "Sara said one of your cuts reopened. Some of the stitches seemed to be torn out."

"Oh." She folded her arms, touching her wrist in the same place his fingers had.

"Oh?" He tapped his pen against the page. "That's not a trivial thing. I don't want you to get an infection. In the future, hurting yourself in any way counts as breaking your promise."

She held in a sigh. "Okay."

"Overall, however, do you feel like your compulsions to hurt yourself have been less since you've been ill?"

She considered. "I think so. Maybe I'm already in enough pain to feel like my outside matches my inside."

"You don't feel like your outside matches your inside?"

"Everybody sees me as good." She dropped her hands to her lap and pressed slightly against her belly. "I'm not."

"Because of things you don't feel you can talk about with your mother or brother?"

"I suppose."

He shut the notebook. "Have you written anything in your journal yet?"

"No."

"Remember, you don't have to let me read it. If you want to share something from it, that's okay, but it's to help you. Next time you want to hurt yourself, write about whatever's making you feel that way."

"I'll try." She'd intended to say, *You must take the book back. It means too much to me.*

"Before I go," he said, "I want to ask you one more thing."

Her heart jumped. She was afraid he was going to bring up Naomi again. Gripping the blanket in her fists, she waited.

"Dawn told me you'd mentioned wanting to join St. Cecilia's Convent."

She relaxed her hands. "That was Naomi's and my dream."

"Do you still want to go?"

She hadn't formulated the question to herself so directly, but she knew the answer. She had bargained with God, and he had denied her. He had let her friend and father die. She searched the doctor's face. Although she wanted to confide in him, it might do more harm than good. He didn't need to know the role he played in her struggle. He didn't need to know she was losing her faith. It would only encourage his unbelief, and she didn't want to be responsible for a single lick of hellfire singeing him. "I don't know. At least I wouldn't be allowed to sin there."

"You would still have the same thoughts you fight against here. Do you want to know what I think?"

His eyes caught her. They were shining, intense, transformative. She felt like a beam of light shooting through a prism. She nodded slightly.

"I think you want to escape what has been a very difficult situation and replace it with one you believe will please your god. But there will be tighter requirements on you there. You might feel even more guilt and want to hurt yourself again. They might encourage you to hurt yourself."

"I'd only be sharing in Christ's sufferings," she said.

He thumped the notebook against the bed as he spoke. "I don't know exactly what goes on in convents these days, but I believe you're still forced to take a new name. Do you want your identity to be taken away? To say goodbye to all your personal hopes, the chance to love someone, have children, travel the world?"

Sudden heaviness oppressed her, and the current that passed between them faded. "I'm not fit for the convent anymore. I know that. I just wish I knew what to do when I get better."

"That's a good subject for your journal. You have a lot of possibilities."

She shook her head and looked away.

"Whatever you decide, you have time."

"How much?" Her breath snagged, but she refused to weep in front of him. Once she was better, she knew she wouldn't be able to see him again.

"Sara will start doing more exercises with you, and we'll see how your body responds." He picked up his bag and settled the notebook inside. "I estimate you'll be able to attend church again, if you want, in a couple of weeks."

Fear rose in her eyes. Church meant Dennis Gentle, and she no longer trusted God to keep her safe from him.

He must have seen her change of expression, for his brow wrinkled. He leaned forward to say something, but just then the door behind him swung open.

Sybil advanced into the room like a cool breeze and asked, "How is the convalescent?"

Bag in hand, Dr. Graham stood. "Convalescing. She's doing well, and I was just telling her that Nurse Ellington will try some new exercises with her today."

"Good," Sybil said. "I like Nurse Ellington, although she's a Methodist. She and her group should join our church. Home churches can go all sorts of heretical ways."

When Sybil mentioned *churches*, the doctor glanced at Ada. She schooled her face into calm. "I'll be back in a few days," he said.

Sybil moved to the side and beckoned to the door. "I'll see you out."

"Goodbye, Miss Williams," he said.

Her heart was too full to reply, and she was afraid Sybil would notice something in the tone of her voice. She picked up her devotional and pretended to read as tears pricked her eyes.

She heard them go out, and then her mother returned. "Can I get you anything, my angel?"

"No, thank you." She was glad she no longer needed assistance to visit the bathroom.

"Dr. Graham seems very involved in your case."

Ada stirred uneasily. "Tetanus isn't very common anymore, and it can lead to complications."

"Well, I just wonder sometimes, if your father would have allowed him in the house so much. Besides the fact that he's an atheist, it might give the impression that we don't trust the Lord with our health."

Ada didn't like to think that seeing Dr. Graham would have displeased her father. The doctor's visits were the only bright spots in her weeks of recuperation. "The Lord uses means, Mother. You've said that. Without Dr. Lansky's antibiotic, more people would have died in the epidemic."

"That was prayer first and modern medicine second," Sybil said. "You should rest now. I'll be back with some soup in a bit."

Sara arrived later in the day and helped Ada through her new exercises. All the while Ada fought the panic that sought to close her throat. Sybil would allow one, maybe two more sessions with Dr. Graham. Perhaps she sensed something between them, or Ada's vulnerability to him.

Thinking about never seeing him again, or only in passing if she visited Dawn, made her want to hurt herself. She felt so very weak, and lying in bed most of the day left too much time for her mind to work. Her thoughts circled like vultures and fed on the carrion of her fears.

Then again—if she saw him only a few more times, it meant fewer times to stay firm and fewer opportunities to sin. She could do it. She would not admit her feelings to him.

CHAPTER FOURTEEN

"You are well enough now for me to bring up something unpleasant," Dr. Graham said as soon as Sybil left the room. Ada heard her mother switch on the radio, and her heart fell. She would have no excuse to delay the conversation in case Sybil overheard.

She told herself she was a fool for thinking he'd forgotten about Naomi's abuser. The familiar anger at herself was almost comforting; she depended on it to defend her from sin. "Haven't you already brought up many unpleasant things?" she asked, drawing her clasped hands closer to her stomach. "Isn't that what our sessions are about?"

"I'm sorry if it seems that way. Being a doctor requires that I face unpleasant things daily, and that distorts my perception of reality. I never forget that any treatment I provide is merely temporary." He allowed a self-deprecating smile. "All my patients eventually die."

"I would think," Ada said to distract him, "that that would drive you to something permanent, such as the strength and eternal goodness of God."

"It might, if so many people didn't use their belief in a god to make this world harder for others. To my view, all too often faith gets in the way of helping people."

Ada thought of her mother's reaction to the epidemic. Resentment gnawed at her as she remembered how Sybil refused to let her visit Naomi on her deathbed. Ada told herself Sybil had been feverish, but she found it hard to forgive her mother. Not that Sybil asked to be forgiven.

"It is belief in God," she said, "that allows—no, requires—us to view each man with dignity, for we are all made in God's image. Without that truth, we would be animals, creating codes of behavior randomly."

"In nature, seemingly random processes result in complex designs. Think of the flight of birds, the balance of predator and prey, the inner workings of a hive, or the sweep of galaxies."

She studied him as he shifted his weight on the hard wooden chair. His doctor's bag sat unopened at his feet. She could almost feel the heat of the sunlight that illuminated his torso and neck. She wished his eyes weren't in shadow. He followed her gaze to the window and got up to open the shade completely. The light was so dazzling it made her eyes ache, but she didn't complain. Enough time in a dim room. Earlier she hadn't been allowed light because it might provoke an attack of tetany.

"I don't believe they are random processes," she said. "They are glorious designs fashioned by the Creator."

He gazed out the window. She knew the view so well she pretended they were looking together over the rolling, treed landscape. "Some are less glorious and more vicious," he said. "Entire species disappear. Natural disasters, diseases, and disorders would point to a different kind of god."

"Those problems are the result of our sin." Her throat was dry, and she picked up the glass from her nightstand. It was empty. She was acutely aware that they were together, alone, in her bedroom. "Of our evil."

"Evil might be another name for chaos," he said. He took the glass from her. His fingers brushed hers, sending color to her cheeks. "Too much chaos leads to destruction, but a little is necessary for change and creativity."

"Chaos is not a good thing," she said. "God is order. He doesn't change."

"In the Bible, if I remember correctly, he changed his mind several times."

"Our limitations are such that we describe him in human terms."

He smiled. "You have an answer for everything, don't you? What about this: If he is all-powerful and completely ordered, how can he allow chaos? To believe that he is separate from it is to divorce him from our world." He filled the glass from the pitcher and handed it back to her. His choice of words could not have been worse.

Divorce. Her hands went numb, and the glass slipped from her grasp. Water splattered her arms and lap and soaked the bedspread.

"I'm sorry. I let go too soon." He put the glass on the stand, then tossed her the rag beside the washbasin. His hands twitched as if he wanted to dry her off himself.

She couldn't ask him the question foremost in her mind, even if it meant he would return to the purpose of his visit. Was he divorced? Was her sin as bad as she feared? She balled up the soggy cloth and handed it to him without looking.

"I like discussing these ideas with you," he said, folding the rag across the washbasin. "I think your mind is full of questions, which this town, and certainly your church, doesn't encourage. But questioning is how we come to knowledge, so don't be afraid of it." He refilled her glass and set it on the stand. "And so I have a question for you, related to something we both agree is evil."

No use to pretend not to know what it was. "I promised not to tell."

"But he could hurt someone else! Now that Naomi is ... gone, he will find another victim. That's how these people work. Tell me his name."

She couldn't meet his eyes. "I can't."

"Of course you can. I already know he's someone from your church. I'm guessing he didn't die during the outbreak, which if your God had any sense of justice, he would have arranged."

She didn't disagree with him there, but she shook her head.

He sat on the chair and stared at her. "What can be your reason for protecting his identity now that Naomi can't be hurt anymore?"

"She can be hurt!" Ada clenched her fists until her nails bit into her palms. "How would everyone remember her? How many people and how many details would become public to make a case?"

"There are more important things than a reputation, and it would be his, not her reputation that would be ruined."

"In a perfect world maybe." She scowled at him. "You should know that one doesn't have to commit a scandal, only be near it to share the blame."

The line on his forehead deepened. "I understand that perfectly. Worden is filled with petty people, but that's what they are—petty! Their opinions matter very little."

"To you," she said. He didn't comprehend the situation, or how it would affect the church. She hated to think how selfish her silence must seem to him.

"I'm trying to understand," he said, "but I can't. Don't you worry that he will hurt someone else?"

"Yes."

"Then what is it? Has he threatened you?"

"It doesn't matter."

He bent forward. His hand moved toward her face. For a moment she thought she'd missed a droplet of water he meant to flick away. Then his warm, full fingers touched her cheek. "Of course it matters. We'll find a way to protect you."

"That's not what I meant." His contact lit up the dark places inside her like will o' the wisps in the forest. "It doesn't matter, because no one will believe you. They'll turn against you."

"The person is that highly placed?" he asked.

"It would be useless." She reached for his hand. As she did, shock at her behavior rippled through her. She grabbed his wrist so her own rested in his deep palm. She looked into his eyes. The blue-gray irises were nearly swallowed by his wide pupils. "Please don't ask me right now."

He cleared his throat. "Ada ..." He disentangled his hand from hers and moved back. "Miss Williams, I should let you rest. But the subject isn't closed between us."

The persistent soreness in her stomach intensified, and she doubled over in pain. The contraction was small and soon over, but she felt ashamed. She cupped her eyes against the brilliant sunlight.

His hand brushed her back. "You're getting better. I'll come again next week. Until then, will you promise not to hurt yourself?"

"Fine," she said.

"And think about what I said. I have connections too, you know."

At the door, he turned to look at her. She felt the intensity of his gaze, but she didn't meet his eyes.

♬

As usual, Ada spent the next week looking forward to the doctor's visit. Sybil brought her breakfast and dinner. Sara came every other day at lunch to check her vitals and supervise her physical exertions, which consisted of stretches and laps around the room. In the evening, Jon usually visited for a few minutes.

Ada was sick of her books, and she had no concentration to read, but she kept her Bible or devotional open in her lap. She wished, vainly, to return to the girl who had found comfort in them. Each time she looked in her hand mirror her face grew more unfamiliar. Sometimes she wondered who was getting better, the old Alameda who wanted to please her family and God, or the new Ada who fantasized about cutting herself so deeply Dr. Graham would compel her to live with him so he could supervise her properly.

Whenever anyone asked, she said she was doing better. By the time she realized that that was not quite accurate, that only part of her was recovering, she had said it so many times that it seemed pointless to correct. It was true; she was recovering physically, but she felt further away than ever from God and her life before the epidemic. Her last meeting with the doctor had triggered something inside her. For the first time she sensed he might return her feelings for him.

"Michael really wants to see you," Sybil said as she brought in a tray of pudding and cut-up boiled egg.

"Does he?" She thought morosely that he was her best friend now. She ought to learn her lesson from Naomi and value him more before it was too late.

"I told him you are moving about the house now. Perhaps in a few days you will feel well enough to visit with him in the parlor."

She nibbled a piece of rubbery egg and made a noncommittal noise. Somehow she doubted talking with him would relieve her perpetual boredom.

"He is helping us in this terrible time of transition," Sybil said. She tidied Ada's tabletop and fluffed the tissues on Michael's card. "His sermons are inspired. You know, it wouldn't hurt to show him a few scraps of kindness. Now that your father has gone to his reward, our circumstances are going to change."

"How so?" Ada asked, interested at last.

Sybil shrugged. "I don't want to burden you while you're not feeling well. We'll talk about it later."

"Mother——"

She raised her hand to stop Ada's argument. "Just think about what I said."

Two days later, Ada bent to Sybil's wishes. For the first time she dressed herself completely and shambled to the living room. She was grateful and a little surprised when Michael arrived with his mother. Mrs. Donner brought cookies that were too hard for Ada to eat, but her presence kept the conversation light. Ada realized that Sybil must have kept the details of her illness a secret. Her mother looked radiant during the visit. She had never been much of a hostess, so Ada marveled at the change. Jon had warned her, but she hadn't seen it until now. Michael was pleasant and divided his attention equally among the three ladies, as was proper.

While Sybil saw them out, Ada shuffled back to her room. After the loud conversation, the quiet of her room was almost aggressive. As she put on her gown, she surveyed the scabs on her stomach. Their dark pink creases told her they were nearly healed, and she felt a wave of loss. As the scars faded, so did her identity. She didn't know what she'd be left with.

♫

At the sound of the doorbell, Ada straightened. She smoothed the front of her peach shirt, which she'd chosen to divert attention from her pallid color. Legs crossed neatly at the ankles, she perched atop her freshly laundered bedspread.

"She's doing so much better, Dr. Graham," Ada heard Sybil say as they came down the hall. "Just look at her, and you'll know. I have a feeling that your visits have fulfilled their purpose."

"I'd still like to see her alone if you don't mind," the doctor said.

Ada blushed as he walked into the room. At the doorway, Sybil flashed an artificial smile and then disappeared. Ada heard the office door close.

"You do look better," he said. He opened his bag and took out a blood pressure cuff and stethoscope. "How do you feel?"

His tone was professional, almost cold. Ada shrank into herself. She wished she hadn't worn such a colorful shirt. "Fine, thank you."

"Have you hurt yourself since my last visit?"

"No." At his gesture, she extended her left arm. He wrapped the cuff above her elbow and pumped it full. She hated the sensation, like her arm was being swallowed by a giant snake.

He released the pressure steadily, watching the dial and listening through his stethoscope. He unwrapped the cuff and put it away, then recorded the results in his notebook. "Your blood pressure is a little low. Don't try to get up suddenly."

She dropped her arm to her lap.

His eyes darted about the room, never settling on her. "Have you experienced any more muscle spasms?"

"No, only soreness and discomfort."

"Excellent." He cleared his throat. "How is your attitude, focus level, that sort of thing?"

"Fine," she said, pricked by his formality.

He sat across from her and finally looked her in the eyes. "I don't want you to depend on me for your mental health, Miss Williams. You can still contact me in case of an emergency, but from now on, you need to rely on your family. If you feel like hurting yourself, please consider telling them. Jon seems like a very nice, rational young man."

Ada wondered what had changed since their previous session. He acted different, like God was watching. She remembered grabbing his wrist, and she felt sick. She had been too forward. She had revolted him.

Her breaths were fast, but she couldn't seem to get enough air. She buried her trembling hands in her lap.

"I think you can consider resuming your old schedule," he said. "Avoid major housework, but things like sweeping, cooking, and teaching lessons should be fine." He slapped his hands to his knees and stood.

She bowed her head to hide her quivering lips. "Thank you, Dr. Graham."

"It might be challenging for you to form a new routine, but I think more activity will be good for you." He sighed. "I want to see you for a follow-up in one month at my office."

"Very well." One month was an unimaginable length of time. It meant nothing to her.

"Until then, promise me you'll stay away from the kitchen knives."

She thought a hint of humor eased his words, but she didn't look up. "I promise."

"Goodbye until then." He left the room. Ada heard him knock on the office door and discuss the specifics of the follow-up appointment with her mother. Sybil thanked him profusely as she led him to the door. She tried to sound sincere, but Ada doubted she convinced anyone.

CHAPTER FIFTEEN

As Ada resumed her old activities, she discovered how much she had changed. Although her jaw had loosened, a generalized fatigue remained, and she was unable to accomplish as much work in a set amount of time as she had previously. Her mind played tricks on her, and she forgot where she'd put her cup of flour, or she set the table for four, or she started teaching Meg's lesson to Harry. The strangest trick, however, was in how time passed.

When she was by herself, time crept by most extremely, so that five minutes in her room seemed an hour. She moved slowly and had to concentrate not to drop things, and sometimes she spent fifteen minutes comb in hand before touching it to her hair. She felt stagnant, a pond rimmed with scum. When she was with others, the conversations around her seemed irrelevant, like dialogue in a dream.

It was only when she thought of Dr. Graham that time passed quickly and the armor of apathy between her and the world clanged to the floor. She replayed every conversation with him, except their last. Those were the only minutes that mattered to her, and as just punishment, they rotted even as she tried to savor them. In the middle of her sweet memories, a sour one ruined her mood. His callous words taunted her in her sleep.

Whatever metaphysical qualities this temporal anomaly possessed, its main effect was to make her yearn for pain. She thought if only she could cut, time would even out. If she could cut, it wouldn't hurt so much that Sybil and Jon were gone so often, or that her father's favorite chair was empty.

She felt so alone in the house that she was almost relieved when Sunday came. She told herself that Dennis couldn't hurt her in God's house. She pretended that he'd forgotten about her, that he was so busy preparing for his wedding he wouldn't notice her.

The empty seats in the pews around her gave her a curious feeling that she was indeed worshiping with the church invisible. Naomi and the others couldn't be gone completely, not when their spaces remained unfilled.

She heard Michael's sermon, or rather, what ought to have been her father's sermon, coming from the wrong mouth. Sybil had helped craft it, Ada thought, and it was grotesque that she performed the same service for Michael that she had for Silas. Ada wiped the bitter expression from her face and bent her head in prayer.

"It is good to see you again, Alameda," Michael said, coming around her pew. "I am overjoyed that God saw fit to restore you to the land of the living."

She almost dropped her book. Time had warped again. Only Mr. Donner and Dennis Gentle remained to count and record the offering. Nearby, Sybil tidied the hymnals. Jon must have already left. Hadn't she stood for the benediction? She remembered now. Michael was not qualified to give it. He'd read it instead, and the congregation had stayed in their seats.

Her legs ached as she rose to her feet and tugged on her skirt.

"I don't mean to be impertinent," he said, "but what did you think of my sermon? I mean, do you think your father would have been pleased by it?"

She didn't want to talk about her father with him, and certainly not about whether he would have been pleased. "He might have given it himself. Surely you know that."

"What do you mean?"

She decided mentioning Sybil's role would be churlish. "Preservation of the saints was one of his favorite themes."

"Indeed. Would you please take a stroll with me?"

His change of subject disoriented her, and she accepted without thinking. The weather was so mild outside she hardly noticed the shift in her surroundings. Keeping an eye out for Dennis, she nodded absently as he talked.

"There has been so much death around us," he said, "that it would be a blessing to hear of God's grace. Worden has lost part of its flock, a holy tithe to the Lord. Now he will multiply us tenfold, as he did Job. Our families will grow. I want to grow with you, Alameda."

Grasping her hand, he turned her to face him. They were at the gate of the churchyard. She saw St. Dominic's in the background and remembered Pete O'Connor had something for her. Now Michael took both of her hands and transfixed her with his stare. She blinked, cast into his brown eyes and unsure what they held in store for her.

"Alameda Williams, will you be my wife?"

"What?" She looked around. No one in sight, not Jon to call out to, or Dennis to terrify her, or Sybil to tell her what to do.

"A pastor should have a helpmeet," he said, "and you have all the qualities I'm looking for. You want to please God and minister to others. You are honest and true. It can't have escaped your attention that I admire you."

She untangled her hands from his and looked down. She mumbled the first excuse that came into her head. "You know I've been considering joining the convent."

"Oh." His lips puckered in distaste. "I thought you had grown past that. Sybil—Mrs. Williams—told me it was a childish phase. 'When I was a child, I thought like a child, but now I have put away childish things.' 1 Corinthians 13:11."

Her heart beat rapidly, and her lungs drew in more breath than she needed. She gulped air. "How can you ask me this, now, not three months since my father died?"

"I discussed it with your mother. We agree that this is a special time, where God's will supersedes etiquette. The flock is distressed and decimated; healing, growth, and love are needed. You must see that too."

"I don't." Behind him, she spotted Mr. Donner, Dennis, and Sybil exit the church building. Sybil locked the door.

"No, Alameda, you must. You will. If the timing is hard for you, I can wait a week. Just consider my proposal."

"I need more time," she said.

"How about two weeks? You can't put me off longer than that."

"Excuse me, I must go." She wheeled away abruptly, in the opposite direction as Dennis.

"Wait a minute!" Michael ran after her, cutting off her escape. "Let me walk you and your mother home."

"How kind," Sybil said. Ada turned slightly, waiting for her to join them. At the edge of her vision, Dennis Gentle waved at her. She trembled.

Sybil took Michael's arm, and he offered his free arm to Ada. It would be rude to refuse, so she allowed herself to be chained to him. Sybil and Michael had no difficulty creating conversation, so at least she was spared that torment. When he had delivered them to their house, Sybil waited only for the door to shut before grabbing her arm.

"Michael is a godly young man, don't you think?"

"Yes, he is."

"He has been a good friend to you."

She nodded.

"His passion for God reminds me of your father." Sybil let go of Ada and strolled into the living room. She set her Bible on the coffee table. "I have been thinking, perhaps you never wanted to be a nun."

Ada bit her lip. Her insides twisted in anxiety. All she wanted was to be alone in her room. "Why would you say that?" she asked, her voice half an octave higher than normal.

"Your wish was to dedicate yourself to God and his service." Sybil shuttered open the blinds and gazed outside. "How could you want to convert? No, my angel, you can do what you wanted to do, as a pastor's wife. If you doubted, your friend's death was a clear sign that the convent is not in God's will for you."

Ada could not believe her mother was using Naomi's death as a bargaining tool. Lowering her head, she hung her cardigan in the hall closet.

"I have found that my life as a pastor's wife has enabled me to influence others and help them understand God's word better," Sybil continued. "When Michael asked me for permission to court you, well, I realized God's plan for your life in an instant." She paused, awaiting a signal that Ada agreed with her.

Ada forced a nod. "I didn't realize I was being courted."

"You are, by the best man in Worden. Probably the best man in Montana! His love for God is his highest qualification. You two have that in common."

"I'm too tired to think about that now. I need to rest before lunch." Ada left the room and her mother's exultant smile. She wandered slowly and purposelessly down the hall. When she was alone again, she searched her drawers for the knife. It was gone, she recalled after a few minutes. She had washed it and replaced it in the kitchen drawer. Still, the search gave her something to do, a chance of relief. When she had exhausted the wardrobe, she turned to the desk. A pencil. She jabbed at her arm. It wasn't sharp enough. She sat on the bed and pounded her upper legs with her fists. It gave her little easement, and her arms were exhausted before they had inflicted enough damage. She fell across the bed and sobbed.

Her mother's words haunted her. They felt wrong, not harmonious and appropriate as they usually did. Ada was the reason for the change. Her mind had grown so thick with sinful thoughts that Biblical advice jarred. Or was the advice itself twisted, a dark growth on the strange designs of reality? Such a thought was heretical. What was not heretical, what struck true, was the idea that she was not elect. She was Esau, not Jacob.

It was impossible to know what she believed and truly wanted in the maelstrom of opinions, advice, and information around her. At the same time, she felt stripped of all façade. She picked up the mirror and studied herself with brutal clarity. How she hated that weak face and those empty eyes. A pimple had started in the hollow of her right temple behind her eyebrow. Her mouth looked sad and dry, and her brown hair was lank, although she'd washed it that morning.

As she scrutinized herself, a double image formed. The second face had lustrous hair, full lips, and a confident gaze. Ada looked from it to the duller image. One was Alameda that had been; one was the Ada that was becoming. She stilled her mind, suspending judgment of the figures.

Ada-in-the mirror smiled. Color rose in her cheeks, and she stepped away from the mirror's frame to reveal a scarlet dress with a flaring skirt and sweetheart neckline.

The old Alameda wore a gray robe and carried a heavy cross around her neck. Her shoulders stooped forward. She looked at Ada-in-the-mirror and clutched her cross. Her upper lip curled in disapproval.

Ada-in-the-mirror laughed. A knife appeared in her hand. She sliced it through the old Alameda's robe, into her belly. A ribbon of red blotted the gray fabric. Ecstasy sparked in the old Alameda's eyes. The cross turned bright gold, and the room smelled of singed flesh. She fell to her knees. In an instant, her hair and clothing flared with fire. She glowed red-orange like a candlewick right after the flame is extinguished. Then she burst into ash.

The dusty snowflakes covered Ada-in-the-mirror's dress and veiled her dark hair. She dropped her knife, and ruby droplets spangled the ground. She held out her hand, but it wasn't to Ada, it was to a man in a doctor's coat.

The reflection of the man split into two. The second man wore a jacket and a brick-red tie. Now it was his hand she was holding, not the doctor's. The man twirled her around and gazed directly out of the mirror at Ada. His blond hair sparkled like the sun on water. He had emotionless blue eyes.

Ada dropped the mirror in shock. The glass smashed against the floor. She rubbed her eyes and peered into the cracked glass. Dennis's face no longer mocked her.

Her grandmother's mirror! Ada cried now at the tragedy of her loss. The glass could be replaced perhaps, but she wouldn't know how to explain her carelessness.

She carried the mirror to her garbage bin and rapped the frame against her hand to dislodge the broken glass. All but one shard fell into the bin. Using an old shirt to protect her fingers, she pulled loose the long, slim shard. She hesitated a moment above the garbage. Wrapping the glass in the shirt, she took it instead to the wardrobe, where she had kept the kitchen knife.

♫

Before Ada knew it, the summer break had arrived, and she was freed from tutoring the Smythes. Last year she had used the extra time to perfect a recipe, sew clothes for Naomi's baby sister, and memorize the Franko cadenza. This year she used it to sleep. She slept much later than usual, and some days Sybil knocked on the door quoting Proverbs to rouse her. Other days she couldn't sleep at all, and she would sit in her room, rocking back and forth and trying not to think, until dawn signified that it was an acceptable time to arise.

One early morning she discovered that Jon had forgotten the lunch she'd packed him the previous evening. She stood at the icebox for several minutes considering the problem. Then she knocked on the office door to alert her mother, who consistently survived on five hours of sleep.

"Mother, Jon's forgotten his lunch. I'll take it to him this morning."

"The station's a good five miles away," Sybil said, looking up from her sermon notes. "Are you well enough for that? I'll call the Donners and see if Michael is free to take you."

"I'd prefer to walk. It's only one way. I'll take the car home, and Jon can walk or find someone to give him a ride."

"I don't like you driving," her mother said. "You hardly know the gear shift from the emergency brake."

"If I drive poorly, it's because I have too few opportunities to practice my skills. I can do it."

"Are you sure?" Sybil pushed her reading glasses to the end of her nose and squinted at her.

"I'll be careful. If I have problems, I'll walk to Donner's Grocery and wait until Michael can drive me home."

A wide smile spread across Sybil's face. "That sounds like a plan."

Leaving the house and slipping into the slightly misty morning was like relaxing into a cool bath during the heat of summer. Ada didn't know how to tell her mother, or even if she had the right to feel, that the house was a rotten apple—bright and clean on the outside, but inwardly crawling with pain and death.

Ada could have chosen a path that skirted the factory and crossed the hospital, but instead she walked straight to the origin of Worden's stench.

It was nearly a rite of passage for every schoolgirl and boy to tour the meatpacking plant. Ada had gone during a school trip in eighth grade. She remembered the staining coal exhaust billowing from the pipes. The large complex of buildings had been a maze of conveyor belts, glistening steel hooks, and stacked tins and crates. Caps and gloves ensured the anonymity of the workers as they hacked, packed, and froze meat and bone.

She paused at the livestock pasture just outside the slaughterhouse. Leaning against the fence, she reenacted in her mind the drama of death.

The steers lowed and flicked their tails. Sometimes their backs, flanks, or entire bodies were crusted with mud or coated by dust, depending on the season. They were herded into consecutively smaller corrals, where they bellowed in earnest. Their cries changed in pitch as the workers slapped them with willow whips to urge them up a metal ramp.

"Too stupid to know where to go," the tour guide had said. He wore a cowboy hat like he was from Texas.

Too smart to want to die, Ada had thought. She stared into a steer's gentle, brown eye, which up close was an alien landscape. She didn't understand why no one else spotted the intelligence inside.

"That's where they get dunked," the guide said, pointing to the ramp. A space of water glistened in the gap between the downward and upward incline. "We try to help them through, but if they're too weak to get up the other side, that's not meat you want to eat anyway."

A steer balked before the pit of water. The cattle that lined up behind him pushed him into it. He bawled as he splashed into the dark liquid. His forelegs struck the opposite side, and he lurched forward. A worker with a long-handled pole helped him find the grooves with his hooves and then smacked his hindquarters until he skittered forward in panic. Up another ramp into the slaughterhouse.

Today no herds were being processed, and a chemical taint cut through the meatpacking stench. A calf grazed in the largest corral, and a heifer chewed her cud nearby. Ada put her hand through the fence and called to them. The calf approached and snuffled her palm. She patted his knobby head.

"That's a cute little fellow," Dr. Graham said behind her.

A thousand cold needles drove into the back of her head, neck, and shoulders. She pressed her hand below her collar, calming her heart.

"I hope they don't plan on killing him," she said.

"Not anytime soon, I should think." He walked to the fence and smiled as the calf kicked its heels and skipped back to its mother. "The inspector is inside. There's been an inspection every week since the epidemic."

"Did they figure out how it started?" she asked.

"Yes. It was a highly mutated form of *Escherichia coli*. The inspectors traced it to a specific batch and threw out all the meat. The plant was shut down for a fortnight, and the only reason it opened again was that there weren't any previous health violations. At least no official ones."

She turned to him. "So the plant will keep processing—killing—cattle?"

He rested his foot on the lower rung of the fence. "Unless the inspectors find anything wrong or the people of Worden unite to shut it down, I suppose so."

"I wish they would."

"Shut it down? I do too, but it's the town's financial backbone. Mr. Smythe and the Worden heirs would fight a closure with their lives. It's the source of their fortunes."

She squeezed the warm wood of the post with her fingers. "If something like the epidemic couldn't shut down the plant, what could?"

"People like you, who are changed by it." He stretched his back and looked up, as if drawing energy from the sun. "You probably won't enjoy hamburger in the same way again."

"I'm not sure I could eat it at all. Could you?"

"I don't eat meat as a rule, except if someone gives it to me."

"Is that true of all meat?" She flushed. "I can't believe I brought you roasted chicken."

He propped his elbow on the post next to hers. "It was delicious, and Dawn and I enjoyed it. What I can't abide is veal, when a young calf dies, or any animal being sacrificed before its time for the sake of the consumer." He gestured to the factory. His face was dark, and she felt his mood dip like a change in weather.

Ada abruptly remembered the lunch box at her feet, containing a ham-and-cheese sandwich. She shouldn't linger anyway. This kind of talk was dangerous. At least she would have a new memory where he was nice to her again.

"I have to walk to the railroad depot," she said. "Jon forgot his lunch."

"You walked from your house? That's a bit far." He frowned. "Can I give you a lift? I just finished my business in the Meatpacking District, and I spotted you as I was walking to my car." He pointed. "I wanted to make sure you were all right."

"I appreciate the offer," she said, "but I will be fine. I was planning to drive our car back from the station."

"Then safe driving to you." He tipped his hat to her and turned. "I'll see you soon."

Watching him walk away, she wished he had insisted on driving her. Then she remembered the last time she'd been in his car, and the desperate feeling slithered away to make place for guilt.

Head down, she trudged to the depot to deliver Jon's lunch. She felt like a rusty puppet and wished after all that she hadn't decided to journey so far on foot. She only ground the gears a few times as she drove home.

CHAPTER SIXTEEN

Ada considered canceling her appointment with Dr. Graham but hesitated the few times she approached the office telephone. Whenever she thought about not seeing him again, her soul flickered like a candle about to go out.

She expected to have to walk to the hospital, but as she tied her shoes, her mother knocked on the door. "Alameda, Michael is here to take you to your appointment."

Michael? Ada had not arranged or foreseen this, but it struck her as so much did these days—flatly, causing minimal reaction. She was glad she wore her plainest brown dress.

Michael opened the passenger door for her, and she said thank you. She buckled the seatbelt and folded her hands in her lap. Buildings and yards kaleidoscoped by without significance. Struggling to breathe, she cracked the window. The air was unseasonably crisp like a sour apple.

He escorted her to the waiting room. There, at last, time focused. She sat on a padded chair and watched Nurse Brandt breeze through files behind the counter. She was plump, blond, and young, perhaps five years older than Ada. She and her husband went to St. Dominic's. Ada wondered whether they were happy.

Nurse Ellington opened the door to the waiting room. "Miss Williams?"

Ada looked around. She and Michael were the only ones waiting. She stood. Her legs felt unsteady. Michael gave her an encouraging smile, but she couldn't return it.

As Sara took her vitals and asked her questions, Ada prepared herself to see the doctor for the final time. Sara took several vials of blood, a process that usually fascinated Ada, but today Ada felt only agony building inside her heart. When Sara left, the door shut too loudly. Ada winced.

She glanced around the examination room. A strange impulse seized her. To make this moment, and her future memories of it, real, she would take something. She got down from the table and pulled at the cupboard handles. The doors stuck, and she thought they were locked, but when she yanked harder, they flew open.

Flasks, empty, full, and in between, faced her like a bouquet of glass flowers. She read a few labels, but only one name meant anything to her. The small vial with colorless liquid fit easily inside her purse. Was stealing truly this easy? Her pulse pounded as she resumed her seat. Now she would never forget.

The door swung open. "Miss Williams, what a pleasure to see you again. How are you?"

Her heart leaped. He was cheerful again, as he had been outside the factory. "I am better, thank you. How are you?"

"Encouraged by your progress. I don't have to ask if you've kept up your exercise."

They shared a smile. Ada's toes tingled.

"Your jaw is completely normal?" he asked, jotting notes on a clipboard.

"That's correct."

"No more muscle spasms?"

She shook her head.

Keeping his eyes on her, he sat on the stool. "How has your transition to a regular schedule been?"

"I've been cleaning and cooking and practicing as usual," she said, lowering her head and darting glances at him, "but I feel very tired."

"That's to be expected. Not only is your body recovering, so is your mind. You lost a lot during the epidemic."

"So did everyone." She didn't want to talk about it again. Not on their last day together.

He clipped his pen to his coat pocket. "What about your promise? Have you cut yourself?"

She bit her lip. She recalled the useless pencil and punching herself. The bruises had taken weeks to fade. "No, I haven't."

"Good." He hesitated. "We'll test your blood to make sure the infection is gone, but I have a good feeling about it. I don't think you'll need to make another visit here for a long time!"

She felt as if her organs had congealed. Although she had known it was coming, he announced the news so happily that the idea of his absence in her life must not affect him the way it did her. She struggled to contain the emotions hurtling inside her; they were presumptuous, irrational. She was glad she had stolen the vial.

"We have one piece of unfinished business," he said, "and when you're ready, I want to hear it. You know you and I can talk about anything."

She stared helplessly at him, wishing he could read the signs in her eyes as easily as he read those in her body. Was wanting to know about Dennis the only reason he'd been kind to her? "I can't." She ground the inside of her lower lip with her teeth until she tasted blood.

"Yes, you can. And you need to. It's the right thing to do."

"Stop trying to tell me what to do!" She pressed her palms into her temples and twisted away from him. "Everyone keeps telling me what to do."

"I'm sorry." She heard him stand, but he moved toward the door, not toward her. "I can't force you to tell me anything; I just don't want anyone else to get hurt. If it bothers you so much, I won't ask you again."

"Thank you." He handed her a tissue, and she wiped her eyes. She shouldn't feel disappointed. She wanted Dennis to be punished, and she had hoped to tell Dr. Graham the whole story eventually. It was only that it was their last visit together, and she didn't want the memory marred by Dennis, as the play in the mirror had been.

"I'm counting on you to do well for me, Miss Williams," he said. "Can you do that?"

"Yes." She slowly met his outstretched hand and shook. Did his fingers linger an instant before he let go, or was time playing games with her again?

"Sara will call you with the results of the blood test. If luck is with us, you won't be seeing me again."

She nodded numbly. He didn't want to see her again. As she made her way back to the waiting room, she recognized how foolish she'd been to think differently.

"How did it go?" Michael asked.

"They're running one more test, but they think I've fully recovered."

"Praise God!" He said more, but Ada ceased listening. She replayed her conversations with the doctor. All along he'd wanted to know the identity of Naomi's abuser. That was how they'd met; that was why he had attended the spring festival. That was probably why he'd nursed her back to health, and now that he believed she wouldn't tell him, she meant nothing to him. He didn't care about her, not even as much as a doctor should care for a patient.

With sinking spirits she realized she was no longer under oath to Dr. Graham not to hurt herself. Since he didn't expect to see her again, keeping her from hurting herself was no longer his responsibility. Perhaps he thought she had gone so long without cutting that she no longer battled the compulsion.

Or maybe the omission was intentional, and he wanted her to hurt herself.

She would cut herself, and he would be sorry. Ada tried, but it was too late to stop the fantasy. She imagined blood slicking down her legs, staining her skirt. Her face would blanch as she and the stained knife dropped to the ground. Dr. Graham knelt beside her. He touched her wrist and then her neck for a pulse. In horror and panic he peeled back her clothes to examine her wounds. His wet fingers brushed her white flesh with scarlet, and his body hovered over hers …

The image of Naomi shrinking from her uncle's advance intruded in Ada's mind. Revolted, she thought she might vomit. She abhorred Dennis. He ruined everything. She envisioned picking up the slick-with-blood knife and cutting off his erect penis. Unlike a starfish's ray, it wouldn't grow back.

"Alameda, are you all right?"

She had forgotten about Michael, although he sat in the driver's seat across from her. They had arrived at her house. "No, sorry. I feel faint."

"That's right, they took your blood. I'll help you inside."

Sybil was waiting. Michael turned Ada over to her and clasped Sybil's arm briefly. "Make sure she eats something. I'm very sorry I can't stay longer, but I have to return to the store. I'll see you on Friday?"

"Of course. Thank you." Sybil returned his gesture with a squeeze of her own.

When he had gone, Sybil busied herself in the kitchen. She cut a loaf of bread and slathered it with jam. She put on the kettle for tea.

"I'm feeling better," Ada told her. "It was only a moment of lightheadedness. I'll finish the tea and bring it to you in the study."

"My angel." Sybil hugged her. "You think only of others."

When she was gone, Ada set two teacups and the sugar pot on a tray. She tried to ignore the bread knife. It lay on the counter, a silver serpent tempting her. It had been so long. She'd been good for so long, and it hadn't mattered.

She took the tray to her mother and unloaded the teacups. She selected the plate with the heel of bread and picked at it without hunger.

"Your father would have been proud of Michael's progress in expounding the Word," Sybil said. Her eyes glistened as she replaced the sugar spoon.

"I'm sure Michael appreciates your help."

"He is humble enough to allow it, and I am glad to feel useful. Don't tease your food like that. You're dropping crumbs on the carpet."

"I'm sorry. I'll vacuum tomorrow."

Sybil nodded. "I suppose I'll let you, now that the doctor has declared your recuperation is over."

Ada blinked, keeping her eyelids closed for several seconds as she reasoned away the tangle of anger in her belly. Why was she so irritable lately? It was the doctor's fault for not caring about her. No, it was hers for perseverating on her licentious thoughts. She hated who she was becoming.

After tea, Ada took the tray back to the kitchen. She washed the knife and put it away, then went to her room.

Consuming, inexpressible rage fueled her as she unwrapped the shard of mirror. She stared at the glass, and Ada-in-the-mirror glared back at her. Ada shrugged off her dress. She looked at the rows of healed scars on her stomach and legs.

Just one cut. She would open one scar. Dr. Graham deserved it, for he had tricked her. She thought of him now with anguish. His soft-edged body matched the kindness of his face and voice. His eyes were intelligent without being sharp, and he exuded good humor and conviction in all he did. The only obstacle was, and it was also her salvation, he did not care for her.

The pointed glass slit her skin without effort.

So much had been taken from her—her father, Naomi, the convent, and now Dr. Graham. What kind of a life did God expect her to live? Michael cared for her, but she couldn't imagine kissing him or allowing him to undress her.

She didn't have to accept it. She didn't have to wait for every option to disappear and see what she was left with. For once, she would take what she desired, and she desired Dr. George J. Graham.

She drew the shard deeper across the same scar. Blood slid down her abdomen, and Ada-in-the-mirror grinned. She felt delightfully wicked. She couldn't force the doctor to love her, but she held one thing over him—the secret that had drawn him to her.

Although Ada-in-the-mirror wanted more, Ada cleaned off the glass and put it away. Waiting for her cut to crust, she lay on her back and pondered her situation. The solution didn't come, but bits and pieces did.

After a while, she got up, bandaged herself, and went to the kitchen to prepare dinner.

♫

Saturday dawned cloudless and hot. Ada rose early and left a note on the kitchen table. She had to leave the house, had to clear her mind, and walking would help. She thought of the countless times she and Naomi had hiked to the Cow's Head. It would have been a perfect day to cool their legs in the water.

She didn't eat breakfast. The darkness inside her was heavy and wet, a black river carving out her joy. She didn't walk to the pastures but headed toward the Meatpacking District. Not many people were up yet. Shops were just opening.

Because she couldn't help herself, she passed the hospital and the doctor's house. Meandering past the front yard, she paused to examine the thorny rose bushes. Had the enigmatic Mrs. Graham planted them? They were so well established, they must have been put in at least a decade ago.

The doctor asked her many questions during his visits, but Ada rarely had an opening to make inquiries of her own. She had learned, however, that he had been quite young when he married. She thought he must have regretted his choice. She wondered if he found solace anywhere. If he had not dismissed her from his life so readily, she could have offered him some.

Without intending to, she wandered toward the place of one of her happier memories of the doctor. The heat of the day intensified the acrid smell. Walls stained gray from the factory exhaust lost their shabbiness in the brilliant gold of the sun. Plumes of smoke blurred the air around her like a dream, and she coughed. She roamed past the corrals where she had spoken with Dr. Graham. Brown cattle crowded one pasture, and she tried not to look at them.

A railroad crossing dinged and flashed. She walked to the crossing and waited for the train. It whirred and whistled, blasting her as it passed. For a moment, she wondered what would happen if she shook off her lethargy and threw herself at the passing cars. Her long recuperation in bed had made it clear that the outside world functioned as easily without as with her. Her jaw tightened, and her body swayed. The click-clack of the wheels on the rails slowed as it approached the station. The opportunity had passed.

Someone touched her back. She jumped and turned at the same time, a scream rising in her throat.

"Ada, I've never seen you here before. What are you doing?" Pete O'Connor pitched his voice over the screech of the train's brakes.

The train whistle drowned out her answer. She waited for it to finish and noticed that Pete wore work coveralls and carried gloves. He must be headed to the depot.

"I'm out for a walk," she said.

"Does Jon know you're here?"

"He's still sleeping. He works the afternoon shift today."

He nodded. "That's right. I knew that."

She cleared her throat. "Jon said you had something for me from Father O'Connor?"

"Yeah. Do you mind walking with me? I don't want to be late for work."

"Of course." She was glad he didn't offer his hand, instead taking giant steps through the crossing. The cars had passed, but the lights were still flashing. She ducked under the guard as it returned to its upright position and scrambled after him.

"That sure was a bad bug going around," Pete said. "I heard you got sick too, though with something else. You're all better now?"

"Yes, thank you. I am so sorry that your uncle died."

"Yeah." He kicked a broken cobblestone. "He wasn't the only one. Makes you think about what you really want in life."

He kept his head down as he walked, so Ada couldn't read his expression.

"You still want to go to St. Cecilia's, huh?" he asked.

"I don't think so."

"Well, that's progress." He flashed her a smile she didn't quite like. "Maybe you won't want what Uncle Aubrey left for you."

"What was it?"

"A letter of recommendation for you to the convent. He wrote it right before he got sick."

"Oh." An icy fist closed in her stomach. Reading it would make her feel too guilty. The old Alameda was dead, and the letter had been intended for her.

"It's in the church office. You can pick it up whenever you like."

His path was erratic, and his steps were too fast for her. Ada panted for breath and touched his arm to slow him. "Why didn't you just give the letter to Jon?" she asked.

"Because I wanted time alone with you." He curled toward her and gripped both of her arms. Before she could react, he dragged her behind a building. In the background, she heard the din of moving crates, rasping metal, and panicked cattle. The odor of cow dung overpowered all else.

"What are you doing?" She wiggled in his arms, struggling to free herself.

"Don't fight me," he said, bending his head to hers. His breath scorched her ears. "I want to help you out. Teach you to have fun."

"Stop it!" She tried to pull away. His rough hands chafed her skin. Only now did she realize how early it was, how far away she was from help. Even if she screamed, no one would hear. If this was God's punishment for planning to seduce Dr. Graham, it wasn't fair. She had already paid, because he didn't love her. If he cared for her at all, he would have sensed her danger. He would come around the corner now. Ada strained to see, but he didn't come.

"I won't hurt you. Stop kicking me! Listen, one kiss, and if you don't like it, I'll stop. Just calm down."

She screamed and kicked him again. He forced her wrists behind her back and seized both of them in one hand, then clamped her body to his with his other hand. Through his pants, she felt a bulge at the level of her waist. She retched.

"I'll tell Jon," she cried. "He'll kill you!"

"No, he won't, because this isn't a big deal, and you touched me first. Now be quiet." His face dropped to hers, and he mashed his mouth against her lips. Sharp stubble grated her chin. She tasted his tongue, vinegary and fleshy, inside her mouth. Fighting to breathe, she chomped her teeth together. He wicked his tongue away with a yelp. Blood spotted his lower lip.

"Geez, O'Connor, leave the lady alone!"

Pete sprang away from Ada. She dropped to the ground, pressing herself against the side of the building. Her body rocked back and forth with dry heaves. Hot tears blocked her vision, and she wiped her eyes with the hem of her skirt. She needed to see her rescuer. His voice—

"I'm sorry, Mr. Gentle. I wasn't going to harm her, I swear."

"Pressing unwanted advances on a lady like her is harming her. Get to work."

Using the building for leverage, Ada lifted herself to her feet. Before she could call out for him to stay, Pete dashed off. She wanted to do the same, but her entire body trembled. If she attempted to run, she would tumble to the ground.

"What about that?" Dennis Gentle said with a laugh. "I'm your knight in shining armor, except I ride a train, not a horse."

She spat bloody saliva onto the ground. "You're nothing."

"I could take you now," he said, "and pin it on that patsy. He'd be run out of town."

"God will protect me."

"Will he? He didn't protect Naomi."

She swallowed. She knew that, and Naomi had deserved more help than Ada did. She bent her head. She should have realized that in God's nasty universe, if she wanted the doctor, Dennis was part of the deal.

He stepped close, scraping his boots deliberately against the pavement. "I like your fighting spirit. Don't give up now. When the time is right, you will come to me."

She shuddered. When she looked up again, he was gone.

CHAPTER SEVENTEEN

"Perhaps you would knock on your brother's door," Sybil said. "I am determined we shall have Sunday breakfast together, just as always." She grabbed the woven hot pad from Ada. "I'll take care of that."

Ada moved away from the oven. She walked mechanically to her brother's room and rapped on the wood.

She didn't blame Pete for his aggressive lust. He had seen a weakness in her to exploit, something hypocritical that he had tried to peel away. Thoughts she couldn't stop cycled in her head. If anyone in the church knew what she had done, what she fantasized doing, they would reject her as the vilest sinner. "St. Alameda," some of them had called her for her acts of kindness. In retrospect, her benevolent deeds felt desperate, a way of convincing herself that she was good, not only in God's eyes but her own.

Ada-in-the-mirror was not good. Not good at all.

The door flew open. Her hand darted to her throat.

"What is it?" Jon's dressing gown hung sloppily about his shoulders.

"Breakfast." She cleared her throat. "Mother wants us to eat together."

"And then go to church together. No thanks. I can't stand another second of Michael's preaching."

"He is trying to be a good preacher." She wondered why she felt the need to defend him, then remembered. "He asked me to marry him."

He jerked back his head. "Whoa, please tell me I'm still sleeping. Of course you said no?"

She shrugged. "I have to consider everything. I told him I needed more time."

"Well, consider yourself first. Michael is a pansy, and if you don't like him, don't do it. Michael as a brother-in-law ..." He pantomimed banging his head against the doorway.

"Then come to church." Emotion skimmed the pool of her apathy. "Don't leave me alone with him."

"Okay." He scratched his arm. "By the way, I can't think of a guy good enough for you. Pete O'Connor, who used to talk nonstop about you, told me yesterday he was seeing Kathy."

A cold sensation swept through Ada. She turned away to hide her face.

"So we shouldn't expect to see her at church anymore," he said. "I guess she's used up all the guys she can in the Protestant fold. That'll be the next scandal, I'm sure, even though the townies expect that kind of thing from meatpackers."

Without comment, Ada returned to the dining table. She adjusted the napkins and then lowered herself to the chair. The breakfast casserole steamed in its dish.

"Is he coming?" Sybil asked, taking her place at the foot of the table.

"Yes."

Time slowed again, and the next thing Ada knew, she was in the hard pews of the church building. The service was over. Jon flicked her collar.

"I agreed to be your shadow, Sis, but I can't sit here all day. Let's go talk to Dawn. Quickly, before Michael gets here."

"What? Dawn's here?" She glanced around the thin crowd. Dawn had come to church? She couldn't believe she hadn't noticed. And if Dawn was here, then the doctor … She urgently scanned the room.

Jon leaped out of the pew. "Wonder of wonders, I know."

She saw Dawn at the front of the building, a smirk on her face that she somewhat tried to hide with the back of her hand. She wore a yellow dress, and she was alone.

Recalling their previous encounter, Ada pulled back and whispered, "No. I don't want to see her."

Jon threaded his arm through hers and hustled her forward. "Come on. Look, would you rather talk with Dawn or Michael?"

She followed his nod to see Michael purposefully approaching. Another peek showed Dennis watching her while in conversation with the Templetons. Meeting her eyes, he slightly shook the offering bags in his hands and stroked the wooden handle. Fury and embarrassment rose in her cheeks.

"Miss Graham!" Jon called. "May we have a word before you go?"

"Of course," Dawn said, coming out of her pew. Her face was rosy, and her blond hair was done in sausage curls.

"Have you taken up religion?" Jon asked. "The balance of the world seems so shifted that maybe I should give it up."

Ada stared at him before realizing it was a joke. At least she hoped it was. Now that she was the bad twin, she needed him to be good.

Dawn laughed. "Could it be that I missed my friends? I haven't seen you in months, Ada, and I know you would never miss a sermon by choice. I can't believe Michael is preaching. He was just a couple years ahead of me in school."

Ada glanced at Michael again. He had changed his trajectory and spoke with Sybil and Mrs. Smythe instead.

"I'm here to keep Ada safe from him," Jon said.

Ada scowled at him.

Jon chuckled. "Fine, I won't say more, but Dawn isn't a gossip, not near as bad as I am, anyway."

"I believe that's true," Dawn said with a smile. "Maybe you can tell me the rest of the story later."

"Sooner's better than later," Jon said.

"You're right. Why don't you have tea with me this afternoon? Ada, what do you say?"

Ada glanced at Jon. "I'm not sure my mother would—"

"She's not asking our mother." He tapped his toe against her shoe.

Ignoring his signal, Ada looked at the wooden floor. It needed sweeping. "I have chores," she said.

"That's not a good excuse, especially on a day of rest." He gave Dawn an apologetic look and bumped Ada's shoe again. "I don't think Ada has quite forgiven you for that shot."

"I have," Ada said, moving her foot to stop his irritating tattoo. "It's really Dawn who needs to forgive me for what I said."

"What, for calling me a bitch?" Her laugh echoed against the wall. "Don't shush me, Jon. I might be talking about dogs, for all these biddies need to know. Don't worry about it, Ada. You were under a lot of stress."

"I had no right," Ada murmured.

"Frankly," Jon said, "I'm impressed you know the word."

Dawn winked at him. "With you around? I'm not surprised. Now let's prove we're friends again. Have tea with me after church, Ada. You can bring *him* if you like."

"We'll go," Jon said. "What time?"

"I'll expect you at three sharp. And don't bring anything. Besides yourselves, of course." She grinned and turned on her heel so her skirt flared up.

As Jon stared after her, Ada elbowed him in the ribs. "You shouldn't have told her yes until we checked with Mother."

"I know our birthday was eclipsed by an epidemic this year, but we are eighteen now. We're adults in the eyes of the State."

"Living in our parents' house," she said. "We must honor them."

"Our mother's house," Jon corrected, "and I am. I also intend to move out once I know you'll be okay."

"Move out? But we need you. You're the man of the house."

"For now," he said. Ada followed his gaze to Michael. It was partly the black suit, but also Michael's growing beard that intimated he was more mature than an average lad of twenty-two. As she watched, Mr. Smythe thumped him on the shoulder. Michael made his excuses to the ladies and followed him to the front of the church.

"I told you," she said, "I don't intend to marry him."

"Have you told him?"

She flushed. Nettles of anger stung her. "I'm tired. I wish you hadn't said we'd go."

"It will cheer you up." He grinned. "*I* wish Mother could see your face. Then she'd stop calling you 'angel.'"

"I'm sorry I was impatient. Forgive me."

"Gee, you don't have to apologize all the time! Come on, I'll be the one to tell Mother." He strode toward Sybil, who was deep in conversation with Mrs. Smythe. Ada noticed her mother's anxious expression. Jon, perhaps, didn't. As soon as Sybil paused and looked at him, he told her of their plans. He embellished Dawn's interest in the sermon and said she had requested they explain it to her.

The line between Sybil's eyes sharpened minutely. "I wish you had asked me before agreeing," she said. "Miss Graham would do better discussing the sermon with an elder."

"My husband would be more than willing, I'm sure," Mrs. Smythe said with a fake smile, "but it does seem more appropriate that Miss Graham ask someone her own age, since her father is not … spiritually qualified."

Sybil glanced at her. "Of course. Well, Jon, since you're going into town, perhaps you will drop me by the Donners' on your way. Mrs. Donner and I have some matters to discuss."

"Of course." Jon bowed his head and excused himself. "See," he told Ada, "simple as that."

What were the matters Sybil and Mrs. Donner needed to discuss? She remembered her mother was keeping something from her. She didn't think she and Jon had won as easily as he imagined they had.

The doctor's car was in the driveway, so Jon parked against the curb. The roses were in full bloom, with giant white- and pink-edged gold, vermilion, and magenta petals. Ada looked at them but didn't dare touch or smell the frilly cups. Someone had weeded the front bed recently. She couldn't picture Dawn kneeling on the grass with leather gloves and a bucket, but then, the idea of Dr. Graham doing it was odd too. Maybe it was a way of dealing with his empathic pain, as he had hoped writing in a journal would be for her.

"I'm so glad you could come," Dawn said, opening the door and ushering them inside. Ada slipped off her shoes and remembered how hesitant Naomi had been entering the house. Now Ada was the hesitant one. Jon sat in the chair nearest the kitchen and rested his feet on the ottoman. Ada shook her head at him, but he disregarded her.

"Shall I help with the tea things?" Ada asked, after she had assured herself that the doctor wasn't there.

"If you like."

Under Dawn's direction, Ada retrieved four teacups and saucers from the cupboards.

"In case my dad joins us," Dawn explained, "but I'm not sure he will. He was still sleeping when I came home."

"Oh." Ada's expression must have been comical, because Dawn laughed.

"He has strange hours," she said. "Sometimes I swear he's a cat with all his naps."

Ada felt too warm. She didn't want to think about Dr. Graham stretched out on his bed. Even handling the china gave her a peculiar, buzzing sensation.

"The tea's ready," Dawn said. "I'll take in the tray if you grab the sandwiches."

Croissants. Ada's mouth watered. As she set them on the coffee table, she tried not to think of how much they had cost. She did not deserve croissants. She would not take one unless pressed.

"I didn't know you could pour tea without spilling," Jon said.

Dawn shot him a glare. "You'd better not break the china with your big hands."

Ada made a sudden connection. They were flirting, and she should have noticed it much earlier. It made her feelings for the doctor even more awkward.

"How are you and your father spending the Fourth of July?" Jon asked.

"We haven't decided yet. I want to be here for the parade and everything, but Dad keeps harping on a vacation. He wants to spend time together before I start at Radcliffe."

Ada's teacup rattled against its saucer.

"You're still intending to go?" Jon asked.

Dawn passed him the plate of croissants. "What, did you think if you gave up Kathy I'd give up college and medical school?"

Jon met Ada's eyes with a shame-faced grin. "I think you've shocked my sister."

Ada lowered her gaze. She felt like a hypocrite.

"I'm sorry, Ada," Dawn said, "but I can never say the proper thing. And I'm sorry, Jonathon, but I'm going to Massachusetts this fall."

"It's all right," Jon said. "At least knowing someone on the East Coast will give me an excuse to visit. I've always wondered what would happen if I slipped inside one of the crates we freight out." He polished off the croissant and grabbed another. Dawn took the platter and offered it to Ada. She refused politely.

"You could become a hobo," Dawn said.

Ada blinked.

"Sounds fun," Jon said.

"Really," Dawn told Ada, "you don't have to save them all for him. We ladies deserve the best too."

"Thank you, but not now." A knot formed in her stomach. "Perhaps later."

"You're such a suffragette, Dawn." Jon dipped his sandwich into the tea. "It's a waste you were born in this century."

Dawn tossed her head. Her curls swung like coiled springs. "There's plenty left to accomplish in women's rights. We shouldn't be consigned to be secretaries, teachers, nurses, or baby factories."

"And on and on." Jon sighed. "This is why we shouldn't see each other very often. Nothing cools a man's passion as quick as feminist talk."

"And nothing provokes a woman to feminism like a chauvinistic male."

"Then I guess I'd better sweeten my approach. At least if I want honey."

"You can't get honey from a wasp."

His smile was wider than a summer sunrise. "Well, I wouldn't mind a sting either."

"Did we forget about your sister again?" Dawn asked. "The tales she could tell your mother."

"She won't say anything." He cocked his chin at Ada. "It would only cause trouble, and St. Alameda is very good at making life easier for others."

"I'm good at being silent," Ada said. She didn't mean it as a reproof, but it came across as one.

There was a pause. "I'm sorry," Dawn said. "I'm afraid we've been a little rude. I've been meaning to tell you about Radcliffe, and—and everything, but you were sick for so long. That's why I went to church. Your mother wouldn't dare turn me away from that door."

"You tried to see me when I was ill?" Ada asked.

Dawn nodded. "I went to your house the day after you were discharged from the hospital. Your mother said I wasn't an influence she 'desired for you' during your vulnerable state, and that you needed to focus on getting better."

"Oh." Anger stirred in Ada's belly. She remembered the stretching hours of boredom on her sickbed and thought Dawn's presence would have relieved them somewhat. Still, she couldn't reprimand her mother, for if Ada had been a better Christian, she would have turned both Dawn and Dr. Graham away herself. Closing her eyes, she struck the top of her left foot with her heel.

Jon gave a disbelieving chortle. "That's Christian hospitality for you. At least Ada's well enough to make her own decisions now."

"I wonder if that's a good thing," Ada murmured under her breath.

Dawn cleared her throat. "Speaking of decisions, what are the two of you planning for the Fourth of July? If I'm in town, I'd like to spend it together."

And with Dr. Graham? Ada's heart beat furiously. "I have to help with the church float for the parade," she said. "They always want music."

"You could say no," Jon said.

"Seriously," Dawn said, finishing the last of her sandwich and speaking through her bites, "Independence Day is the time to rebel. I'm sure your mother won't disown you for shooting off some fireworks after I ply you with liquor."

"Your birthday's not until July 11," Jon said.

She winked. "I have a feeling that won't matter."

"Ha! There are fireworks for sale near the train station. Let's walk there and buy some."

"Sounds good to me. Let's go. Ada, what do you think?"

Ada shut her eyes, remembering herself powerless in Pete's hold. His acidic tongue raked across her teeth. She heard again Dennis's heavy boots shuffling against the pavement. *When the time is right, you will come to me.*

"Ada?" Jon asked.

She pressed her hands together and dug her fingernails into her right palm. "That sounds lovely. I wish I weren't so tired. Why don't you two go, and I'll clean up?"

"Don't you dare clean up," Dawn said. "If you're tired, you can take a nap in my room. I'll show you."

"Thank you; that would be nice."

Dawn started down the hall. "And don't worry, Dad won't disturb you. When he's in his room this late, it usually means he's caught up in a medical journal. I'm glad we left one sandwich," she looked significantly at Jon, "in case he comes out to forage."

Ada trailed after Dawn, feeling uncomfortable as she entered her room. She doubted Dawn would be so welcoming if she knew Ada's feelings for her father. Surrounded by Dawn's personal belongings, her sense of unease grew. She sat on the navy blue bed and waited until she heard the front door close. Once she was alone, she exited the room to the hallway. As she entered the living room, she caught sight of herself in the long, golden-framed mirror by the fireplace. Something inside her quivered, struggling to break free. Now was not the time, she told Ada-in-the-mirror. She hadn't thought through everything yet.

She sank into a chair. The four-limbed starfish drew her gaze from the photo on the mantel.

Muffled footsteps sounded behind her. She stood and whirled around, surprising Dr. Graham halfway to the kitchen. He wore a rumpled shirt and slacks and hefted a soft-bound journal in one hand.

"Miss Williams, I didn't know you were here."

She took a step backward. "Dr. Graham. Excuse me."

"I heard them go out. I thought … I didn't want to disturb you." He lowered the book to his side.

"You didn't. I'm the intruder." She tried to gauge his mood. She thought to herself, what would Ada-in-the-mirror do? "I was too tired to go with them."

"Where did they go?'"

"The train station." She spotted the last croissant on the platter and offered it to him. "Here, we left you a sandwich."

"Thank you." He took the plate and sat awkwardly across from her. She tried to breathe normally and hoped her grumbling stomach wouldn't betray her.

"Dawn told me Michael Donner is the interim pastor," he said. "How long do you suppose it will be until the church finds a replacement?"

He wanted to talk about church? Ada swallowed her disappointment. "I really don't know."

"How are you adjusting to everything?"

He'd asked something similar during their final appointment, but this time she sensed that he really wanted to know. She met his eyes and recognized his expression. Empathy. He *did* care for her, at least a little. "I'm adjusting."

"Is the convent still in your future?"

The question caught her off guard. She hadn't fetched Father O'Connor's letter from the church office yet. "No. It was something I should have done with Naomi." Her voice caught.

He set the platter on the table beside him. "Did she want to go as much as you did?"

Sadness lumped in her throat. She was ashamed to admit that at the end, Naomi had wanted the convent more than Ada. "Yes. We always knew we were different. We thought God had called us."

He shifted in the chair, and she was afraid he would get up. Instead, he asked, "How were you different?"

She faltered, but his kindness broke her resistance. "We never liked boys the way other girls did," she said at last.

"What about girls?"

She went scarlet. She had thought he, of all people, would never ask that. *I love you*, Naomi had said, caressing Ada's hair. Paralyzed, she stared at the sprigs of wildflowers patterned in her skirt.

"It's okay," he said gently. "I don't mean to pry, but I want you to know that whatever you answer is fine."

"No, it's not." She studied his face—the strong jaw, the laugh lines, the ever-present dark patches beneath his eyes. Desire made her neck heat, and she pinched herself through the folds of her skirt. "Not in God's eyes."

"If you're afraid of going to Hell, think about how you feel right now." As he leaned forward, his pant legs bunched a little so she saw an inch of shin above his black socks. "You're already in hell. I've read of this before. Other people have reacted to strict teachings in similar ways. It's called scrupulosity, and it's not your fault."

"It is, because I can't handle the truth of this world. Because I'm weak and sinful."

He covered his face with his hands. "Ada, please. Have you been hurting yourself again?"

She wished she had something to do with her hands besides wring them together, rasping and rubbing her dry skin. "You didn't ask me not to last time."

"Oh my god." He jumped up and began to pace. "I thought you were getting better. I thought you were finding other ways to express yourself."

She thought of the seagull journal, which was still empty. "I only did it once. You don't understand what it's like." Her voice sounded flat and hollow. "The world isn't right. I'm not right. I've changed, and I can't go back to how I used to be."

"Did you clean the cut?" He walked toward her, then stopped. "Would you let me look at it?"

She imagined lifting her shirt as he watched. He might even touch her stomach. When she looked at his face, however, she saw only his medical stare. Her throat constricted. She blinked her eyes rapidly so she wouldn't cry. "No. I'm not your patient anymore."

"But we're still friends," he said.

"You want to be my friend?"

"Yes. I'm sorry I tried to force you to talk with other people about how you feel. I can tell that you're very depressed, and I don't understand your situation enough to know who you can or cannot trust."

"*Whom*," she corrected. She stood and walked toward the mirror. Ada-in-the-mirror looked back at her and said something. Ada tipped her head forward to hear, "Let us sin so that grace may abound." It wasn't like Ada-in-the-mirror to quote scripture.

"Well, at least you still care about grammar," Dr. Graham said.

She felt his presence behind her. She imagined spinning toward him and throwing her arms around his solid body. Ada-in-the-mirror looked ready to leap from the glass.

"I care about a great many things," she said. "Too many things."

"You can tell me anything." He appeared in the mirror too. Although he was several feet from her, their reflections looked like they were touching. "Tell me what's troubling you."

Ada-in-the-mirror gave a sardonic grin. Ada frowned and turned her back to her. "I know what you want from me," she told the doctor. Panic surged as she realized it was Ada-in-the-mirror speaking. "You want to know his name."

His eyes widened, and he spread his hands. "Yes, I do. I won't deny it, but that's not why I want to be your friend. There are so few people like us in Worden."

"What are we like, Doctor?" Ada-in-the-mirror feigned innocence. Ada shouted at her to stop, that she would ruin everything. Ada-in-the-mirror twitched her fingers in annoyance. "What do you think of me?" she insisted.

"You are a good person." He took a step closer. "You think deeply, and you feel deeply. It's not your fault that the world you live in is wrong. You'll find a place that's right, that matches your wisdom and beauty."

When he said *beauty*, Ada-in-the-mirror closed the distance between them. Touching his arm, she lifted her face to his. Their mouths met. His lips were unexpectedly soft and warm. At the sensation, Ada-in-the-mirror trembled, and Ada took control of her body again. Although she knew she ought to, she couldn't move. For a moment, his arms were reassuring and strong.

Then he pulled away. "Ada ... I don't—please don't—Forgive me."

She lurched from the mirror and stumbled to the fireplace. She put her hand on the mantel. Her head sang like a down bow on an open string. As she turned around, her hand brushed the picture of the Grahams and the starfish. She caught and steadied the frame before it could fall.

"Dr. Graham ..." She looked around. He was gone. She pushed out her tongue just enough to taste where his lips had been.

CHAPTER EIGHTEEN

Ada had composed herself by the time Dawn and Jon returned, and she summoned mild interest as they displayed and explained each incendiary purchase. They had more tea, this time with shortbread and fruit. Dawn placed the shortbread on each plate, so Ada didn't have the chance to refuse it. It was delicious, and Ada told Dawn she was impressed by her baking.

"It was actually a present from Sara Ellington," Dawn said. "She is always bringing in goodies for Dad."

The shortbread turned to ash in her mouth. She put the rest of it on her plate, then reconsidered. Not finishing it might offend Dawn, and it was wrong to waste it. She forced it down with the rest of her tea.

"Look at the time!" Jon said. "We've got to pick up Mother. You'll think about what I said, Dawn?"

"Sure, I'll think. I'm glad you believe I'm capable of that at least." She rolled her eyes at Ada.

Inside the car, Jon sighed. "Why are women so maddening?"

Deep in her own thoughts, Ada emitted only a sympathetic shake of her head.

"They tell you one thing," he said, "and when you do it, they say you should have done the opposite."

She shook herself from her reverie. "Jon, what are you talking about?"

He gripped the steering wheel. "I know she's your friend, but if she tells you anything that's not in confidence, you could help a brother out."

"I don't think that would be—"

"Forget it. I know what it is. She thinks I'm too young for her. She has her whole life planned, and she doesn't want to be tied to someone who's still trying to figure it out."

"What are you trying to figure out?" she asked.

"Life." He honked at a dog in the road. "But I guess you know about that too."

131

Her pulse quickened. What was he implying? She told herself she was reading too much into his words. The events of the past months would shake anyone. She let his comment pass without reply.

The tall brick building that was Donner's Grocery loomed in front of them. Jon parked next to the curb. "Don't worry, I'll go in with you in case they're planning an ambush."

To Ada's relief, their stop was short. Sybil was ready to leave, so Ada exchanged only a few words with Michael and his parents.

"How was your tea?" Sybil asked once they were in the car.

Ada waited, but Jon didn't speak. "It was nice to see Dawn again," she said. "How was your visit?"

"Slightly disconcerting. I'm glad you are both here. We need to discuss something as a family."

Ada wished she could see their faces from the back seat. She caught glimpses in the rear-view mirror of her mother—a pucker of worry, lines deepening near the mouth.

"This morning, Mrs. Smythe told me that the consistory has called another minister, Rev. Lloyd Abel from Caldwell. He and his wife have four children, and they will arrive next week." Sybil exhaled loudly. "He will deliver two sermons, and the congregation will vote on whether to retain him. If the church approves him, he will be given the parsonage."

"Where's that?" Jon asked.

"That's our home," Ada said. She immediately understood that this was the news Sybil had been waiting to share.

"I thought we owned the house," Jon said.

"No." Sybil fanned herself with an old bulletin. "When your father was called to Worden, he was given the house on the understanding that he would fill it with a family."

"Enter you, a beguiling meatpacker wanting to change her future," Jon said.

"I am not a meatpacker!" Sybil dropped the bulletin into her lap. "I worked there for less than a year. But you're right; that's how people see me now. Forget how I ministered to the congregation beside my husband— they'll toss me out of my home."

"Maybe," Jon said. "They might not like Rev. Abel."

"Eventually, someone will be called to stay." Sybil wiped her brow. "Charlotte and I and a few others want to prevent things from changing too much. Sometimes new pastors try to stir up controversy in the community. We don't want that."

"God forbid," Jon said.

"Don't be flippant," Sybil said. "We have a plan, which Eric Donner will present at the consistory meeting this week. When another minister is called, Michael will become the assistant minister. He deserves that position at least, for his efforts after ... for his efforts."

Ada's stomach turned.

"The Donners just bought the lot next to theirs—the Asian market that went out of business. It has a living area above the store, just like their lot does. They'll expand the grocery into the store downstairs, and we'll move above the new market space. Michael will join us once he and Alameda are married."

The car jerked, but not as much as Ada's heart. Dr. Graham's kiss still burned on her lips. She couldn't think about Michael without feeling sick.

"They're getting married?" Jon cried.

"He's asked you, hasn't he?" Sybil half turned to the backseat. "He told me he had."

Ada's heartbeat pounded in her ears. "I did not accept!"

"Why not?" Sybil gripped the seat. "I feel sure God has called him for extraordinary things, like your father. This is your opportunity to dedicate yourself to God."

"And to a life of misery," Jon said, "if she doesn't love him."

"I'll thank you to keep quiet." Sybil shook her finger at him. "Alameda knows her duty, and she desires our Savior to speak the words 'well done, good and faithful servant' to her."

"I didn't think it was appropriate that he asked so soon after Father's funeral," Ada said. More than anything, she wanted to reject this notion as easily and forcefully as Jon did.

Sybil nodded. "It is sudden, but we both agree the timing is of God. Your father would have agreed. His heart's desire was for you to be established in a godly home as mother and wife."

Ada clenched her fingers. "I didn't realize that."

"Then you weren't paying attention." Sybil sighed. "Perhaps we responded to your notions about the convent too calmly when you brought it up as a child. When we discovered you were still considering converting, your father told me how dismayed he was. He thought we had failed to demonstrate Christ's grace to you."

"You didn't fail," Ada said. "I don't care about the convent anymore."

Jon raised his eyebrows at her in the mirror. Ada glanced down.

"I'm relieved to hear it." Sybil fanned herself again. "The wedding doesn't have to be immediate, but there's no reason to delay the engagement. We'll move as soon as the good news is announced."

"Now hold on," Jon said. "What about staying at the motel?"

"The motel is not a permanent residence," Sybil said. "Besides, it's seedy."

"Because the people there are down on their luck? Jesus consorted with prostitutes and adulterers."

"Yes, but he didn't live with them."

Ada's fingernails dug into her skin. "I don't love Michael," she said. "Does he know that?"

"Love doesn't matter as much as respect. A man whom you respect you can grow to love. Men have passions almost from the moment they're born, but women need to be wooed and gently introduced to the mysterious way of a man with a maid. The fact that you need such introduction proves your virtue."

Ada avoided looking in the mirror. She felt her mother's eyes on her just the same, and she went hot with embarrassment.

"We can set a wedding date within a reasonable time frame," Sybil said, "perhaps six months. Once you're able to see Michael every day, though, I'm sure you'll be begging to move the date closer."

"I'll think about it," Ada said. She didn't have to see her mother's smile to know it was there. Victory and happiness radiated from Sybil's pores.

"Why doesn't anyone ask me what I think?" Jon demanded. "I don't want Michael as a brother-in-law."

"He will be a good influence on you," Sybil said.

"Not if I can help it. If you and Ada move to the Donners' new place, I'm moving out."

"No," Ada whispered. She couldn't lose him, not after losing Naomi and her father.

"Where would you go?" Sybil asked him.

"The Meatpacking District."

Sybil gave a cry of pain and faced the window. "I am so disappointed in you, Jonathon. You must reconsider."

"I'll reconsider if you do. We don't have to move in with the Donners. We could leave Worden and live with your parents."

"Never." The word was icy in the warm car. "I swore not to see them again. They would not welcome me back, nor would they welcome you. I don't even know if they're still in Pennsylvania. I'm trying," she reached for his arm, "to keep you from making the same mistakes I did. You don't understand the guilt I felt before Jesus cleansed me."

"I suppose not."

As Ada listened to them bicker, she closed her eyes. Change was being forced on her. Action was being forced on her. Did she believe in predestination simply because she was afraid of what having free will meant?

She had a way out. It was there, in the cramped space of her mind, waiting for her to stop ignoring it. She must try every other door first, not allow herself to weigh the option, for it had a sweetness to it that frightened her. It was an alien choice in an alien mind. That choice was not possible in her reality.

In whose reality? Ada-in-the-mirror hadn't hesitated to plunge her knife into the old Alameda's heart. Ada knew what God wanted her to do, what he decreed was real, and what her place was in his kingdom. She had been taught it all her life. If God would rather she enter Heaven maimed and blind, even reeking of hellfire's smoke, than not at all, then a final deed of selfishness and despair could also be the supreme act of self-sacrifice.

The solution was there, in the cramped, chaotic space of her mind.

It was Sunday, the first time Rev. Abel would preach. Every church member was present, and there was a new contingent of meatpackers. Jon sat with them, and Ada's eyes stung as she studied the group. She missed seeing Jim Reeves' dark face among the white congregants. His presence had given her the silly notion that God was pleased with the church and that his word spoke to all men, regardless of culture, class, or color. Like so many things she had been taught, it wasn't true.

Michael officiated for the first part of the service, and then he took a seat as Rev. Abel hobbled to the pulpit. A sufferer of gout, Rev. Abel favored one foot, but this didn't impede his sailor-like swaying as he preached. His wife and four children sat bolt upright on the pew in front of Ada and Sybil, the pew that no one ever occupied. The three boys with sandy hair and matching ties and the small girl with red hair kept very still, sucking on mints. Mrs. Abel had red hair too, pinned haphazardly under her green hat. She was as tall as her husband, and more generously sized.

"The pains of death surrounded me, and the pangs of Sheol laid hold of me; I found trouble and sorrow." Even though the Bible was open in front of him, Rev. Abel recited the psalm by memory, looking straight ahead. His eyes were small, leaving doubt as to their color, and his light eyebrows were almost unnoticeable in his wide forehead. "I believed, therefore I spoke, 'I am greatly afflicted.' I said in my haste, 'All men are liars.'"

His voice was lilting, hypnotic. Ada felt herself slipping further and further away as if in the swells of the ocean, and she saw his head as a bobbing buoy near the shoreline.

"Precious in the sight of Jehovah is the death of his saints. O Jehovah, you have loosed my bonds."

How would her bonds be loosed? The problem, which had robbed her of sleep for the past week, floated beside her. It had five arms like a starfish. Not just one arm would do; she needed to chop them all off.

"Let us sing number 219," Michael said.

Ada startled awake. She wiped her chin discreetly in case she had drooled. Caught in her observation of Mrs. Abel, Sybil didn't seem to have noticed anything. Ada felt more awake than she had for months. She knew what to do. With the daydream had come her decision.

When the service was over, the back of the church congested as members swarmed Rev. Abel. Ada headed in the opposite direction and took out a bag of chocolate candies that Michael had given her on Friday. Although chocolate was a special treat, she hadn't permitted herself to taste them.

"Mattie, would you like a chocolate?" she asked.

The little girl smiled and stuck out her hand. "Thank you, Miss Will'ams!"

"No fair!" Kathleen stumbled out of a pew, dragging Billy by the hand. Ada handed them both a sweet, and soon she was surrounded.

"One for me too, please!"

"Get back, you greedy pig!"

"Gentlemen, watch your language," Ada said. She noticed that Hezekiah Gentle scowled at her from the edge of the group. He stuck his hands in his pockets, and when his sister Christabella tried to hand him a chocolate, he shook his head.

"Naomi used to give us candy," Mattie said. Her lip trembled. Ada picked her up and hugged her. The child's fast pulse matched her own accelerated heartbeat.

"Why don't you share the rest with the Abel children?" She set Mattie down and pressed the bag into her sticky hands. "Go on."

"Mattie!" Dennis called to her. "Give some sugar to your uncle."

His niece ran into his arms. He kissed her cheek and accepted the candy she handed him, all the while glancing at Ada with a defiant grin. Mattie smiled and then wriggled down, headed for the Abels.

For a long moment, Ada's eyes met Dennis's. If he wanted to read fear in her stare, she hoped he was disappointed. Then his gaze shifted to Christabella a few yards away. Christabella had Naomi's heart-shaped face and slight build, although it looked like she would grow taller than her sister. Dennis looked back at Ada and smiled. Alarm ripped through her as she recognized his threat. She had assumed she was his next victim, but now she saw she was only one of his prey. Dennis would never stop with one, or two, or three girls. Her mouth tightened.

"Come along, dear." Edith Templeton laid her hand on Dennis's sleeve. "Lydia and I were discussing parade floats, and you have to settle a question for us." She ignored Ada as she had since the spring festival. At least she had never followed through on her promise to bring up Ada's accusations about Dennis to the elders. Dennis must have counseled her against it.

"What? You weren't discussing the 'able' sermon we just heard?" He laughed, flashing his even, white teeth.

"I've already heard that joke," she said, "twice."

After they left, Ada waited in a nearby pew. Tension spiked through her body, and she shuffled a hymnal, straightening the corners of the creased pages. She flipped through one of the forms in the back, the funeral service that had been read so recently for her father and friends. At last she saw that Michael was free. She caught his eye and rose.

They met at the door and walked out together. Michael's white collar was spotless in the sunshine. Ada was ashamed of her overly bleached, thin shirt.

"I'm glad you're still here," Michael said. "I wanted to talk to you about the message. I have not been entirely at peace with this transition in leadership, but that sermon humbled me. I can learn from Rev. Abel. What did you think of it?"

She tried to remember the salient points of the sermon, but she had not been present past the reading of the psalm. "It was very … enlightening."

"That's the word! I prefer to be reminded that a minister has been to seminary—that he knows how to parse Latin, Greek, and Hebrew, and not merely preach from the heart."

"You have a heart," Ada said. Her lack of sleep was showing in her thoughts and speech, but she didn't care. She just wanted it to be over.

"I do have a heart." He cleared his throat and brushed his finger through a strand of her hair. "I thought you hadn't noticed."

His touch elicited nothing from her, no interest, no desire, not even revulsion. She gestured at the courting bench a few paces away. "Look where we are."

"Where I should have proposed."

She bit her lip. "You might try again."

A sharp intake of breath. Claiming her hand, he knelt. "Alameda Williams, will you be my wife?"

She stared down at him. He warded off the sun's glare with his right hand and reached into his pocket with his left. The sight of the ring caught her like a blow, but she forced a smile. "Yes, Michael, I agree to marry you."

He slid the ring over her finger. The gold was brassy and warm, and so flimsy she wondered if it was from a cereal box.

"I've been carrying this since the last time I asked," he said. "I'll buy a real one soon."

"There's no reason to waste money on such a trifle. Use it for God's work instead."

He stood and embraced her. His mouth pressed against her cheek. "Of course you're right. Oh, I'm so pleased! I'll go make an announcement."

She pulled away. "Not now. Look—a lot of people have left already. Let's do it next Sunday, with the pre-service announcements."

"Whatever you want, my angel." He took her hand in his and kissed it.

Her palm felt numb; her skin hardly registered his caresses. He might have done anything to her then, and she wouldn't have noticed. Instead, she faced the sun and shut her eyes. Through her eyelids, the light was orange and pink, an illuminated womb she hoped she was strong enough to escape.

CHAPTER NINETEEN

*T*he following Sunday, Michael and Ada's engagement was formally announced, and Rev. Abel gave the second of his trial sermons. Ada made out less of his message than she had the previous week, perhaps due to her new seating arrangement. The Donners had moved into Sybil and Ada's row, and Michael sat beside Ada, brushing her arm whenever he retrieved or replaced the psalter hymnal. He didn't allow her to hold her own book but took it in his hands and slanted it so she had to lean close to see the page. Since she had long since memorized the harmonies and text, she sang looking straight ahead and didn't give him the satisfaction of sharing.

After the service, she and Michael formed a receiving line with the pastor at the back of the pews. She suffered through the handshakes of several families, all the while dreading when Dennis's bland face would appear. There he was. One arm touched Edith's waist, guiding her in front so her dress skimmed his khaki slacks. Edith congratulated Michael but ignored Ada. She toyed with the strap of her purse as she waited for her fiancé to shake hands. Her heavy perfume coated Ada's hypersensitive nostrils with plum, cinnamon, and buttery, briny oakmoss.

"Congratulations on catching such a virtuous woman," Dennis said as he shook Michael's hand. He turned to Ada and lightly pressed her fingers. "Best wishes to you, Miss Williams."

Struggling not to snatch her hand away, she looked down. A stream of vile language twisted through her head, and she clamped her teeth together to keep from spewing it at him. She was shocked she could think such things.

"When's the wedding?" Dennis asked.

"Next spring," Michael said. "Earlier if I can convince *this one* not to overtake the marriage with wedding planning." He squeezed Ada's arm and laughed, making it seem a joke. She frowned.

"Edith and I will be an old married couple by then," Dennis said. "We'll have to invite you over and compare newlywed life."

"Perhaps our ladies would want to discuss wedding details before then," Michael offered.

"That sounds extremely entertaining," Dennis said. "Meanwhile, you and I could shoot whatever is in season."

"Dennis!" Edith's frown morphed into a smile like a snake slipping into grass. "You have already promised so many visits, I am afraid we shall not be able to keep them all. Please consult with me first."

"My dear." He patted her arm, and her cheeks flushed at the patronizing gesture. "I was merely being polite."

Michael watched them go. "I wish you had helped me set a date to visit them. A pastor should be among his flock, and it seems that Miss Templeton could be a good friend for you."

"She doesn't like me," Ada said.

"Why not?"

"I said something unpleasant once," Ada said, "and she thought I was lying. I will set it straight soon."

He pressed her hand and nodded. Ada's insides contracted.

The next night the congregation gathered for a special meeting and voted to call Rev. Abel as their new minister. Michael was given a position as assistant minister. Afterward Ada and Sybil visited the Donners, and Sybil and Charlotte arranged moving plans. Michael sat next to Ada with his pale, long-fingered hand perched near her knee, but she kept her hands in her lap. His hopefulness grated her nerves.

On Tuesday Jon didn't come home after work, and when he stopped by the next day he announced he'd found a place to stay. He helped them box up the kitchen and parlor and emptied out his room.

When he carried out his last box, Ada ran after him.

"Please don't go, Jon," she said, touching his arm. He was real and solid, but more and more she felt like a bubble about to float away and burst. "At least not until we move out."

"You can break the engagement," he said. "You can stay with me."

"I can't leave Mother."

He set the box on the front seat. "I know you believe that, but it's not true. She could move to the Donners by herself."

"She would never allow it, and I couldn't see her at church knowing I'd broken her heart like that."

"Then don't go to church. I won't."

"Oh, Jon!" She hugged him. She feared for his soul more than for her own. She had already accepted the possibility of Hell for herself, but she couldn't imagine her twin being tormented eternally.

He held her tightly, then stepped back. "I guess I shouldn't blame you for being so weak."

His reproof stung. She was weaker than he knew, but not for the reasons he supposed. As she watched him drive away, a tear fell to her cheek.

On Wednesday Sybil called Ada to the phone. Ada held the receiver to her ear for half a minute before she had the presence of mind to introduce herself. Relief washed through her when she heard Dawn answer. She was glad her mother had allowed the call and given her the privacy of the office. The engagement must have made her generous.

"Jon told me that he moved out," Dawn said. "How are you doing?"

"I miss him, but maybe it's for the best."

"Have you seen his new place?"

"No."

"I haven't either, although he asked me to." She giggled. "Sorry. I know it's what's best for Jon, but I'm worried about you."

Ada shook her head. She couldn't afford to attract Dawn's attention, not at this point. "That's kind of you, but I'm fine."

"I hear you're marrying Michael Donner?" She pitched the end of her sentence high, as if in disbelief.

"We are engaged, yes."

"I thought you didn't like him."

"I respect him. Anything else is not your concern."

A pause. "Jon says you're doing it so your mom will have a place to live. There are plenty of other places available."

"Tenements in the Meatpacking District, you mean." Ada braided the phone cord through her fingers. "We can't afford to rent a house."

"The church should help you! Didn't your father have life insurance?"

"No. He trusted God to provide for us, and God is helping us through the Donners. According to my mother, this is the ideal plan."

"Maybe for your mother, but not for you. You're the one making the sacrifice."

Ada glanced through the office window. Sunlight streamed through the clouds like she imagined it would when Christ returned, igniting a halo of golden fire around his divine body. "It's okay, Dawn. I've accepted it."

"Don't you know what exchanging your body for material goods is called?"

Ada shut her eyes. Patterns of chromatic light played on her eyelids. "That's unfair."

"You're right. I'm sorry. I just feel like you're being taken advantage of."

"I know what I want." Ada's forehead prickled. "Do me the courtesy of believing that."

Dawn sighed. "I'm telling you as a friend, you will regret this decision if you go through with it."

"Then you're not my friend." Something inside her collapsed as she spoke, but she needed Dawn to leave her alone. She couldn't risk her getting in the way or kindling doubt in Ada's mind.

"Please don't say that." Dawn's voice was small. "I only want to help."

"You can help by leaving me alone." Ada clicked down the receiver. The first of many endings, she told herself.

♫

On Thursday Ada drove to the hospital. Sara Ellington gave her a doubtful look when she entered. "Do you have an appointment, Miss Williams?"

"No, but I need to see Dr. Graham today. I don't mind waiting."

"You might have to," she said. "Take a seat."

"Thank you," Ada whispered. The nurse's critical expression made her reconsider her decision. No. If she didn't act now, she might never have another chance.

Ada chose a chair away from the other patients. As Sara worked through them, calling them back to the examination rooms, Ada secretly studied her. Dawn's anecdote about the shortbread had fired Ada's jealousy. Although Sara was unusually tall and thin, she carried herself with dignity and grace. The severity of her hairstyle brought her irregular facial features into relief. She was not beautiful, but she was striking. Working with Dr. Graham every day must draw her close to him. Ada's heart dropped into her stomach.

She waited nearly an hour before her name was called, and it wasn't by Sara. Dr. Graham opened the back door and uttered it quietly. As she stood and walked toward him, her legs felt as jiggly as the blackberry jelly she'd opened for her mother's breakfast that morning.

Dr. Graham took her to a small room she hadn't noticed before. She didn't see any medical equipment except for a stethoscope on the desk. A coat hung on a hook by the door. His office. It must be his office.

He entered and shut the door haltingly behind him. "What brings you here, Miss Williams?"

"I was hoping to talk with you. I didn't realize it would be so busy." She fidgeted with her hands. This was more difficult than she'd anticipated.

"What do you want to talk about?" He looked sick, like someone expecting bad news.

She glanced down. He wasn't helping her. "What happened at the house."

"Ah. I thought that might be it." His back pressed against the door in a painfully straight pose. "I apologize again. Please forgive me."

"You don't have to apologize."

"Yes, I do." He shook his head. "I took advantage of you and the situation. I am your doctor, and you are my patient. That is our relationship."

"I told you, I'm not your patient anymore."

"Yes, but even in … similar cases, a decent time should pass before a doctor and his patient can—can—"

"You did nothing wrong," she said emphatically. She judged her own actions more harshly.

He folded his arms. "Dawn tells me you are engaged to be married."

She reddened. "That's true, but I wasn't engaged when we kissed."

"Why?" He cleared his throat. "Why are you marrying him?"

"My mother needs a place to live. The church voted to call Rev. Abel as the new pastor, and he accepted. The Abels will move into the parsonage as soon as we can pack our personal belongings."

He looked intently at her. "You're marrying him for your mother's sake?"

"I'm not marrying him at all." She watched his face. "I'm going to break the engagement."

"You are!" He grabbed the back of the chair and sat heavily on it. "I don't understand."

"There's nothing to understand. I'm breaking my engagement on the Fourth of July."

"Independence Day." He dug his hands into his coat pockets. "Is that intentional irony?"

"It's not your concern," she said. She didn't want to offend him, but she didn't want him prying into her motives either. It would hurt him too much, later.

"The Fourth is only a week away, so why not end the farce now? You'll just have to move again. Where will you and your mother live after that?"

"I don't want to talk about it. Please." She didn't like the frown settling behind his eyes. "I hate disappointing you."

"You don't disappoint me; you mystify me."

"I know I haven't told you everything about my … situation." Not daring to face him, she took a step toward the door. She heard him stand and scoot the chair toward the desk. "I want to tell you everything."

"Maybe that's not such a good idea."

She turned. "What do you mean?"

He straightened a stack of folders. "I don't want to repeat what happened at the house. I'm sure it confused you, and I have my reputation to consider."

"I'm not confused, and you've said before you don't care what other people think."

"It's more what I would think of myself, ethically. I'm forty-one, and you're only eighteen. I was wrong to think we could be friends—just friends. You mean too much to me."

Her heart thumped, and she lowered her eyes. "I thought I was alone," she said, "in feeling this way."

"Damn it, Ada, you're making this hard for me." He wiped his forehead with his sleeve, then took off his doctor's coat and laid it across the chair. "You are in a vulnerable psychological state."

"I was," she corrected. "Part of that was the way I felt about you. It upset me because I always thought I wanted to be a nun."

As if pricked by a thought, he looked up. "Is that why you hurt yourself? Because of me?"

She considered the question, aware of the delicate balance between them. At least she no longer felt the strong sense that he wanted her to leave. "When I'm with you, that's when I want to hurt myself least."

"See? *That.*" He shook his head. "That kind of talk is why I can't be with you. I shouldn't have so much power over your state of mind."

Her stomach felt empty and twisted, making her want to double over and clasp her arms about herself. She nodded, hoping he wouldn't sense her misery. She had thought, since he was an atheist, she wouldn't have this much trouble convincing him. How long would she humiliate herself? "If you think that way, if you don't feel a connection ..." She couldn't finish the sentence. She rushed for the door.

As she turned the handle, she felt his hand on her back.

"Ada, wait." He arrested her arm and turned her toward him. If God saw fit to strike her dead, he should do so now, because feeling the doctor's grip dissolved any final resistance about what she planned to do. "You affect my mental state too," he admitted reluctantly.

"I know we can't be together forever," she said. "I'm not naïve. You're probably still married."

"I'm divorced." His hand slid down her arm and clasped her palm. "Ianna and I thought that would be easiest for Dawn."

Dawn. Ada felt foolish. How could she have dreamed she could seduce him? A queasy feeling hovered in her throat. Her only comfort was that he still held her hand. "I hoped—I thought—"

His fingers brushed the back of her wrist. "Maybe you're right. Maybe I'm too worried about other people's opinions. However, you can't deny that there's an imbalance of age and experience between us."

Hope warmed her. "There is—was—a twelve-year age difference between my parents. Fifty years ago, twice that age gap would have meant nothing. Even today it is not so unusual. And I'm ... I'm only asking for a day."

He released her hand. "One day?"

She'd made a mistake, she saw that now. "One chance," she corrected, "for us to spend time together. You'll see that I know my mind, that I'm mature enough to match wits with you."

A grudging smile creased the corners of his eyes. "You're asking me on a date?"

She ducked her head in embarrassment. "Yes, as soon as I break my engagement to Michael."

"What goes on in that head of yours?" He extended his hand, hesitated, and then touched her cheek. Her breath caught. "When do you want to meet?"

"Will you be in town for the Independence Day parade?"

He nodded. "I have to keep an eye on Dawn. I have a feeling she's planning to make trouble."

He didn't know the half of it. "Let's meet after the parade ends. Your house isn't far from the Town Hall. We could walk there together."

"Are you sure this is what you want?" he asked. "You have your reputation to consider too."

"Let me worry about my reputation," she said in a teasing tone. "Just meet me there."

On Friday, men from the church helped Ada and her mother move next to the Donners. As the car pulled away from the parsonage for the final time, Ada saw the Abels' moving van roll in. Not even the house would have the opportunity to miss her.

CHAPTER TWENTY

*A*da wiped beads of sweat from her face. Her white robe itched and clung to her skin and clothing. The gently rolling float was plastered with cotton and white feathers in an attempt to evoke the angelic, but Ada felt more like a giant chicken than a heavenly being.

"Let's play *Yankee Doodle* again," Gail Keller said. Her robe swarmed the piano bench and covered the piano legs tied down in the middle of the float. A garland of red and blue stars matching the decorations on the piano and truck sat crookedly on her head. She looked much younger than her thirty years.

"I want to hear *When the Saints*," the three Abel boys chorused. Two of them peppered the crowd with toffee wrapped in paper that had been scribbled over with Bible verses. That had been Mrs. Abel's idea. Sybil had wanted to hand out pamphlets and penny bangers as a play on hellfire.

"*When the Saints* it is." Ada fiddled a few notes in introduction, and Gail joined her. The neck of her violin swelled in the heat, and she struggled to tune her notes. It worried her that the instrument might be damaged, but the parade was nearing the Town Hall, so she could put it away soon.

As she played, she scanned the crowd for Dr. Graham. She was self-conscious about her costume, but knowing that he was waiting to meet her was worth a little embarrassment. As the float rolled on and she didn't see him, her stomach churned and she lost her concentration, fumbling the familiar melody.

A few floats behind them, the mayor preceded the Miss Independence float in his Cadillac Le Mans. Mrs. Templeton and Dennis Gentle waved from the car; Edith sat next to Miss Independence with a white parasol and a brilliant smile. This year, Katherine Heath was Miss Independence. Her dress was a shocking shade of red. Ada couldn't help but think of blood, and between songs she scratched her wrists with her fingernails. If the doctor wasn't here, it wouldn't matter. She wished she were home with her shard of mirror.

146

They had passed Jonathon and Dawn. Neither greeted her with a gesture or smile, but she guessed they would forgive her if she joined in their day of fun. More than anything, Ada wished she could have a moment alone with her brother. She hadn't talked with him since he'd moved, and she hated how they'd parted. Her posture stiffened. Making up with Jon wasn't part of her deal with God. Once she put herself completely into God's hands, her twin would realize she wasn't weak after all.

"Ada!"

She scratched her bow against the string.

"I have something for you." Pete O'Connor ran up to the float. He thrust an envelope at her feet and darted back to the side of the road.

After the song finished, Ada bent over and retrieved the envelope. Her heart thudded in her throat.

"What was that about?" Gail asked.

"It's from Father O'Connor." Her eyes smarted as she opened the letter, so she folded it again and hid it in her waistband beneath her robe.

"I thought he was dead."

"You're right; he is. Let's play another song."

"I want to hear *For the Dear Old Flag!*" the oldest Abel boy shouted.

"No, *Camptown Races!*" the youngest protested.

Ada sighed. "You choose, Gail." As she retuned her strings, she noticed that the varnish on her violin was sticky. Although she knew she should put her instrument away before it cracked, she no longer cared. The world was wrecked, and so was she. It seemed appropriate that her violin suffered as well.

When they reached Town Hall, she placed the instrument in its case and shrugged off her sweaty robe, hanging it over the truck's side with the other costumes. All the while, she searched for Dr. Graham. Where was he? A dark voice taunted he would never come.

Perhaps he was late, delayed by an emergency. She could wait longer. The Donner's Grocery float had yet to arrive, and the mayor was preparing for his speech. Dr. Graham might be running up to Dawn this minute.

Dennis strolled back and forth in the crowd, fetching chairs, adjusting the sound system, shaking hands. He whispered something in Edith's ear, then in Mrs. Templeton's, and they smiled as if charmed. At last he seemed to sense Ada's gaze. Their eyes met, and he touched the brim of his straw hat. She walked to a less crowded spot by a cluster of trees and tipped her violin case against one of the trunks. Less than a minute later, he was there.

"You should move closer to hear the mayor's speech," he said behind her.

"Actually, I was hoping to miss it," she said.

"A true patriot! And what would you be doing instead? Making your fiancé happy?"

She pushed her hand against the tree bark. "I might miss the fireworks tonight too," she said after a moment. "I won't be with Michael then."

He stepped closer, tugging one of the branches. "It's an interesting game you're playing, Alameda Henrietta Williams." He snapped off a twig and scraped it against the tree near her hand.

If he thought saying her whole name gave him power over her, he was wrong. She picked up the violin case to hide her trembling hands. "I'll be at Naomi's favorite spot," she said. "No one will be there tonight." She marched into the hot sunshine. Her legs shook.

No Dr. Graham yet. Now she was relieved; she hadn't wanted him to witness that conversation. The last of the parade arrived, and she saw Michael help Sybil from the grocery float. She moved forward to meet them.

The mayor tapped the microphone. "Hello? Hello?"

The crowd cheered.

"Happy Independence Day, Worden!"

The mayor mopped his face and launched into his lecture while the crowd stirred and pulsed like coalescing and collapsing waves. Michael and Mr. Donner put up the folding chairs, and Sybil and Charlotte sat gratefully. As Ada wavered, still searching for the doctor, Michael took the violin case from her.

"Sit right there," he directed. "Let me get you something to drink."

She complied, and Michael fetched tall glasses of icy lemonade from the stand. As Ada sipped hers, she glanced around. Where was he?

"Who are you looking for?" Michael whispered into her ear.

"Jon," she said. Then she put her hand to her mouth. She had just lied!

"He's over there, with Miss Graham. I fear your twin has fallen from the path of righteousness, my sweet."

"Shh! Lovebirds!" Sybil giggled. "Listen to the mayor."

Ada couldn't. The heat was overpowering. Her palm throbbed where she had scraped it against the tree bark. Where was Dr. Graham? Had he changed his mind? She had to find him.

"I'm sorry," she said to Michael. "I have to talk to him."

Pursing his lips, he nodded slightly. She picked her way through the crowd toward her brother. She bowed her shoulders as she approached, sensing the hurt in Dawn's eyes and the reproach in Jon's.

"How are you?" Ada asked her twin.

"Better than you look. What's wrong?"

"Nothing." She swallowed. Another lie. "I thought your father would be here, Dawn."

"Something upset him," Dawn said. "He wouldn't tell me what, but he refused to come with us."

"Oh." She pressed her hands against her stomach.

"Maybe you should sit down," Jon said, staring at the stage. "Michael's holding your seat for you."

She stumbled back to Michael and Sybil. Her legs gave out as she reached the chair.

"What's the matter?" Sybil asked.

"It's the heat," she whispered. "It's too much for me."

"I'll take you back to the house," Michael said. "It's just a block. Can you walk that far?"

She nodded. He threaded his arm under her shoulders and helped her. She couldn't breathe. Where had the air gone? It was all muggy heat, oppressive and clawing at her like a devil.

Halfway to the store, she collapsed. Michael swung her into his arms and carried her the rest of the way. He strode upstairs and without a modicum of propriety deposited her onto her mattress. He fumbled at the buttons around her collar.

"It's okay." She fended him off. "I can breathe now. Thank you."

Michael swabbed his forehead with a handkerchief and sat on the mattress. "For goodness' sake, Alameda. How could you worry me like that?"

"I just need to rest," she said. "I'll be all right."

"You need something to drink." He left the room for a minute and returned with a glass of water.

"Thank you," she said. "I'm sorry to be a burden. You should go back."

"I'd rather stay."

"I don't want you to miss the rest of the speech on my account. Besides, there's my mother. She's probably worried."

"You're right." He touched her arm. "You always think of others."

She grabbed his hand. "Please, Michael, take care of her. It's hard for her, not being the minister's wife anymore."

"You don't need to worry. According to my mother, she was born to be a shopkeeper." He lifted her fingers to his lips, but she pulled her hand free before he could land a kiss.

"Just take care of her."

"Of course." At the door, he looked back. "Are you sure you'll be all right?"

She nodded.

As soon as he was gone, she sat up. She couldn't stay here speculating about what had kept the doctor. If he had second-guessed himself, she would make him tell her in person. She had convinced him at the hospital, and she could do so again. Going to the desk, she selected a pen. Her hand was steady as she jotted her note. *Dear Michael, I've gone to find Jon and watch the fireworks.* So many lies. They were harder to write than to say.

In the bathroom, she squarely met her reflection as she washed her face and fixed her hair. Primping like this was worse than useless, but she couldn't help herself. She went downstairs and locked the shop door behind her. An empty wrapper skittered across the road in the breeze.

Her shirt was soggy with sweat when she reached the doctor's house. As soon as she saw the front drive, she stopped. It was the roses that arrested her, kept her from running the last few feet. Canes strewed the lawn like cracked bones. She peered closer. Pale gashes marked where the bushes had been hacked violently and repeatedly.

She sidestepped the floral carnage. At the front door, her hand wavered on the knocker. She clanked it, twice. Again, louder. It was still softer than the pounding of her heart.

The door scraped open. "What is it?" Dr. Graham asked. His eyes were red and slightly unfocused, and he shielded them from the light. She smelled something fermented and sour on his breath. He blinked. "Ada? Damn it. Come in."

Uncertainly she crossed the threshold. All the shades were down.

"I'm sorry about the mess outside." He lumbered to the sitting room. His gait was a little impaired, and Ada hung back.

"What happened?" she asked.

"What happened? What happened? I destroyed her roses."

The dead feeling inside her grew. "Whose?"

He walked to the mantel and picked up the photograph of his family. "I got a letter from Ianna yesterday. After ten years without a word, she wants to see Dawn and me again."

The air thickened. She choked in a breath. "She's coming here?"

"No. She wants to meet us at the seaside. She wants to spend Thanksgiving or Christmas with us there."

Ada sat in the nearest chair.

He laughed in a low voice. "She loved those roses, and I took care of them all these years. My thanks for the gift she'd given me in Dawn. She couldn't stay with me in Worden, she said, but she could give me Dawn. It would be better for both of us if she never saw us again. And now. Now!"

"She wants to be with you again?"

He replaced the frame and turned around. "I don't know. She didn't mention Julie in her letter."

Ada remembered Julie, Miss Shoemaker, who had played the church organ so masterfully. A sense of unreality settled over her. Dr. Graham's life detached from her own. His education, family, and experiences separated him from her and all she thought he was. He was incontrovertibly other, and she was isolated, alone, pointless. The room blurred, and the objects in it telescoped away from her eyes. Even the doctor's face, as she watched it, receded in her vision until it was as distant as a doll's. She was conscious not only of herself watching him, but of herself watching herself.

"I know I need to tell Dawn about the letter," he said. "We can make a decision together. I've coped rather poorly, drinking and destroying, and I apologize. I completely forgot about our meeting."

Their rendezvous was not the sort of thing one forgot. She dug her fingernails into her legs, but it didn't help. "Perhaps it would be best if I left."

"Do you want to?"

She stared at him. The circles under his eyes were lilac smudges of twilight. His inner energy sang out and resonated within her being. It didn't matter that their paths diverged in the past and the future. They crossed now, and that was all she asked.

"Only if you want me to go."

He sighed. "No, stay. I need some coffee and a meal. At least I can offer you that much."

"I'll make us something," she offered, although the thought of food turned her stomach. She hadn't eaten all day.

"Thank you. That would give me time to take a shower." He swayed across the room.

In the kitchen, she grated potatoes for hash browns, fixed a fruit salad, and started a mushroom omelet. As she held the knife, she went dizzy with need. Her desire was too strong, and now she doubted he would ever touch her. She didn't bother to roll down her stocking. She sliced into the flesh above her left knee, a messy cut she didn't try to define. The fresh pain eased her disconnected perception and returned her to the moment. She could breathe again. She wanted to cut more, but she didn't have time. The hash browns were already crisping. Letting her skirt fall without cleaning the wound, she tended to the meal.

A tear leaked down her cheek as she slipped from the kitchen to straighten the table settings. A bowl of pine cones and berries the color of dried blood was centered on the dark, wooden table. She nudged it one way then the other, but it didn't look right.

"You're very precise, aren't you?" Dr. Graham leaned against the doorjamb. "My mother was like that, only more so. She would remake my brother's bed or mine if she saw a single wrinkle—sometimes many times in a row."

She turned her back to him and wiped her eyes. "At least she didn't make *you* redo it."

"I know. I think she recognized that her obsession with symmetry was pathological, and she tried not to pull us into it."

She adjusted the bowl again.

He laid his hand on her arm. "It looks perfect, and whatever you made smells fabulous. Can I help with anything?"

"You can help me bring the food to the table."

They sat across from each other. She served him and then returned the utensils to their platters.

"You're going to eat too, aren't you?" he asked. "Let me help you." He scraped half the omelet onto her plate and heaped hash browns and fruit next to it.

"Stop!" She smiled unwillingly. "I could never eat that much food."

"Follow my example. I'll teach you soon enough." He winked.

To please him, she forked a few bites and chewed without tasting.

"While we're eating," he said, "perhaps you wouldn't mind telling me how your parents came up with your name. It's unusual, especially in Worden."

"It's simple enough. My mother saw the name on a street sign somewhere between here and Pennsylvania, where she's from. She liked it, and my father came up with using Ada as a nickname. St. Ada was a French abbess, the niece of St. Engelbert, who was renowned for her piety." She spoke without inflection. It was the old Alameda's story, not hers.

"A Roman Catholic saint?" He wiped his lips. "Wouldn't that be a reason not to use the name?"

"She was from the seventh century, so it was acceptable. The pre-Reformation church was still the church."

"Still, I wonder if it didn't send mixed messages to you."

She set down her fork. Always the doctor, analyzing her ailments. He hadn't asked if she'd broken her engagement with Michael. He had probably forgotten this was supposed to be a date. Nevertheless, talking with him in the cool house was better than waiting alone at the Donners'. He could afford an air conditioner, unlike many other families in Worden.

"Dawn told me she once heard someone call you 'St. Alameda,'" he continued, "and she said it was merited. You might have broken many hearts if you weren't as good as you are beautiful."

Her face warmed. "I'm not good, Dr. Graham."

"I'm not your doctor, remember. Please, call me George."

"I'm not good, George," she repeated. His name felt like a weapon, and it hurt her to say it.

"Why aren't you good? Give me one reason," he challenged with a smile.

Shrugging, she hunched forward. "I cut myself today."

"Oh, honey." He creased his napkin in half and set it by his plate. "Why?"

"I thought it wouldn't matter."

"It always matters to me. How bad is it? Let me see."

She shook her head.

"Ada." He stretched across the table and tipped back her chin until she couldn't avoid looking at him. "I think you're beautiful, with or without cuts. Now please come to the bathroom with me. I have a kit there. I can clean it properly."

"Are you drunk?" she asked.

"A little," he admitted, "but I'm hoping this won't require major surgery."

Straightening her posture, she followed him to the bathroom. As he washed his hands, she shivered and was glad she hadn't eaten more. When he asked, she shyly raised her skirt and showed him the cut.

"You did it just now?" he asked, bending over her knee. He tugged down her stocking, working it free from the dried blood. His fingers prodded her tender skin.

"Yes. I'm sorry."

"It's okay. Just let me clean it." He washed the cut with a wet cloth, rubbed on antiseptic, and then bandaged it. His hands were steady, and she coaxed breath back into her lungs. He was being professional, that was all. When he was done, she dropped her hem to cover her leg.

Near the sink, their bodies touched. She heard him panting too. Then he took her in his arms, and she knew her wait was over.

CHAPTER TWENTY-ONE

*H*er back pressed against the porcelain countertop as he crushed her with a kiss. Then he hitched her off her feet and carried her to the bedroom. They sat side by side on the hard cotton mattress, so close they touched from shoulder to hip. Through his clothes the heat of his body warmed her, as if he were a strange fire whose properties she had yet to learn.

"Are you sure this is what you want? It doesn't frighten you?" He leaned close, his breath sizzling her ear.

"Should it?"

He smiled. "No. But mothers have been known to say all kinds of things to make sure their daughters stay pure."

"I never needed convincing."

"I'm sure you didn't," he said with a chuckle.

She put her hand to his close-shaven chin. Her fingertips traced the lines of his face. She removed his glasses and placed them on the nightstand next to the bed. "I like it when you laugh."

He put his arm around her shoulder and nuzzled her cheek. Her heart beat so loud and fast she thought it would bound from her chest into his lap. She shut her eyes as he caressed her with his hands and lips. He energized each part of her face, her shoulders and arms. The warmth spread down her body and centered at her thighs. She opened her eyes as they lay back across the bed.

"You're so lovely," he said. "Your eyes are like a startled deer's."

She touched the softness of his neck. "It's strange. I worried that my guilt would ruin this moment, but now I'm only worried that being with me will disappoint you."

"Ada, no." He bent over her and kissed her. The weight of his body exhilarated her. She wrapped her arms around him and slid her hands up the back of his shirt. She felt the muscles padding his spine, the movement of his scapulae as he massaged her body.

"I'm the one who doesn't want to disappoint you," he said as she pulled off his shirt. "Most people would call me a fat old man."

She reached for his shoulders and drew his head down close to hers. "When I look at you, all I see is your heart—your soul—vast as the ocean."

He kissed her again and left a trail of flames down her front, unbuttoning as he went. She remembered Michael's scrabbling fingers on her collar, like insects she wanted to brush off. George's touch fueled an internal blaze.

"What's this?" He plucked Father O'Connor's letter from her waistband.

"It's a letter of recommendation for St. Cecilia's Convent," she said, "from Father O'Connor. Pete gave it to me today." She took the letter from him and set it next to his glasses. "It's not important."

"Is it because of me," he asked, "that you decided you didn't want to join the convent?"

"Partly."

"I'm not sorry," he said. "You have a gift with your music. It should be shared with more than a convent, more than a town."

She shrugged. "All I cared about was sharing it with God."

"There's a sense of holiness about you," he said. "Being around you, I feel connected to sacred things. I only hope you'll learn how deep that connection is and that the rules of the day have nothing to do with it."

"I feel connected to you," she murmured, "to life, and to death." She put her arms around him, stopping the conversation. Despite the air conditioning, she was feverishly hot. A shooting star of sweat flashed across her scalp. She marveled that her skin didn't ignite.

He stroked her shoulders, then the tops of her breasts above her brassiere. She arched her chest toward him. His kisses were coals that made her body spark and burn. She yearned for more. He unbuckled her bra, then tugged the straps down her shoulders.

"Your skin is so soft," he said, "and so warm." His hand touched her forehead. She lifted her chin and nipped at his fingers.

"Don't you dare take my temperature, Dr. Graham."

His fingers retreated, sliding down her abdomen. He slowed as he passed her rows of scars. His fingertips pressed slightly against the ridged flesh as if reading braille. When his lips dipped to her belly, she rolled to her side to stop him. She didn't want to feel his pity or regret for what she'd done.

Drawn to the source of his heat, she unbuttoned his pants. He sat up for a moment to yank them off. Although muscular, his legs were pale and hairy. They looked nothing like hers. His olive green boxer shorts hardly disguised the extent of his pleasure. She reached for him, but he caught her hands.

"Not yet," he said. He knelt at the foot of the bed, captured her left leg, and kissed the curve of her calf. He reached beneath her skirt to the tops of her nylons and slowly drew them down her limbs, taking extra care where he had bandaged her cut. Slick with sweat, the nylons resisted. It felt like he was peeling away a second skin that she'd been unable to shed by herself, and finally she could feel the air around her. Her hairs prickled, thrusting toward him.

His lips scorched her newborn flesh. A vein of fire pulsed at the apex of her thighs. As his mouth climbed her legs, the pulse intensified.

He lifted her hips free of the skirt and flung the rest of their clothing to the foot of the bed. She felt his need as he pressed his nakedness against her. They were two cords of wood feeding the same fire.

He wound her around so she lay above him on the mattress.

"Tell me if it hurts," he whispered.

She quivered reflexively as their bodies united. Her insides ached for a moment, but she appreciated the unexpected pain. It made the moment real. Already the hurt evaporated in a blaze of sensation. Moaning, she tightened her legs around him. Her imagination had failed in this respect; she had never conceived of anything feeling this good.

Her lungs swelled with air. Like bellows to a fire, the breath combusted her senses, and conscious thought melted away.

When Ada woke, his eyes were on her. He circled her shoulder with his broad hand and played with her hair.

"How do you feel?"

Content in his embrace, she smiled. She didn't want to think about what came next. It was already so different from what she had imagined. She had anticipated waking with a feeling of dread, but this trembling happiness was much harder to confront. "What time is it?" she asked.

"About seven thirty. Do you have to go?"

"Not quite yet." She nestled in his arms, resting her face against his chest. She hoped he couldn't feel the steady tears leaking from her eyes.

He kissed the top of her head. "I can't help feeling there's something wrong."

She closed her eyes and pressed herself against his warm skin. He ran his hand down her body, and she shivered with aftershocks of passion.

"I was afraid you would hate me forever for letting Naomi die," he said.

"I don't blame you." She felt safe here, able to tell him anything. "I should have been a better friend to her, but I was afraid of what she wanted from me. I was afraid of what was happening to her." She rubbed his arm repetitively.

"What did she want from you?"

"I don't know." She wiped her eyes and rolled away from him. "I think maybe she loved me, and she felt guilty about that, besides about what her—her abuser made her do."

He moved closer to her and kissed her neck. "Ada, why won't you tell me who he is?"

She blinked. She had known he would ask again. "I will," she said. "Soon."

"Good. I promise it will be okay."

A promise he couldn't keep. Another tear escaped to the pillow. "Nothing can ever make up for what he did to her. He made her want to die. I was with her once, during a storm at the Cow's Head. She wouldn't leave, just stood on the dock. She wanted God to kill her. Sometimes I think ..."

He rested his hand against the small of her back. "What?"

She should stop now, tell him nothing, but somehow she couldn't. "I think that would have been the perfect place to die. That's what she was trying to tell me. We both could have gone then, before anything else happened."

"What didn't you want to happen?"

She folded her hands and hid her face behind them. "This," she said, feeling how she hurt him with the single word.

He dropped his hand from her back. "You regret it?"

"No." She rolled toward him. "It's the best of everything that has happened since. But the old Alameda would never have done it. I changed, knowing that I risked God's wrath."

His hand skimmed her arm. "God isn't angry with you. It's just what you've been taught by people who want to control you."

"No, you're wrong. They love me. That's why there are rules; that's why there are consequences." She sat up restlessly, clutching the sheet around her breasts.

"Sweetheart, don't go." He moved next to her. "Can you stay long enough for me to make us some dinner?"

She nodded, and he got up. She watched him dress, but only after he left the room did she reach for her shirt. Her body seemed to vanish as she draped it with clothes, and for a moment she doubted what had passed between them. There were no scars to remind her of the doctor's gentle touch. The hands that had cut down Ianna's roses hadn't surfaced. She shut her eyes against a sudden vision—Dr. Graham returning from the kitchen, knife in hand. He would make this next part easy for her. He would understand what she had to do.

No. He wouldn't understand, and she couldn't tell him. She finished dressing and made the bed. The sea-green coverlet lay crumpled on the floor like a discarded dream. She pressed out every wrinkle and fluffed the pillows. She wanted to make his mother proud. Etching each detail into her memory, she studied the room. Foamy white lace covered the nightstand and chest of drawers. Sea shells were assembled in a silver bowl. A giant print of a ship in a storm roiled across the cerulean wallpaper. Nothing might have changed since Ianna had left. Ada wondered, if she looked in the closet, would she discover a dress or a slip left in haste that Dr. Graham couldn't bear to throw away?

There was a pen in the top drawer of the nightstand, but no paper. She took Father O'Connor's letter and turned over the envelope. She scrawled a few words on the creamy brown paper. It would have to be enough.

"I love you," she whispered into the room, and felt it breathe back to her.

She tiptoed down the hall toward the front door. She could hear him humming and opening cupboards. The smell of garlic and toasted bread made her stomach grumble. For the first time in many days, she was hungry.

More than anything she wanted to tell him goodbye, but the time for self-indulgence was over. She shut the door quietly behind her. Dusk was close. Her excitement and fear sharpened every color and sensation. She observed the shapes of the bushes, the silhouettes of the houses, the cracked pavement beneath her low-heeled shoes. The scents of sweat, spilled gasoline, and bovine death were almost tangible on her tongue.

As she walked, she relived her moments with Dr. Graham. Her nightmare and her fantasy were one and the same—that he would sense what she planned and come running after her, proving their empathy. He would drive her to the seaside where they would trace disappearing patterns in the sand and roll together until the warm smell of their bodies mingled with the stinging salt. They would wade through the aching coldness of the waves to the up-thrusting rocks and discover the creatures that clung to them. He would place a starfish in her palm and sweep back her hair with an ocean-wet hand. Together, they would study the perfect sea star. But when she put it down, she cut herself on a shell. Orange-red blood sprinkled the rock. Dr. Graham caught hold of her hand and dipped his fingers into the wound like an artist dips a brush. He peeled back her damp clothing and painted her goose-pimpled flesh in vivid cerise. Passages from the Song of Songs ... Judgments on the Whore of Babylon ... pagan poetry and occult symbols ...

She shuddered and uttered a prayer. It couldn't happen. It shouldn't happen. He hadn't saved her from Pete, and he wouldn't save her now. Already she was near the parsonage. She wondered how the Abels had filled it, and if they kept it clean.

The sky darkened. She should have brought a flashlight. She hurried through the back field and the Smythes' acres toward the lake. A cow lowed restlessly at her as she summited the final hill.

She was there first, she could tell. The lake was deserted except for a group of mallards. She bent near the dock and dug in the sandy earth with her fingers until she found the glass vial she'd buried there earlier. She pocketed it and walked onto the dock. Water lapped at the scuzzy timbers. The last crimson streaks in the sky dimmed.

Short, heavy steps boomed on the dock behind her. She turned. He didn't speak. He would make her say it. Her anguish surged into a sudden sentence.

"I want you to kill me."

Dennis gave a sharp laugh. "I knew you liked to hurt, Baby, but death? I don't know. A secret is one thing to hide. A body is another."

"It's what you threatened to do if I talked," she said.

He advanced to her, grabbed her arm with bruising strength. "Did you?"

"No."

He let go. "I can't say I haven't thought about it, but don't you think death is the easy way out? It would be more fun for both of us if we played with it a little."

"I'm done playing." She yanked up the bottom of her shirt to expose a row of cuts. "This is how much I hate myself. This is how much I want to die."

At the flash of flesh, excitement kindled in his eyes. "It's got to be my way. My timing."

"If you don't do it now, I'll tell everyone what you did to Naomi!"

He seized her arms. She didn't resist. "You're serious, my little saint?" His expression was predatory, inhuman.

"I can make it easy for you," she said. "There's a bottle of chloroform in my pocket. I took it from the hospital. Use it in case I struggle when I'm underwater." As the Apostle Paul put it, the spirit was willing, but the flesh was weak.

"You want to go by drowning? An effective, if simple suicide, provided you can't swim."

"I can't. I never learned. Everyone knows that."

"You cunning bitch." He let go of her and scratched the front of his leg. "God knows it would feel good to teach you some respect. And no one will know."

She massaged her arms. She remembered how her neck had purpled from his grip. "No one will know. It will look like a suicide."

"Your poor fiancé will be devastated. Perhaps he will blame himself. And your mother ... what a blow."

He looked as if he enjoyed the idea, which Ada told herself was good, according to plan. She tried not to think what would happen afterward to those she loved. It was better for them if she never grew into the evil thing she knew she was becoming.

"Everyone has a fundamental choice," she said, "whether to live in a world perverted with beauty and pain, filth and joy. We're told it's more courageous to live, or that it's our duty, or that the good will eventually outweigh the bad, but the people who tell us so haven't been where we've been. It's only when an individual recognizes his peculiar destiny that he or she can make an authentic choice."

"You're a damn philosopher, half cracked like they all are. That's what happens when there's no man around to show a girl what her peculiar destiny is."

She spread her arms. "I await the lesson."

He laughed. "The first lesson is that you don't always get what you want, or the way you want it."

She had guessed this was coming, this, her final punishment for her time with Dr. Graham. She would take it as she must, without fear or anger. Sometimes, that way, pain could transform into catharsis, or torment into pleasure. She wanted to ask him to use the chloroform now, but she was afraid to show weakness.

"I bet you wanted to die like the Virgin Mary, immaculate." He fingered something in his pocket. Withdrew it.

She didn't reply. Her gaze was transfixed by what he held in his hand. A knife.

"I'm glad you cut yourself," he said. "I guessed it, way back at the church dance. A shot in the dark of course, but I've learned to trust my instincts in that area."

"You sense the pain in others," she said, "and you exploit it."

He shrugged. "I want to watch you cut."

"Where?"

He jerked his chin. "Where else?"

She had been prepared, and yet she wasn't. His hands pulled around her waist, forcing off her skirt. He pushed her, and she stepped out of the circle of cloth with a little cry.

"Go on," he said. He slapped the knife into her hand. "Just a little one, right there."

She dipped into her skin.

"Now under your panties. More. Deeper!"

Blood slicked her fingers. She ached. The pain was different, terrible. She felt like she were vandalizing a statue or cutting off a limb. All of a sudden, her nerves failed her.

"No!" She threw down the knife. "I can't do it."

He was on her, tackling her to the hard dock and crushing her with his weight. "I suppose I shouldn't be surprised. No matter how much a woman cries for a man to stop, she wants him to do it. Being with someone who will take charge shows her how the world's supposed to work." He didn't bother removing his pants, just coiled them at his ankles. He lay on top of her, pinching her hands with his knees.

Blood seeped from her lacerations as she struggled. She screamed from the pain, screamed for the chloroform, but he didn't falter. He pounded mercilessly at her like a railcar engine. His aggression surged beyond her swollen, agonized body, and she felt him inside her mind, violating her. It was worse than she had predicted, much worse.

"You little whore." His humid breath touched her ear. "You liked that, didn't you?"

She whimpered and twisted her knees together. He had defeated her. She was ready to die.

He pulled up his pants and then hitched the skirt back up her legs.

"Get in the water."

She tried to stand, but her legs buckled, and her knees bashed against the wood as she fell. He watched her crawl the few feet to the ladder at the end of the dock. She gasped at the steely temperature of the lake. The dirty, dark water seeped into her thighs and removed the evidence of his penetration. It saturated her clothing, slowing her movements.

At his command, she let go. As the water towed her down, she reached for the rung. She found Dennis's foot instead. He braced himself against the top of her head and shoved her below the surface.

She flailed wildly for something to hold onto. The water was dark and empty as a void. Captured in a rush of bubbles, her screams were silent. She choked. Her lungs throbbed with fire. She felt weeds in her hands, and then the gravelly bottom of the lake against her feet. She pushed against it with all her might.

Her head broke the surface. She spat a lungful of water and managed a wild shriek and half a breath before he clapped a handkerchief over her mouth. A smell of overwhelming sweetness eroded her strength. Her head lolled back, and she gazed upward as she sank. Through the water, the sky erupted in a burst of light. Fireworks to celebrate her coming freedom.

Dennis's face shimmered above her. For the first time, he looked at her with genuine emotion—the curiosity of a child drowning a kitten.

Then he disappeared, fading into darkness.

CHAPTER TWENTY-TWO

𝒜da coughed and vomited simultaneously. She was on her belly, and the contents of her stomach splashed her face.

"Ada! Oh God, Alameda."

It was his voice, and that meant probably his hand that thumped her back.

"George," she croaked.

"What did you do?" he said. His voice sounded broken. "What did he do to you?" He rolled her onto her back. All she could do was gasp like a fish for breath. Above her, patterns of blue, yellow, red, and green played out a firework display. The pops of noise confused her.

"She was drowning!" Dennis's voice was defiant, even offended. "I was trying to save her."

"Then why'd you run?" That was Officer Reynolds.

Ada glanced over. Her neck was stiff. Dennis knelt in the grass, hands cuffed behind his back. His hair and shirt dripped.

"I was going to find help," he said. His sanctimonious tone exploded something inside Ada's head. She struggled to sit up.

"You're lying," she rasped. Each word agonized her throat. "You raped Naomi and threatened both of us. You were trying to kill me!"

"Do you hear that?" Dennis asked. "She's crazy. If you want the truth, she asked me to come here, to pin this on me. She did it all to herself."

"You bastard!" Dr. Graham closed the distance between them and punched him in the jaw.

"George, there's no need." Officer Reynolds grabbed Dr. Graham's arm and moved between them.

"Like hell there's not!"

Dennis laughed, showing bloody teeth. "I might have guessed. You were sleeping with a patient, George Graham."

"Shut up!" Officer Reynolds barked. "Get on your feet. Start walking."

Ada coughed. Dr. Graham came back to her as Reynolds led Dennis

162

down the hill. His shirt and pants were soaked, and he was missing a shoe. He must have jumped into the lake to save her.

"I told you I had connections," Dr. Graham said. He sniffed and wiped his eyes with the back of his hand. "I wish you had trusted me much, much sooner. Let me look at those cuts."

"He said he'd kill Naomi." She retched again. Her lungs felt like ripped cloth. "He'd kill Naomi and me if we talked."

"Did you mean for us to catch him after you were dead?"

Ashamed to answer, she sank against the cool ground.

He sighed and knelt next to her. Lifting the wet fabric of her skirt, he probed at her wounds. The muggy air warmed her cold thighs. "These are bad, Ada, especially the ones on your, on your ..." His voice caught. Tears streamed down his face. "What did it mean to you?" he asked. "Our time together? Were you using me? Were you making yourself feel guilty enough to go through with your plan? Did you even consider how it would make me—all of us—feel?"

"I didn't mean to hurt you." Her voice slipped away from her like mist.

"I'm sorry. I shouldn't blame you." His hands on her arms kept her upright. "But we were almost too late! If I had waited another five minutes before going to my room, or if I hadn't realized that Cow Lake was significant to you and told Brent, you would be dead."

She remembered her letter. *Dennis Gentle hurt Naomi. Goodbye.* But for the goodbye, he might never have questioned her absence. That he had questioned it meant something, she was sure, yet her head was so fuzzy it was hard to think.

"Help me," she said.

"I can't!" He folded her into his arms. "Tonight has shown me that. If you can go from me to him, and plan it so perfectly, I can't help you. For your own good, I have to send you away."

She leaned into his chest. How different it was now than it had been hours earlier! His body shook against hers. "Please don't."

"What can I do? I don't trust you not to hurt yourself."

"I won't." She could breathe now, although her heart ached more with each second. "I thought God wanted me dead. It would be better for my father, for Naomi, for my mother, for Michael, for the church."

"Shh. Shh." He cradled her head and rocked her gently. He was crying. "You're safe now."

"I don't want to be locked up. I couldn't stand it!"

His palms spread across her back so she sensed his sturdiness and strength, but none of it diffused to her. "Oh, Ada, I can feel your pain. This is the only way I know to fix it."

Tears squeezed from her eyes. She wished she could caress him, but her hands were hooked into fists. "No one can fix it," she said.

His hands moved up to her hair, her neck, her ears. "I know a good place. You won't be there forever, I promise. You'll get better, and they'll let you out."

"I can't face her," she whispered.

"Your mother? I understand. I can talk to her for you."

"What are you going to tell her?" Tears dripped from her nose.

"I'll tell her that you tried to hurt yourself and I'm sending you somewhere to get better."

"And ... Dennis?"

His grip tightened. "That goddamn sociopath will pay. You'll have to make a statement to Brent, but the whole town doesn't need to know the details. We'll make sure it's a closed trial."

"I have to testify?"

"When you're ready." He brushed her cheek with his thumb. "Don't worry about it now. Because of my involvement, it might be better to call in another doctor—"

"No." Panic suffocated her, swallowing her words. "I can't let anyone else ... touch me."

"Honey." He paused. "Did he rape you?"

Her throat squeezed in on itself. She could barely murmur, "I let him."

"No!" He held her at arm's length and stared her in the eyes. "It's not your fault. You're not well. This town made you sick."

She had been ready. She had suffered and come close to being delivered. Now she must suffer more. He had saved her so she could suffer. She sobbed hopelessly, drowning again. Her breaths were ragged. She sank against him, pooling onto the ground.

Even the crunch of footsteps meant nothing to her.

"George," Officer Reynolds said, "let me help you with her."

She felt her body lift.

"I hope that little shit's accusation won't reach the sheriff," Reynolds said, "but if it does, what will you do?"

"Two scandals might be too many for me. If not, I'll stay here."

"This place is poison to you. Why would you stay?"

"To help people like her."

Ada had stopped crying by the time they laid her in the back seat of the doctor's car, but her body quivered. Someone covered her with a blanket. She was too numb to feel its texture or warmth.

"Will she be okay until you reach the hospital?" Reynolds asked. "I called it in, so the roads should be clear."

Dr. Graham nodded. "She'll be fine. Thank you, Brent."

Ada didn't think he was right. She would not be fine. She concentrated her energy and lifted her head to look into the rear-view mirror. No one stared back at her. She had no reflection. Everything, even Ada-in-the-mirror, had been taken from her. Curling herself into a ball, she let her awareness ebb. Quietly she dissolved into the vinyl upholstery.

Her mind was a womb, and she drifted inside the easy blankness. She winced at the noises outside. Her world was one she created, a reverie she stepped into, and external stimuli threatened its solidity.

After a while, the soft colors around her settled, and she unfolded from herself to explore her surroundings. She walked barefoot through a dark forest. The whispering of trees and the buzz of insects soothed her. Moss and grass formed a velvet carpet for her feet. Thought evaporated, and she was no longer a person. She was the birch tree, and sap sang through her veins. She was the forest, each tree a cell of consciousness communicating with the earth. She was the world, suspended in a void of possibilities. She was the universe, everything and everywhen.

Light surrounded her, and she laughed. She chased a silver ray that skipped across the tunnel of light. As she pounced on it, the ray collapsed into a shard of mirror.

She held the mirror in her hand. It resonated with pain and familiarity. She glanced down the bright corridor. Only joy and pure being awaited her there. She set the mirror on the floor and took a step into the light.

A fragment of memory made her turn back. The silver mirror glinted on the ground. She approached it again. As she bent over it, she saw a strange girl reflected inside. Another woman dressed in white held two oval pills to the girl's mouth. She saw the girl swallow the pills, then drink from a paper cup held to her lips. The girl had empty, mud-brown eyes, short, dark hair cut above her small ears, and a thin, vulnerable neck.

As if from another life, she recognized the girl. She met her eyes. Their gazes locked, and anguish vibrated between them, shaking the mirror into a channel of silver light. She tilted upside down and slid through the light into the girl's eyes.

"Have you been writing in your journal?" Dr. Graham asked across the table in the room reserved for visits, which were allowed Saturday and Sunday afternoons at three.

Ada fidgeted. She glanced at the other inmates gathered in small groups.

Like hers, their conversations were quiet. An atmosphere of dullness, only partially induced by drugs, glazed the hospital.

"I wrote my name in it," she said. "Alameda Henrietta Williams. Henrietta after my paternal grandfather. I'll never meet him, because he's dead."

"That's progress," he said. His smile was much too encouraging for what she'd done. "I heard Jon met some of your other relatives."

She nodded. After she had been admitted to the asylum, Jon left Worden. He rode the train all the way to Pennsylvania, where he met Sybil's parents. He sent Ada a postcard about them, not caring that family gossip was scrawled without an envelope to cover it. Sybil had a sister, whom she had never mentioned, a scientist and an atheist. Their grandparents were evangelical Christians whose hearts had been broken when Sybil stole money from them to run away with a man from the circus. She had written them once to say she was no longer with the man, God had punished her by killing her baby before it was born, and she was going West to do penance.

There was more to the story, Jon promised, that he would share when she came to visit him.

"Nothing about visiting me," she muttered.

"Of course I'll visit you again," he said. "Dawn was sorry she couldn't come down this time. She left for Cambridge yesterday."

She shook her head, clenched shut her eyes. "I'm having trouble ... focusing."

"It's the medication. I'll talk to your doctors. I think they need to reduce it."

She looked at him. He believed in her so much, yet he was the one who had locked her in here. She was at turns angry and ashamed when she thought of him. His attitude to her was impeccably professional. He hadn't touched her since he and Reynolds had put her in the car, at least not as far as she remembered.

Dr. Graham told her she had lasted to the police station, given her testimony fully and unemotionally, and told the saga from Naomi's birthday to a few hours previous, excising only that afternoon with him. She didn't recall any of that. He'd said that when Sybil came to pick her up ...

"Honey, don't scratch yourself." He reached for her wrists, but drew back before touching her.

... Sybil's blouse had been damp with sweat and tears. "I don't understand," she said. "Why would you try to hurt yourself? Did you do all this so you wouldn't have to marry Michael?" To the doctor, when Ada didn't respond, "Why were you the one who found her?"

She didn't hear her mother's questions or what he answered. In the doctor's car, her body had trembled like a terrified rabbit, and she'd closed herself to outside influence, turned in on herself, and let what would, happen.

For a time, she'd left herself. It had been a relief then, but now it hurt to remember that world of shadows and soft sounds, where consciousness did not mean pain. She recalled the sensation of tipping into her body, and how she had tried to turn back at the end. Her decision came too late, and she disintegrated like sand into an hourglass until she was spent.

Her awareness had returned, slowly and agonizingly. At the asylum, not everyone's did. The walls around them imprinted upon their minds, and the halls became a puzzle they could never solve.

"It's all right," she said, hiding her arms under the table. "It's just this place."

"Would you like more visitors? I'm sure your mother—"

"No." After learning how Sybil left her own parents, Ada refused to feel shame for telling the doctor in charge of her case not to admit her.

Dr. Graham exhaled heavily, drawing Ada's attention. She met his eyes with as much clarity as she could summon. She wanted to feel his fingers on her skin, his lips on her hair, something to demonstrate that he didn't consider everything that had passed between them a mistake. Something to convince herself she was real. In here, they wouldn't let her cut. They wouldn't even give her a pencil unless they were watching.

He blinked rapidly, then looked down. "I didn't know if you'd heard … I suppose I'm the only one with news from home?"

She nodded.

"The trial is over. Even though you weren't able to testify personally, your statement was read in court, and Dennis was convicted. Well, we couldn't prove the charges for what he did to Naomi, but we did prove your charges, and he was convicted for rape and attempted murder. Another investigation found that he'd been stealing from the church. So he'll be locked up for a long time."

She didn't want to be the first to touch him, no matter how strong the urge. She was surprised she didn't cry. It was the medication. It buffered her from everything.

"Thank you," she said at last.

"There's something very wrong with him," he said, shaking his head. "I hope he'll get help, although I wonder if someone like him can be helped. He didn't react at all when the sentence was given."

"Christabella?"

"She said he never hurt her. And Edith is moving to New York to live with relatives." He peered at her. "Have you thought where you might like to live when you are released?"

She sank into her chair. The floor had a peculiar type of gravity these days, and she thought longingly of her mattress in the small cubicle she shared with another girl, who spent most of the time sleeping. "I don't want to be released."

Another sigh. She hated how sad he looked, and the masking brightness he faked.

"You won't want to stay here forever," he said. "You're going to get better, and this place will start to bore you. Isn't there anything you miss about the outside?"

Being able to cut herself. Being alone. Being with him. "My violin."

"There you go." Relief turned up the corners of his eyes. "I want you to think about that, and about where you want to go when you get better. Dawn offered for you to stay with her, and I'm sure your grandparents or aunt would love to meet you. I will make some calls."

"You don't have to do that," she said.

"I want to do it." He looked about to say more, but an orderly announced that the visiting hour was nearly over.

Ada rested her hands on the table, hoping.

"I'll see you next weekend." He stood. "Every weekend I can. There are a few babies that might get in the way, but we're expecting the new doctor in a few days."

She didn't get up. She thought of the hours he would spend on the road, driving back to Worden. Alone, now that Dawn had left. "Please don't," she said, drawing her hands into her lap. "It's easier without you."

For an instant, the anguish in his face made her happy. Then he turned away and put his hands in his pockets, and muted terror that she had lost him forever spread through her body. Although the medication kept the emotion from overwhelming her, her stomach turned acidic. Her chest ached from the never-ending beating of her heart. She stared at the speckled grain of the table, wishing for sleep.

"If that's what you want, I'll stay away." He cleared his throat. "But I'll call you about those places. After a while."

CHAPTER TWENTY-THREE

*L*ike a pesky fly, the thought of what she should do *after* wouldn't go away. Two weeks later, Dr. Graham called to confirm that both offers, Pennsylvania and Massachusetts, were open to her. After that, his calls and visits stopped. Meanwhile, Jon telephoned her a few times. Their conversations were short and usually ended with her twin urging her to join him and their grandparents once she was released.

Jon was seeing a girl called Lucy now. He didn't say what had happened between him and Dawn, but Ada felt that it was her fault. She had always wondered what caused Dr. Graham's change of attitude toward her on his final visit to her sickbed. Perhaps Dawn had told him she was seeing Jon, and he'd been ashamed of his feelings for Ada. Guessing that Ada and Dr. Graham were involved must have caused a similar conflict for Jon.

Dr. Graham's silence, although according to her express wish, confirmed her fear that he'd never cared for her, and that the Grahams had no place in her life. As she was told to prepare for her release, she made the expected decision of where to go. Overjoyed, Jon promised to take care of the details. She didn't share his excitement. Her counselor said one day she would be grateful she hadn't died, but so far gratitude was exactly the wrong word to describe how she felt about life.

Still, her steps quickened as she walked into the sunshine and gazed at the buildings and trees. She had seen them through the window, or over the top of the courtyard wall, and now it was like opening a picture book and jumping through the pages into another world. She brushed her hands through her chin-length hair.

"Ada, you're out early!"

Her heart thumped, and she whirled around.

"George."

His car keys rattled in his hand. "I'm sorry I frightened you. It was supposed to be a good surprise."

"A good surprise, yes."

"I'm going to take you to the train station," he said. "Jon and I arranged it."

She smiled and moved toward him. His eyes were two pieces of sky. God, how she'd missed him.

"If you're hungry," he continued, "we have time to stop for lunch. The train doesn't leave until two."

For the first time in nearly three months, her stomach rumbled. She blushed. "I would like that very much."

He ushered her to the car and opened the door for her. She kept hoping he would hug her or shake her hand, but she no longer felt desperate for his touch. She didn't want to talk about herself, but she hesitated to ask him about his life. She had missed so much, she was sure, that it was hard to know what to say.

Luggage was piled on the back seat. She recognized one of the cases. "My violin!"

"All the bags are yours," he said. "I won't tell you how much trouble it was to get them. I had to bargain with your mother."

"Really?"

He paused as if weighing what to say. "Perhaps I shouldn't talk about her."

"I can handle it." The fresh air through the window and the midday sun that made her squint strengthened her. "I want to see her again, I think. My counselor said it might help me process things."

Showing what he thought of that, he shook his head. "She gave me your things on the condition that I leave Worden. Permanently."

"You agreed?"

He stole a glance at her, and her heart skipped. "Now that Dawn is out of the house, I realize how secluded my life is. I want to move to a big city again, where I can meet like-minded people."

Was that a euphemism for wife? "Which city?"

"I've contacted agencies in New York, Pennsylvania, and of course all over Massachusetts. We'll see what happens."

Had he chosen Pennsylvania with her in mind? "You'll be close to Dawn at least."

"Yes, everything is closer there." He parked the car next to an Asian restaurant; the sign read *Hoang's Vietnamese Cuisine*. "I took Dawn here the last time we visited you together. I think you'll like it."

Before he could come over to the passenger side, she opened the door and stepped from the car. The simple act of independence gave her the courage to ask, "Do you view me as a daughter, George?"

"You know that's not possible," he said, halting in the middle of the street. "I have to beg your forgiveness for abandoning you earlier. I wanted to visit you, I swear, but you didn't seem to want it, and people were talking, well, more than they already were——"

"It's okay." She waited for him to approach and lowered her voice. "It gave me a chance to decide where to live, just for myself."

"I hope you like your grandparents. Jon thinks you will." He held the restaurant door for her with a wink. "Next time you can open it for me."

As the hostess seated them, Ada studied the twisting bamboo plants, the pictures of jewel-blue lakes and strange temples, the paintings of exotic flowers. They were a welcome distraction from the confusion of sentiment that surrounded her thoughts of George Graham.

"I've never been out to eat before," she confessed.

"Really? I wondered. Trying new food is a wonderful way to experience another culture."

She glanced at the incomprehensible menu, then at him.

"The vermicelli is good," he said, "and any of the pho dishes. Just steer clear of the squid."

Pointing to the cheapest of the options he had named, she asked, "Can I get this without the meat?"

"Of course," he said, "although I think they use bones in the broth. The spring rolls are vegetarian, and so is this. And … that." Leaning forward, he ran his finger down her menu. Ada trembled at the memories his gesture spurred.

The server brought a metal teapot and took their order. Before Ada could reach for the small pot, George poured the tea into white cups without handles. Before taking a sip, she smelled the dark-gold brew. A delicate rice aroma. Dried flowers.

"After the tasteless food at the hospital, this is delicious," she said. No longer caring what he thought, she stared into his eyes. She wanted to explore the world, follow him anywhere … but only if he wanted her too.

Their lunch arrived, and they laughed at the messy noodles and guessed at the oddly shaped vegetables. The unfamiliar spices elated Ada, and the heat made her flush. She had never seen the doctor as gay as he was now, chuckling and joking and playing with his food to make her laugh. Before he tried his dish, he asked her to taste it, which she did with a peculiar thrill. She wanted their meal to last forever.

All too soon the waiter arrived with the bill. George paid it, then escorted her back to the car. For a moment he lifted an arm and she thought he would put it around her shoulder, but all he did was scratch his head. The motion of the car calmed some of her frenetic energy, so much so that her head dipped in drowsiness.

"We're here." He had pulled up to the train station. He parked and grabbed the two large bags, leaving the violin case for her.

The sight of the violin reminded her. "The last two weeks I've been thinking, I want to do something for Naomi, for my father and Jim and everyone who died this year. I'm considering playing a concert."

He rested a bag on the pavement. "I think that's a great idea."

"So far, it's just an idea." She shook her head. "I need to plan my repertoire, find a pianist, and of course choose a venue. It seems appropriate to do it in Worden, but …"

"You can do it in Worden," he said. "I think it's the only place for it. Would you want anything else on the program? Something read, or, or prayed?"

She hid her smile, which warred with the rest of her feelings. "Maybe, but I would want you to be there too. You lost friends along with everyone else. You're the one who saved us—you sent samples to Dr. Lansky so he could manufacture an antibiotic. In fact, I'd like him to be there as well."

"Jerome would be more than happy, I'm sure, but I did promise your mother to leave."

"You shouldn't have," she said. "She had no right to ask it of you."

He checked his watch and picked up the bag. "I didn't want to tell you this, but she was going to report me to the medical board. I don't want any black marks on my record. I don't think it would have mattered except that you were … so unstable."

By which he meant she'd been suicidal. Guilt twinged, but she ignored it. She couldn't let it upset her again. She tucked the case under her arm and strode toward the front doors. "Don't worry about it. I'll talk to her."

"Either way, I want to help. I'll tell Brent. His wife likes to organize things. Do you have a date in mind?"

"I'd like to do it this year, but we get so much snow, maybe it would be better to wait until spring."

"Spring sounds good to me. I don't want you going back to Worden before you're ready." He produced the ticket from his wallet and helped her check in. Ada heard the train whistle, and suddenly she was at the railroad crossing. Pete's sweaty lips, Dennis's leer, forever tangled in her head. She shuddered.

He touched her arm. "What's wrong?"

She glanced up. "I don't want you to leave me again."

At last he put his arms around her and pressed her against his chest. She smelled his soapy, musky scent. "What am I to you, George Graham?" she whispered into his shirt.

"Not my daughter. I think we've established that."

"A friend? Is that possible for us now?"

He released her and looked into her eyes. "I don't want to imprison you with a category. Give it time. Get to know your relatives and see the world, and when you and I meet next, we can decide together what we are."

She touched his cheek, resisting the urge to stroke his face. He had promised nothing, except that they would meet again. For now, that was enough.

Over the loudspeaker, she heard the call to board. The crowd around them moved more quickly, bumping and jostling, and she felt as if she were in slow motion. She memorized his rueful grin and turned around with a pang. Too much might change before she saw him again.

♫

As the train pulled into the 30th Street Station in Philadelphia, Ada fumbled with her bags. An attendant helped her carry them to the pavement. Caught in a swirl of stylish jackets, fur coats, and hats, she looked around anxiously for Jon.

"Ada, here!"

She almost didn't recognize him. His hair was curly and nearly as long as hers. More than his new clothes and hairstyle, a sense of confidence pervaded him. Emotion filled her throat as they hugged.

"I like your hair," he said. "When did you cut it?"

"They did it at the hospital." She glanced down. Another thing she didn't remember. "I wasn't caring for it properly."

"Well, it looks great now." He picked up her bags. "I'll flag us a taxi."

Grateful that he handled the particulars, she clutched her case and followed him. Bicycle bells dinged, and car horns honked. A trolley whizzed by. The pace of life here was much faster than in Worden, and after her quiet schedule in the asylum, it was almost overwhelming.

She relaxed once they were in a cab.

"We should be there in about fifteen minutes," Jon said after he gave directions to their driver. "How was your train ride?"

"Long." She didn't tell him she'd felt nauseated and had hardly slept. Despite his optimism and energy, she sensed an undercurrent of concern in his questions. She sighed and looked out the window. Her counselor had warned her that it would take a while to convince others she was better. It would take even longer to convince herself.

"How much did you tell them?" she asked her twin.

He knew immediately what she meant. "I told them you had a nervous breakdown after your best friend died, and that a change in scenery would be best for you."

She nodded. "It certainly has done wonders for you."

"I love it here. I'm on the forefront of fashion, actually." He picked a piece of lint from one of his sleeves.

"You're selling things?" she asked, remembering what he'd told her.

"I go door to door with knives, nifty kitchen gadgets, and news." He smiled. "Housewives love me. It's just for now, until I find something better. I'm interested in doing medical tests, as odd as that sounds."

"What kind of tests?"

"Psychological ones," he said. "Lucy's brother is a psychiatrist who's doing new work on how chemical substances affect the brain."

"That sounds dangerous."

He stretched out his legs. "Naw. Everything's monitored and safe. I'm just excited to meet people who want to change the way things are. No one in Worden wanted to change."

She folded her hands. Her skin was dry and chapped from the cold. "I'm happy that you're making a future for yourself. I need to find something to do as well."

"I'm sure Grandma Ellie will let you do what you want in the house. She's a great cook, like you, and she does a bit of sewing and knitting." He rubbed his ear. "More than a bit."

The prospect of being stuck cooking and cleaning in another house disheartened Ada. She wanted a different life here, not more of what she'd left. Pushing back her fear, she asked Jon about his girlfriend. The subject kept him talking until they arrived.

♫

Jon stayed for supper to ease Ada's meeting with her grandparents before he returned to his apartment. Despite her grandmother's protests, Ada helped wash and dry the dishes in the tiny, shallow sink. When she asked to be excused to her room, she could tell they were disappointed, but they didn't protest.

Not ready to unpack, she sat on the edge of the mattress in their guest room and plaited her fingers through the bright afghan on the foot of the bed. She had opened her smaller bag on the train, guessing correctly that it contained essentials, but she'd left the large bag alone. She'd gone without so many things for so long, she'd forgotten what might be in it. Besides, she hated to think that Sybil had folded and placed each item for her.

At last she unzipped the bag. Although her clothing and books must have shifted during the trip, her Bible was still on top. Next to it was her hand mirror. She picked it up, rubbing the bronze backing where the glass used to be. Her reflection had haunted her. Now the mirror was empty, and Ada felt strangely comforted.

A folded sheet of stationery was pinned to the fabric cover of her Bible. Ada undid the safety pin and unfolded the letter.

It began with verses from Acts, the story of the prodigal son, who left his family, gambled away his inheritance, was reduced to eating scraps with the pigs, and returned to his forgiving father at the end. A tear plopped onto the page, and Ada blotted it with her sleeve. Sybil continued the letter in a similar vein. Ada was running from God and her duty, but if she returned, all would be well. Michael was willing to forgive and marry her. Like the prophet Hosea, he would obey the Lord and join himself to a prostitute.

She crumpled the letter in her hand. Anguish knifed through her, and she wished she'd drowned that night at the Cow's Head. She turned over the pin in her fingers, feeling its sharp point. Her mother's words had stabbed her. It would be fitting to harm herself with Sybil's pin.

She thought of Jon's concern for her. His conversation in the cab and at dinner betrayed his silent plea that she would do better here. She didn't want to be stuck in her habits and unhappiness like Worden was. She wanted to change, and she hadn't given up on Worden either.

Slipping the pin into her bag, she picked up her violin case instead. When she opened it, she felt sick. She had left others to take care of it that fateful Fourth of July, and now she paid the price. The intense heat had melted the varnish, and a crack had started in the back lining near the top block. She plucked a few loose hairs from the bow and tuned the violin as best she could.

Although afraid of damaging the instrument even more, she spread out a few sheets of music on the mattress and began to play. The violin had lost much of its resonance, and she paused every few minutes to adjust the tuning pegs, but she persisted. Pressing the strings against the swollen neck made her fingers sore, but perhaps because of the discomfort, the music eased her need to hurt herself.

After half an hour, she put away the violin and started unpacking her clothes. A moment later, she heard a knock at the door.

Grandma Ellie stood outside. She held a half-knitted cloth in her hands. "Ada, child, was that you?"

"Yes, I'm sorry. I hope I didn't disturb you."

"Disturb? No. That was beautiful." Like a cat, she flexed her fingers round the ball of yarn. "My father used to play second chair in the symphony."

"Was that his profession?"

"He made a decent salary." She smiled. "And he was happy, which was most important. He used to claim he could tell what kind of a person a musician was, after hearing them play just a few bars of music."

"I wonder what kind of a person he would have thought I was."

Grandma Ellie pushed up her thick glasses with the end of her knitting needle and squinted at her. "I think he would say you have a lot to play about," she said.

Ada fidgeted, and her grandmother's face eased into a smile.

"When he passed, he left his violin to me," Grandma Ellie said, "and I think you should have it. Tomorrow I will show you."

CHAPTER TWENTY-FOUR

Ada discovered, along with a beautifully crafted violin of Yugoslavian maple and spruce, boxes of her great-grandfather's records and scores. The timing of this gift was so synchronous with discovering that her violin was damaged that she took it as a symbol of her new life and confirmation that she should prepare a concert for the victims of the epidemic.

With renewed purpose, she restrung and polished the violin and practiced it for hours. When she played, she forgot the constant drone of traffic around her grandparents' snug house. For a while, music soothed her loneliness, but as the cold deepened, so did the ache of her heart. She awoke from nightmares where she was isolated in a dark landscape, yet hunted by Dennis's specter. She wondered if she would ever be completely well.

On Thanksgiving, Grandma Ellie invited a group of her friends to the house, and Ada performed a miniature concert for them before the meal. In the middle of the festivities, the phone rang. Grandpa Russell answered it, then called Ada to the phone.

"Hello," she said, heart fluttering.

"Ada, guess who it is!"

"Dawn," she said with a mixture of relief and disappointment. At least it wasn't her mother. "How are you?"

"I'm with Mom and Julie," Dawn said, "and doing well. I'm sorry I haven't called you for so long. I've hardly had an hour to myself since I started at Radcliffe."

"I'm sure you've been very busy. How is your Thanksgiving?"

"It's crowded. There are painters and professors everywhere, but I miss Dad."

Ada looked through the kitchen at Jon, who sat at the table with his arm slung across Lucy's shoulder. Tall and skinny, Lucy had mounds of red-gold hair and a crooked grin. She looked comfortable and content as she cuddled next to Jon.

"He's not there?" she asked.

"No, he had an interview in Syracuse a few days ago and got snowed in. I talked with him, though. We're all spending Christmas on the coast together."

"That sounds lovely."

"I want you to come. It'll be the first time in almost eleven years that Mom and Dad will see each other. I think having you there will make things less awkward for everyone."

Somehow Ada doubted that. "I don't know. Jon is spending Christmas with Lucy's family, and I'd hate to leave my grandparents alone."

Across the room, Grandma Ellie met Ada's eyes and shook her head slightly. "Don't worry about us," she mouthed. She pointed a knitting needle at Ada's Aunt Simone.

"They'll understand," Dawn said on cue. "You've never seen the ocean, and it's amazing, even in the winter."

"Don't you think—" Ada cleared her throat and lowered her voice. "Don't you think my presence would make things more awkward? Has your father told you … everything?"

"Ada, we don't keep secrets, at least not for long. I'm asking you to come because Mom and Julie are so happy. I don't want him to feel left out."

Ada's stomach flip-flopped. She couldn't believe Dawn was saying Ada made him happy. She couldn't believe she might see him again so soon.

"Having a good friend like you there," Dawn said, "will ensure that no one says anything they might regret. Apparently my parents' split was not champagne and roses." She paused. "Mom gave me the details. It's crazy what you miss when you're ten."

Ada felt panic at the surge of information. "I—I don't know what to say." She swallowed, considering something else. "But your dad will be happy if I'm there as a friend?"

"Yes. He said you made him feel better after Mom sent him the letter last summer. He said you talked, and afterward he realized he didn't want to be selfish about me." Her voice trailed off. "I'm sorry, I forgot that was the day that you … you got Dennis Gentle arrested."

"It's fine." Turning her back to the dining room, Ada stared at her shimmering hands and blinked furiously. "That's actually a kind way to put it. I would be happy to go *as a friend*."

"Excellent!" Ada heard voices on the other end of the line, and the receiver crackled like wrapping paper before she heard Dawn again. "Oh, and make sure you bring your violin. Julie wants to hear you play. Her friend, Dr. Hlavaček, is a music professor who is known for discovering and sculpting talent for the nation's concert halls."

"Very well." She choked out the words. "I have to go."

"Okay. I'll pick you up the Monday before Christmas."

Not breathing, Ada banged the receiver to its hook. Grandma Ellie looked at her, and Ada's face heated. She felt claustrophobic in the congested room. Her head spun, and she swayed down the hallway to her room.

Dawn claimed that she and her father didn't keep secrets, yet George hadn't told her that he and Ada had slept together before she'd gone to the Cow's Head to meet Dennis. He'd said they'd *talked*. Ada made it to the room, shut the door with a massive force of will, and collapsed on the bed. If he told Dawn Ada was just a friend, then that's what he wanted her to be. The letter had reminded him of his ex-wife, and half-drunk and upset, he'd made love to Ada to bolster his ego.

She flushed, this time in anger. He must have regretted that decision! He probably thought she was too weak for him to reject now, that she'd harm herself in despair if he walked out of her life. Well, he wasn't that important to her. She could survive without him. She'd been forced to. She hated the way he'd made her feel, vital and loved, because now it was revealed as a lie.

The compulsion to cut flashed over her. She had resisted so far, but her mind had cataloged a dozen sharp objects in various parts of the house. An old razor blade rusted in the bathroom under the sink. Sharp curved scissors waited like crocodiles in both of Grandma Ellie's sewing kits. Even the excised tops of tin cans called to her.

The thought of her grandparents and the guests outside her door wiped away her anger. They didn't deserve to be ignored simply because they weren't George. They didn't deserve to be punished because of him. She filled again with aching loneliness.

"Ada, are you all right?"

Hearing her grandmother's voice, Ada stopped crying. "Yes," she said. The falsehood eased something vicious inside her. She could still hurt herself in subtle ways.

The door inched open. "We're getting ready for dessert," Grandma Ellie said. "I can tell you're not feeling well, and you don't have to come, but whatever it is, know that we love you."

"Thank you." Ada clenched her jaw. "I feel fine, and I'll be out in a minute. I just wanted to put on an extra pair of socks."

When her grandmother left, Ada took half a minute to compose herself, pulled on the socks as if they were a hair shirt, and opened the door. She refused to be weak. She would face George, and Worden too.

♫

Dawn whistled when she heard Ada planned to go to Worden and crash the next spring festival.

"You've got *chutzpah*," Dawn said. "Do you know when it will be held?"

"It's usually the third Saturday in March." Ada tossed her head and snuggled under the red blanket keeping her warm in the passenger seat of Dawn's Oldsmobile. "I want to shake things up a little. I don't know what people think of me, or what they were told, but it doesn't matter."

"You're going to pull a Miss Passerini?"

"Yes. I'll start playing in the middle of the festival, and instead of putting out a hat, I'll have a sheet printed with the names of everyone who died, and photographs if we can find them, and something else, maybe a poem."

"There are photos of most of them in the medical files," Dawn said, "unless the hospital threw them out. My dad can call and ask."

She nodded. "People need to remember how we acted. Sybil forbade me to take food to anyone in the Meatpacking District. She wouldn't let me leave the house to say goodbye to Naomi. I know we were supposed to stay isolated, but that kind of fear is irrational." She kept her gaze pasted in front of her, straining to see the ocean. Dawn had said any minute it would pop into view. "What I can't understand is that no one blamed the factory or the conditions that Mr. Smythe allowed and Mr. Stone enforced. I can't believe that nothing changed."

"It's such a major part of the town's economy ..." Dawn shrugged. "I guess I can understand it."

"People can find something else to do." She sucked in her breath. "There's always something."

The glittering serpent of the ocean rose below the foggy sky. Blue-gray waves foamed against dark rocks. Ada watched the wide swells rise and release like a great beast's ribs as it breathed in and out.

"You can't say that nothing changed," Dawn argued. "You did." She pulled into a long driveway that ended in a series of bungalows and parked the car. "Look at that beach access."

Ada noticed the doctor's car. And then he and two women spilled out of the bungalow. She folded the red blanket and got out of the car.

Dawn reintroduced her to Ianna and Julie. Ada recognized them even though they varied from her memories. George looked different too, although perhaps it was only her new perception of him. He hugged Dawn and shook Ada's hand. Remembering her determination to be strong, she compressed her lips and met his eyes without blinking.

The bungalow contained four bedrooms, so at least Ada had privacy. After unpacking and freshening up, she went into the main room. Christmas lights and fragrant boughs of evergreen made it impossible to be entirely depressed. A stack of presents near the fireplace drew her attention, and she added her small gifts to the collection.

George cleared his throat behind her. "I'm glad you came, Ada. I missed you."

She couldn't listen to his lies. "I came for Dawn," she said, grabbing her coat and scarf. "I see she's outside. I'm going down to the water."

"I'll go with you," he said.

"If you insist." Not waiting for him, she hurried out the door. A gust of air filled her lungs, and she smelled brine, seaweed, a hint of wet wood. She smiled in spite of herself.

Dawn was more than happy to explore the beach with her, and for that day and the next Ada was her nearly constant companion. She made sure never to be alone with George. Although she felt sorry for treating him coldly, it was the only way she could deal with his friendly overtures. And he *was* friendly. At supper, he handed her the salt and pepper without being asked. He helped prepare most of the meals and wash the dishes, nearly driving her from the kitchen with his attempts at conversation.

On Christmas Eve she performed an etude she had perfected. The rich wood of her great-grandfather's violin sang in the small room, and the new strings on her bow energized her final flurry of fast notes. Her small audience clapped, and Ada curtseyed in triumph.

"I'm going to call Dr. Hlaváček as soon as I get back to schedule an audition," Julie promised. "If he accepts you, you'll have to move closer to Cambridge."

"You'll like it," Dawn said. "It's not as industrial as Philly."

"We'll see." Ada put away her violin. The idea of being independent excited her. Despite her grandparents' generosity, she still felt like a visitor in their house.

"Maybe Ada appreciates her life the way it is," Ianna said mildly. "She's close to her brother in Philadelphia, and family is important."

As if the comment nettled him, George stood from his chair and walked to the large front window. Ada looked from him to Ianna. Her gaze jealously lingered on Ianna's tawny hair and Grecian body. She had noted how George stood straighter when Ianna was in the room and forced laughter when she made a joke. Ada sensed and feared the conflict of his emotions toward her. From Ada's observation, Ianna was overly agreeable to her ex-husband. She described several symptoms and asked for his "expert" opinion. Julie didn't seem to mind how unctuously Ianna behaved, but that suited her relaxed personality. Initially shocked by Julie's mannish pants and posture, Ada now admired her unselfconsciousness.

"Family is important, but so is knowing when to leave," Ada said and was rewarded by Ianna's faint blush. It wasn't her fault if her comment had a double meaning. "I have to balance both sides."

"Knowing *how* to leave is another factor," Ianna said, not looking at

Ada. "Nothing is as embarrassing as an ill-planned, failed exit."

George made a noise at the window. In the background, waves dashed against the horizon.

Ada hoped her cheeks didn't look as hot as they felt. In her cruelty, she had prodded Ianna, and she'd gotten stung in return. Any attempt at rejoinder evaded her.

Julie brushed her hand against Ianna's back. "At least we've all come together today. We should go for a walk tomorrow, on Christmas."

"I listened to the forecast," Ianna said. "There's supposed to be a storm."

"Don't be a wet blanket." Dawn stood from the couch. "We're in, right, Ada?"

"Of course." She wanted to say she didn't mind a storm, but it seemed petty even to her.

"We'll go out after breakfast," Dawn said, "and come back to open presents."

Ada picked up her case and went to her room. While she was tidying her things, she heard Julie call her name. She opened the door with a questioning look.

"Don't let Ianna bother you," Julie said, raking her fingers through her thick, black hair. "She's just being protective."

"Of what? I don't intend to steal anything from her."

Julie's eyebrow quirked in disbelief. "She feels guilty about hurting George all those years ago. Hell, so do I. She can tell he cares about you, and she doesn't want you to hurt him like she did."

"I don't think that's the case," Ada said stiffly. She walked to the table in the corner of the room and picked up a book. She hoped Julie would get the hint that she wanted to be alone.

"What do I know?" Julie drummed her fingers against the edge of the door. "I'm just saying, I think we'll all have a better Christmas if we're honest with each other."

"Tell George that." Ada shut the book with a thud. "I came here as Dawn's friend. If he wants me to be nicer to him, he should have the courage to tell me. I never lied to him, but he hasn't been exactly truthful with me."

Julie *hmm*ed. "Okay. I'll let you read now, or whatever you planned on doing. By the way, those cherry chocolate cookies you brought are delicious. A natural aphrodisiac too."

Ada felt her face burn again. "Thank you."

Julie turned on her heel, but as she closed the door she said, "You were right to leave Worden, Ada. I can't imagine ever going back."

"Wait." Ada stepped to the doorway and grabbed the knob. "Are you sure about that?" She told Julie about her plan for the spring festival. "I would love to have a keyboardist like you play with me."

"That would really flabbergast the locals." Julie smiled. "I'll think about it. I'm not sure Ianna could face them though. What would we play?"

"I haven't decided. I'm working on some repertoire, but nothing feels quite right."

"Maybe you could compose something for the occasion. After all, you were the one with the experience, with the suffering. You can make the pain beautiful through music."

Ada watched Julie saunter down the hallway, and then she slowly shut the door. Instead of going to her book, she picked up her violin. Strands of melody, sharp as coral reefs, emerged from her instrument.

♫

Against her bare toes, the cold, wet sand almost tickled. Ada knew that in a few minutes her feet would grow numb, but she loved skimming along the shoreline like a bird.

"I don't know how you can stand this weather," Ianna said, holding her hood closed. "I have to turn back."

"Come on, Mom! It's a glorious storm. Let's walk into it." Dawn's green eyes sparkled, matching the wild water. Ianna's eyes were a lighter green, Ada noticed, like new growth in the spring. She felt a rush of sympathy for the years Ianna had spent away from her daughter and husband.

"Let's not." Julie's calm, pragmatic voice cut through the wind. "I think George would agree it's bad for our health."

"As a doctor, I agree with Julie." George glanced apologetically at Dawn. "As an adventurer, I still want to go out to that rock."

"We all do," Dawn said. "It's low tide, and there's no one else on the beach. We'd be the first to see whatever's there."

"It will be new again at the next low tide," Ianna said.

With those words, Ada realized why she loved the ocean. It was always new, unpredictable yet constant in its fluctuation. The foam of consciousness cast itself into the beach's form, changing and being changed. A metaphor for life.

"Yes, but I don't want to wait for the next low tide! This is the lowest of the week."

"Dawn, can't you hear your mother's teeth chattering?" Like Ada, George walked barefoot, but the cold didn't seem to touch him. "Why don't you go back with her?"

"You're staying out?" She looked at her father.

He nodded.

"Fine," she said. "We'll open the Christmas presents without you." She linked arms with her mother and headed for the hotel. Julie joggled Ada's elbow, gave her a significant look, and then strode after them.

Ada's heart pounded. She glanced at George, but he said nothing. The shoes she carried wobbled, and in an instant she struck out after her friends.

His hand settled on her shoulder. Even through the coat she felt his urgency. "Wait, Ada. Don't you want to see the rock with me?"

His touch melted her resistance, as she had feared it would. It was Christmas after all, and she could forgive him for an hour. "We've come this far. I suppose it would be a shame not to."

"Good, because there's something I want to tell you." His face looked as stony and resigned as the small cliffs at the end of the beach.

Ada was afraid to hear the truth from him. She dropped her shoes and broke into a jog toward the surf. The rock drew her like a beacon. White swells rose and fell just beyond it. As she approached, she saw it was much larger and longer than she'd thought. Bulbous kelp fastened to its sides.

"Are you trying to leave me behind?" George caught up with her.

She let him wonder and walked around the boulder. The sand dipped near the base, creating a moat of marine life. Barnacles carpeted the rock. At the top, a pair of seagulls squawked at her.

"Look," George said, "starfish."

Clinging to the side of the rock, half submerged in the aquamarine water, a clump of purple sea stars blended into the dark shadows around them. Ada bent across the moat and touched one of the rays. It felt harder and bumpier than she'd expected. With the sensation, she felt her self-indulgent fantasies about the photograph on the mantel dissipate. She sighed with an odd feeling of release.

"There," she said. "Now we can go back."

"Your fingers must be freezing." Before she could say anything, he took hold of her hands. "God, I was right!"

His palms were so hot it almost hurt. Her fingers itched, but she didn't move them. She was rooted to the moment. Her heart throbbed with the desire she had tried to quell since she'd been in the asylum. Her efforts had been for nothing. She felt raw before him, helpless.

An icy wave lapped across her feet, breaking the spell. As she cried out, George lifted her into his arms, out of the seawater's reach. Her body ached, remembering the last time they'd been so near. She lowered her eyes, afraid he would glimpse the need in her soul.

His lips were salty and warm. He heated her face and neck with kisses. He gasped as another wave washed up to his ankles, released her, and stepped back with a splash. She slid to the sand and ran a few feet away.

"You didn't need to do that." She brushed her hands over her cheeks and lips, wiping away his kisses and her tears.

"Ada, I'm sorry. Did I make you cry? I thought—"

She turned her back to him. Thick gray mist bubbled in front of her, hiding the shore from sight. Raindrops spattered her face.

"You don't have to keep pretending," she said. "It's too much that I'm the same age as your daughter. I understand. I'm going back now."

"You can't. That's the storm cloud passing around us. We should wait."

Shielding her eyes from the drizzle, she squinted at the ocean. For the time being, the tide was safely behind them.

He took a few steps forward and grabbed her arm. "And I'm not pretending. How can you believe that?"

"You never told Dawn about us." She shivered as the wind picked up. "You were thinking about your wife the whole time."

He swung her around to face him. "I was *not* thinking of Ianna. I considered telling Dawn, but it was a private thing between us, and I wasn't sure of your feelings."

"That's not true." She reclaimed her hands and stuck them up the sleeves of her coat. "You knew how I felt."

"I knew how you felt then, but that might change when the world opened up to you. It still might." He pushed his hat down more securely and moved so his body blocked her from the wind. "I held myself back because I thought you could find so much more to make you happy. After all, being with me wasn't enough to stop you from hurting yourself." Pain darkened his eyes to cobalt.

She glanced down guiltily. "You can't keep me from hurting."

He sighed and surveyed the surf. Rough gray breakers hurtled onto the sand and dragged back debris with sucking fingers. Ada craned her neck to follow the careening flight of a storm petrel.

"I've lost so many people I love," he said after a moment. "For a doctor, I'm not very good at saving people."

"You saved me," she said. "I don't believe I ever thanked you either."

"I don't want gratitude from you, Ada. I want you to enjoy your life. Is it selfish of me to hope I can be part of that?"

"Do you want to be part of that?" she asked.

He smiled. "Yes, for as long as you'll allow. What I wanted to say is, I love you. This morning I told Dawn how I feel about you. She understands that love doesn't always guide us down an easy path."

Unbelieving, she stared at him. "You love me?"

"You are beautiful, gentle, and a hell of a violinist. It may not be easy for us, but I'm willing to try. I won't let my fear get in the way of our happiness."

She stopped his words with a kiss. "I love you too." Any sensation of coldness left her. It might have been springtime around her, and she stood on a blanket of blossoms.

He unbuttoned his coat and drew her into his body heat. "Is there anything I can do to prove how I feel?"

She leaned into him. "Tell me you bought me a present."

"I did. Gloves, and something else. You'll have to wait and see." He opened her coat and wrapped his hands around the small of her back. His fingers worked past the curves of her rear and down her thighs, then inched up her skirt. She moaned as he touched her. She was glad for the storm cloud hiding them from view. It made her feel wild and part of the sea, like a selkie or a mermaid.

He stroked her panties with one finger. Desire opened her like a flower, and at last his fingers slipped inside. He kissed her ear and whispered words that were lost in the crash of the sea. As he caressed her, her stomach clenched and she bit into his shirt. Love surged through her like a giant wave, forcing a cry from her frozen lips.

"Say you'll come home with me tomorrow," he said. "I was offered a position in Boston. We can start a new life there, together."

She wanted nothing else.

CHAPTER TWENTY-FIVE

Ada waited without breathing as the operator connected her call.

"Donner's Grocery. How may I help you?" The line hummed slightly, but Ada recognized Sybil's voice.

"Mother?"

Sybil inhaled sharply. "Alameda, my dear child, I haven't heard from you since that letter you sent. How are you? Are you still in Pennsylvania?"

She glanced around the small bedroom. George sat at the desk, flipping through files.

"I'm fine, and no, I'm not in Pennsylvania. I wanted to let you know I'll be in Worden in a few months."

"You're coming here? Oh, please say it's for good."

"No, it's just for a couple of days." She scooted back on the bed and drew her knees up to her chin.

"You should be here with me, your mother. Now that Jonathon is gone, I'm all alone. I miss you."

Ada swallowed. "You have the Donners," she said after a moment. "You have God."

"And God is all I have relied on since your father's death. On whom do you rely?"

Sybil's question seemed earnest, but Ada knew her mother would never accept her answer. She put a hand to the center of her ribs, feeling the familiar ache of her shame and shortcomings. "I have my music," she said. "I have friends, and some family nearby." She didn't dare mention George. He glanced at her from the desk, and she nodded she was okay.

"Daughter, for your own happiness, you must cling to Christ. He's the only one who will bring you true contentment and eternal life."

The lump in her throat deepened. Following Christ had only brought her pain. "I know that's what you believe," she murmured.

"You believe it too! I know you do. What church are you attending?

If it's not Reformed, there's probably some heresy of doctrine, like female elders or universal salvation."

In Pennsylvania, Ada had attended church with her grandparents, and although it was pleasantly different from the one she'd grown up in, she hadn't continued the tradition in Boston. Now she spent Sundays sleeping, or walking in the park a little ways off. Wandering from bush to bush and watching birds flit in the trees, she felt more peaceful than she ever had. "I haven't settled on a church yet," she hedged.

"Do not forsake the 'assembling together, as the manner of some is.' Hebrews 10:25. Michael and I struggle with feeling judged by the congregants for your actions, but we still commune with them and serve them. We don't run away from hardship."

Ada sagged forward, her will crumpling like a pile of leaves. She heard the desk creak as George stood. An instant later his fingers brushed her back.

"Don't get caught in the conversation," he said. "Just tell her what she needs to know."

She nodded and spoke into the transmitter. "As I said, I'm returning to Worden. I'll be arriving the day of the spring festival. Marjory Reynolds was supposed to put up a notice about a concert in the Town Hall right after the festival. I'm performing in it."

"I saw the notice," Sybil said. "It looked like some sort of memorial for the plague."

"Yes, it's a memorial for the deceased … and a protest of sorts."

Sybil made a noise in her throat. "What are you protesting? You know as well as I that the plague was God's punishment on us for secret sins."

"The epidemic could have been avoided if the meatpacking factory were more ethical, or shut down. Any donations will go toward that purpose."

"Why should you get in the way of honest men and their bread? Shame on you, Alameda."

"It's Ada now." Tears stung her eyes. She felt young again, a child reprimanded by her mother. George squeezed her arm. "Dr. Graham will be there," she said, leaning into him. "I know you told him never to come back to Worden, but it's just for the concert."

"He is a wicked man, and he will be held accountable to God for his evil advice to you."

"Don't punish him for my mistakes. He did nothing wrong."

"That's a lie, Daughter! He seduced you, and if he sets foot in town, the world will know it."

"He didn't, and no one will listen to your accusations. He has a good position at a large hospital. You can't hurt him anymore." She splayed out her left hand and examined her Christmas present, a gold band with three sapphire stones representing her new family. George kissed her palm. "If you try, you will only hurt me."

"You're hurting yourself by rejecting the Lord. You used to be so truthful, so sensitive to God's will. Now you're doing what you want, not what God and your family want. I didn't raise you to be a selfish girl."

She didn't want to be selfish. Could she explain that doing what her mother considered selfish was how she had learned to survive? The feeling that her mother's words were unfair grew in her chest until she knew she must burst. Hoping that motion would help channel her thoughts into intelligibility, she jumped to her feet.

"How do you know what God wants for me?" she asked, pacing across the thick cream carpet. The phone line buzzed. "I no longer live according to the fear of man but according to my conscience. That takes courage."

"God has made it clear what he requires in his Word." Sybil's voice was loud, and she dragged her words in an agonizing cadence. "If you cannot see that, then sin is veiling your eyes, and you should not call that noble or courageous. Those are rationalizations to excuse your behavior, lies of the devil your worldly counselors have taught you."

Tears slipped down her cheeks. She had hoped she was past crying like this. She had hoped she was past this fragility. "I tried to live your way, Mother. It made me want to die."

"Because you love the lusts of the flesh more than God! I only pray that the covenant of your baptism will prevail. God put his mark on you long before you desecrated the temple of your body."

Ada's hands went numb. Her throat throbbed. She couldn't speak.

"Even if you abandon Christ, he will not forsake you. Isn't that wonderful? He loves you more than I do."

"I can see that," she croaked.

"Why didn't you tell us you were struggling, Alameda? Why didn't you let your father and me help you? It pains me to say this, but I am relieved Silas never witnessed your apostasy."

"Let me talk to her," George said. He uncrossed his arms and stepped toward her. "What's she saying?"

Ada shook her head. She thought of her new life and her dim hope that Sybil might visit one day and celebrate with her. Dashed, like her mood. "I think Father loved people more than he cared about truth," she said. "Truth is too difficult to be sure of."

"You're wrong; nothing is simpler than truth. You either love God, or you hate him."

Ada neared the telephone cradle. "Goodbye, Mother. I'll see you at the concert."

"I'm not sure I'll be there. I don't want to support your rebellion. I just don't know what you're capable of anymore."

She let the phone drop onto the cradle. An instant before it clicked, she heard her mother's voice float up to her, soft but desperate.

"Please, my angel, repent and come home."

♫

The music came to her in flashes of memory. While George worked long shifts at the hospital, Ada scribbled notes at the desk. Time had dulled the sharpness of the images, but less so than she'd thought, and she relived the horrible epic through internal music. Her composition was a way of memorializing what had happened with eternal, diamond clarity.

Now she was to present what she had toiled over in her soul and crafted under the brutal discipline of Dr. Hlaváček. She was glad she had decided to plan a concert rather than spontaneously serenade the festival-goers. Like those who had died in the epidemic, her music deserved respectful silence.

She held the first note longer than she ever had, bowing with increasing intensity. Then came the sudden glissando, the questioning flutter of notes. The perpetual question: Why am I here? Each person carved out a meaning, a method of processing the world. She and Naomi had been so naïve. They wanted to filter the world more minutely, concentrate it into a convent.

Ada returned to the opening note, then began a frantic fugue with jagged intervals. The piano joined her in aggressive pursuit. The upper melody played the theme a measure behind the lower line, snapping at its heels.

The frightened bellow of a calf. Animals that were slaughtered routinely, callously. Their splattered feces spawned sickness.

She jerked on the bow, squealing the strings. The fugue jolted to a halt. In the silence, the piano's keys crashed. Again. Death knells. She could hear the audience breathing. She waited.

With a graceful motion, she brought the bow back to the string and produced a whistle-thin harmonic. The crack in the mirror. You see who you are, but you don't have to like it. She plucked a series of pizzicato notes, each a choice to make, a facet of identity to shed. Choices ended when a person died, but they shouldn't end before then.

At last she rolled a chord, and the piano joined her, easing into a fluid accompaniment to the violin's passionate, obsessive melody. As she played, she broke her rule and looked into the audience. The lights had been dimmed in the Town Hall, but she could see the first few rows of chairs. White face unreadable, Sybil leaned slightly against Michael as if for support. A few seats from them, Mayor Templeton frowned and shifted uncomfortably. At least he and his wife were there; the Smythes were conspicuously absent.

George sat with Grandma Ellie and Grandpa Russell. On his other side were Dr. Lansky and the new town doctor. Dawn hadn't been able to get off the date, and Ianna hadn't tried. The past wasn't something everyone could face, at least not at the same time.

Although she couldn't see Jon, she knew he and Lucy sat with the meat-packers. They filled the hall all the way to the door. Near the edge of the circle of light, Pete O'Connor watched Julie with unsettled eyes and tugged at his suit. All of Worden was represented.

Ada played for the dead. She played for Miss Passerini, who had yelled at her mistakes and trembled with excitement when she'd perfected a phrase. She played for her father, a kind man who had never doubted his faith. She played for Naomi, whose love for her had gone unacknowledged. She played for the old Alameda—the girl she used to be—and for Ada-in-the-mirror, who had helped her change.

It was the final piece of the concert, but Ada didn't end flamboyantly. Instead, her melody faded into the distance, lonely harmonics singing out the ghosts that had possessed her and still haunted Worden.

THE END

ABOUT THE AUTHOR

Tara Pegasus resides in Washington State with her wife, cats, and a variety of musical instruments. She has been writing fiction and poetry since age six. A professional pianist as well as a writer, she earned music degrees from the Universities of Idaho and Washington. She enjoys fermenting foods, climbing trees, and lucid dreaming. Look for *The Seer and the Sphinx*, book one of her upcoming urban fantasy series.

ABOUT PURPLE PEGASUS PUBLISHING

Purple Pegasus Publishing was created in 2014 by Jordan and Tara Pegasus. Their titles focus on consciousness, environmentalism, holistic health, and LBGTQ+ themes. To learn more, follow them on Facebook and Twitter.